TO THE DEVIL A DAUGHTER

TO THE DEVIL A DAUGHTER

A Vivian Summers Investigation

K.H. KOEHLER

The Monster Factory

CONTENTS

1	2
2	6
3	15
4	20
5	22
6	27
7	31
8	36
9	44

CONTENTS

10	52
11	55
12	63
13	66
14	67
15	70
16	75
17	84
18	88
19	92
20	95
21	98

22	99
23	103
24	106
25	115
26	124
27	128
28	136
29	138
30	145
31	148
32	153
33	155

VIII - CONTENTS

34	160
35	165
36	168
37	175
38	177
39	179
40	184
41	187
42	194
43	195
44	206
45	208

46	211
47	216
48	221
49	230
50	236
51	238
52	242
53	249
54	256
55	261
56	265
57	267

58	271
59	272
60	280
61	282
62	289
63	296
64	298
About The Author	302

Copyright © 2019 by K.H. Koehler

All rights reserved. No part of this publication may be reproduced, stored or transmitted in any form or by any means, electronic, mechanical, photocopying, recording, scanning, or otherwise without written permission from the publisher. It is illegal to copy this book, post it to a website, or distribute it by any other means without permission.

This novel is entirely a work of fiction. The names, characters and incidents portrayed in it are the work of the author's imagination. Any resemblance to actual persons, living or dead, events or localities is entirely coincidental.

Paperback ISBN: 979-8-8693-7897-2
Ebook ISBN: 979-8-8693-7898-9

Cover art and interior design by KH Koehler Design

https://khkoehler.net

No part of this book was created using artificial intelligence.

It was a special pleasure to see things eaten, to see things blackened and changed.
—Ray Bradbury, *Fahrenheit 451*

God is love. But Lucifer does that thing with his tongue.
—Online Meme

1

THE SHOP WAS twenty by thirty feet, with a large, fairly modern prep room in the back. It was small—barely large enough to change your mind in—and Sebastian kept reminding me of that fact. But it had plenty of windows that overlooked Broad Street, and the shop was in one of Philadelphia's "revitalizing corridors," so I knew it would get a lot of coverage in the lifestyle section of the paper. I thought it was perfect.

"Where should we start first?" I asked Sebastian as I carried in a box of tools and paintbrushes and dumped it on the floor. I straightened up, stretched my back, and looked at the walls. They were all dingy beige except for the giant mural of a pig on one wall with all of the choice butchery parts outlined in broken lines. My partner Sebastian and I planned to transform this old butcher shop into something spectacular

Sebastian looked unsure. This was the first time he was seeing it "in the flesh," so to speak. Up until now, our shop (I wanted to call it "Confessions") had been nothing but outlines on paper napkins and jots of ink on scraps of notebook paper. "I...well, it's rather small, luv."

He looked worriedly at the pig mural.

I smacked him on the arm. "Look at it!"

He shoved his hands into the deep pockets of his drainpipe trousers. They looked like he'd stolen them off a carnival barker from the eighteenth century, and they exposed his white socks and saddle shoes. His shirt was a froth of cheap, gold-lined lace at the throat, and he was wearing a garish tailcoat of red damask with velvet-trimmed lapels and flaps. I once discreetly snapped a pic of him and posted it to a British message board just to see what would happen. Everyone on the board wanted to know who the cute but woefully outdated Teddy Boy was.

"Sebastian!"

"I'm bloody looking, ya cunt!"

Sebastian Davis was head and shoulders taller than I was and as thin as a whip. He looked my age but talked like something out of Mary Poppins. Well, an X-rated Mary Poppins. He didn't really mean the "cunt" remark, by the way. At least, I didn't think he did. That was just the way he rolled.

While he contemplated the property we'd just leased, I looked over at the glass counter that could be refurbished and filled with fudge, cordials, truffles, brittles, and fondant fancies. Those Sebastian would be in charge of because those are British and what the hell is a fondant fancy, anyway? The hard candy I would be making would go in barrels or behind plates of glass along the walls, optimizing the small space.

My mind started building the store up like some crazy fast-forward CGI sequence. I could see it all in seconds, finished, painted, and presented. It had happened before. Sometimes, I catch glimpses of the future—things that have not yet to come to pass but will. One of the many quirks of being a biological witch.

I heard Sebastian talking but couldn't make out the words. I turned my head and saw his lips moving. Seconds later, the words caught up.

"...okay? Right then, let's carry on..."

"I want to paint a hex over the pig," I told him.

He looked at me like I was mad. "A hex?"

Like me, Sebastian is a witch. Well, sort of. More of a necromancer, though he tells me the PC term is "resurrectionist." (Eye roll.) He can move his essence—what he calls his "selfie"—into other bodies, either temporarily or permanently. He can also "put rise" into the dead, although it's a complicated and screwy process, he says. Sebastian is one of the few who can appreciate the power behind symbols of power.

"Are you sure, witchy?" he asked.

"I am." I'd already seen it completed. A combination of mural and ward to keep the darker things away. And the gods know I needed that in my life.

"It's already painted. I just have to do the work." I leaned over for a small can of blue paint from the box.

"You are one strange witch, witch," Sebastian said as he went over to the display counter and hiked himself up so he was sitting on the glass, his long, long legs in those ridiculous trousers dangling down.

"I take it you aren't going to help?"

"I like to watch you work, you sexy thing," he cooed.

He made it all sound so scandalous, but I wasn't fooled by his display. Sebastian is as kiki as a $700 Chanel scarf.

An hour later, the ward was complete and covered the old pig mural from top to bottom as well as most of the remaining wall. It was a complex hex made up of wards—some well known to various witches and other occultists and a few long since lost to history. But in the middle of it all was a simple but infinitely more powerful symbol only I and one other person in the whole world even knew how to draw.

One long line with a little curl at the bottom and two forked lines at the top.

The bident.
The Morning Star. The sign of my father's house.
The House of Lucifer.
One strange witch. Poor Sebastian didn't know even the half of it.

| 2 |

THREE DAYS AFTER I buried my business partner, Mike Bartholdi, I stepped into the law offices of Butcher & Butcher (what an awful name, I thought peripherally), shook the rain off my coat, and prepared to be slaughtered upon the legal altar.

Mike was dead. Murdered, if you wanted to get technical, and his little Mafioso family was going to rip the club Mike and I owned right out from under my feet. I mean, why wouldn't they? They owed me nothing. Neither did he even though we were more than friends for a short time.

"You can go right in, Ms. Summers," the secretary who looked to be in her seventies and who was likely the Butchers' Sons' mom said with a cheery, apple-cheeked smile that made me want to cringe.

"Thanks." I sounded about as enthusiastic as Anne Boleyn being led away to the royal executioner.

I wasn't in the office more than three seconds when the elder Butcher brother rose from his desk and raced to me, taking my hands as if I was a widow in mourning in a gothic novel. "If you want to sell, I'll be happy to help you with that, Ms. Summers," he said and then followed up with some legalese I couldn't follow but I interpreted to mean that I was now the sole owner of The Loop, the club Mike and I had bought and fixed up three years ago.

Well, Mike had bought it with his family's dirty blood money. I just redesigned the interior because for all of Mike's disposable income, he knew exactly squat about gothic subculture. Turned out, the Loop was mine to run or sell. When I asked how that was possible, the elder Butcher told me Mike's family was honoring his Last Will and Testament, and that I had been named his sole heir and executor.

"It's a clean break," my brother Josh said that night while we sat together on the sofa, watching *SpongeBob Square Pants* on the Cartoon Network as if we were kids again. We used to watch Saturday Morning cartoons all the time while we ate our sugary cereal, at least until the networks yanked them all off. It was our thing.

I sat there, munching on Lucky Charms, the new owner of half a million dollars' worth of failing rave club, and looked over at my brother. Josh had lost his sight while serving in Afghanistan. As always, I figured he was watching TV with me *for* me. He wasn't getting a damned thing out of it, but that was just like Josh, being there for me.

"Is that why you keep taking off? You think it's a clean break?" I asked, referring to all of the times my brilliant but chronically underpaid musician brother hit the road and did a circuit through some godforsaken armpit of the country. Sometimes, he didn't call for days on end."

"Maybe." He slurped his milk.

"You know my dump is your dump," I said, indicating my cheap, chintzy apartment in a renovated and de-sanctified church. And my fortune is your fortune…"

He smiled at that and popped a mouthful of Trix right from the box into his mouth."You want some serious advice, sis?"

"Hit me."

"Unload The Loop and get the hell out of this fucking town. What has Blackwater ever done for you?"

I thought about his words that night and in the days that followed. I had moved here after our parents died. I had gone to school here. Been hunted by angels and terrorized by supernatural cults here. I had found out who I was here. And I had met Nick here.

Nick. Yeah, if I wanted to be honest with myself, it was probably him more than anything else holding me back. And I didn't know why. We weren't going to be together. That wasn't going to happen. I didn't even *want* it to happen. I was *so* done with the walking, talking calamity that was Nick Englebrecht.

But we had a connection, one I didn't feel with anyone else. One I was still reluctant to break.

I still loved him. That much was true, and would probably always be true, but we were not suited to each other. Bad things happened when we were together.

Compulsively, I looked at the witch's mark on my wrist, the one he had given me. Touching it sent a wave of sensual echoes throughout my body. I knew it was the same for him. No matter where I went in this world, I would never be rid of the mark. I would never be rid of him.

Well, then, I thought. What difference does it make where I go?

I owned so little. Some out-of-date club clothes. A few personal trinkets. And all of it was connected to this town in some way. The following week, I sold the club to a developer and put the keys to the apartment into Josh's hand.

"What's this?" he asked. He was sitting at the little two-seater table, feeding his service dog the bacon off his plate. I had made eggs—badly. Burned around the edges. But he ate them anyway.

"It's yours," I said from across the table. "All of it. Even the dresses in the closet. Though I don't think they'll fit you."

He laughed at that. "You're going to do it. You're going on a great adventure."

"You make me sound like a Hobbit."

That made him laugh even harder.

Later that day, the lawyer cut me a check and I came back to pack a single suitcase. A few changes of clothes, some personal items, my business course textbooks, a few old DVDs of Josh and me on our birthdays in a time when our parents were still alive, and a photo album full of pictures of people not related to me but who were my family nonetheless. Sentimental stuff, sure, but I felt I needed to know where I'd come from before I knew where I was going.

I got it all in the back of my jeep, Daisy. Then I got in the driver's seat and closed the door. I laughed. I had no plans. Nowhere to go. Not even a clear destination. So, I flipped a coin. Heads and I would drive out to New Jersey. Tales it was Philadelphia.

Tales won. And, three hours later, dog-tired from turnpike traffic, I checked into a dump that looked like a slightly nicer version of the Bates Motel and threw my bags on the floor before collapsing on the big weird waterbed. I laughed and laughed, shaking the whole bed. I couldn't believe I was doing this. Totally winging it.

I should have been frightened half to death and questioning my suspicious life choices. Normally, I did, even under the best circumstances. But I wasn't.

I was free. For the first time, I felt I was deciding my own future. Going on a great Hobbit adventure, as Josh had said.

Once, long ago, I'd had plans set in stone. Life could only go one way for me, Vivian Summers. But I'd been through so much hell in the last few years. So much had changed me, inside and out. I wasn't that girl who'd wanted to launch her own bakery one day, and all of those old dreams were now dust.

Witches can't bake. All those romance novels about witches running super cute cupcake shops as the front for some secret spell-casting service? Lies and bullshit. The author didn't do her homework, let me tell you. Something about leavening and witches does not mix. And, for a while, I'd been pretty messed up about that. Of all the stupid legends to be true, why that one?

But as I lay there, thinking about how that old dream would never be mine, I remembered something else. When I was eight, my mom would take me to the YMCA for swim lessons, and, afterward, we'd stop at this sweet shop for chocolate pops. They had them in all different shapes. Cats and dolls and even an ice cream cone, which was my favorite.

I sat up as I had my first—but not my last—vision of the future. It was terrifyingly explicit and full of small details. After it was over, I got back into my jeep and drove, and even though it was late and I was exhausted from the long drive, I found myself cruising the streets of Philly after dark, looking at the neon signs on all of the little elicit, after-dark shops. You could watch a movie, buy ice cream, or get a lap dance here. Porn was available on every corner. I liked how limitless the possibilities were.

Eventually, something pulled me to the curb. I got out and walked across the street and found myself standing in front of a dark, boarded-up shop, the second half of a business duplex. I cupped my hands around my face to block out all of the neon lights and peered through the dirty window. I could see a big pig mural on the wall, just like in my waking dream.

The other half of the duplex was a modern Laundromat. I went to peer in there as well, because, as silly as it might sound, I've always loved Laundromats. I find them so strangely magical. The bright blue lights and churning machines remind me of a spaceship or maybe a discotheque from the 1970s.

I stood there a long time, watching the people in neat rows reading two-month-old magazines and feeding coins into hungry vending machines until a voice behind me said, "Oi, witchy, you got some spirits?"

Turning, I glanced around the street. My shoulders stiffened as I prepared to be rushed. But the street on my side was empty. A couple was walking down on the other side, but it was obvious they hadn't spoken. Then I looked down and saw a small brown mouse sitting up on the broken pavement in front of the abandoned shop. It was looking straight at me.

"Ginny will do," echoed the disembodied voice.

I continued to look around, but, after a moment or two, I realized the voice was coming from inside my head. The mouse was twitching its nose and glaring at me intently with its beady black eyes. My attention kept coming back to it. I thought of all of the weirdness I had experienced in my life and figured why the hell not?

Scooting down, I looked closely at the mouse, which did not run from me.

"Oi! If you ain't got no ginny, witchy, just say so."

"It is you," I sighed.

The mouse seemed to look deep into my soul…and then it turned tail and fled down the alley that ran alongside the abandoned shop.

I'd never met a talking mouse before, but I followed it around the bend and down a dark, weedy space. The alley was barely wide enough to get your shoulders through without brushing against the privacy fence that separated the property from the one next door, and the ground was all broken, wet concrete, making it treacherous, but I managed to catch a flash of the creature as it disappeared around the back of the building.

A narrow service alley ran behind the establishment, barely recognizable in the dim moonlight and the yellowish bulb of a single security light from the Laundromat next door. A weathered picket fence encased a large blue dumpster and what looked like the casing for a gas backup generator. Sprawled against the fence was a tall, immensely thin (and rather dodgy-looking) young man. He was bruised and battered and seemed to have a bloody hole in his side. The asphalt under him was damp with blood.

I'm not so stupid as to run up to a potential drunk or rapist, so I hung back near the employees' exit door and watched the mouse scamper over the man and crawl up the length of his body until they were practically nose to nose. I thought for sure the mouse was going to bite the man's face. Instead, the creature kind of shuddered and then fell over, dropping off the man's chest and to the ground, where it squirmed for a few seconds before climbing back to its feet and running off.

The man opened his eyes and turned his head. His eyes looked black like the mouse's eyes, and blood was dripping into them from a deep wound in his scalp. He'd been rolled pretty badly. "Oi, witchy," he said, voice weak. He flexed a hand toward me, "you got that gin for ol' Sebastian?"

"I don't have any gin," I explained.

By then, the man, Sebastian, had passed out again.

I pulled my cell phone out, ready to call for an ambulance, but then tucked it back into my pocket. Except for Nick, I'd never met another witch. Or whatever Sebastian was.

It was stupid, I know. I knew I shouldn't get involved with this strange man. But I really wanted to know what he was. I wanted to know if he was like me.

Approaching him was difficult. I kept expecting him to jump up and scare me like in a horror movie, but he never moved. It was harder still to get an arm around him and maneuver him around into a sitting position. Even though he looked like a bundle of sticks, he was tall and heavier than I expected. There was no way I was getting him down that long alley. That left me with the only remaining option I could think of.

Running back around to the front, I drove the jeep up the service alley, backed up as far as I was able to get to the fence, and then got out. Wrangling Sebastian into the jeep took some doing, but I managed it. I'm a lot stronger than I look. Still, I was left with the dilemma of what to do with him. I had no idea where he lived, and looking for a wallet or cell phone turned out to be useless. If he'd had either of those, the ones who had beaten him had taken it. I realized I had to do something with him before he stank up my car with the old fumes of gin and vomit.

I'd been running on instinct all day. This seemed just an extension of all of that. I drove Sebastian back to the motel room and, because it was late and I was on the ground floor, I managed to drag him in through the door without anyone noticing.

The question remained, though: Now what?

I didn't know if Sebastian was dangerous. Most witches are to some extent. I also didn't know if he would bleed to death if I did nothing. So, the first thing I did was lug him across the room by his shirt and then wrangle him into the big porcelain soaking tub in the bathroom. He filled the whole thing.

I checked out the hole in his side. It looked like a stab wound, but I didn't think it was too deep. I cleaned the blood away as best I could. He probably needed stitches, but I didn't have the skill—or the nerve, frankly—for that. After I got his dirty white dress shirt off—it had taken the brunt of the blood, booze, and vomit, I noted—I used butterfly bandages from the complimentary first aid kit to pull the wound closed and then, finally, bound the whole sordid thing with some toilet paper. Next, I cleaned the wound in his scalp, though that had long since stopped bleeding. When I was done, I closed the bathroom door, stuck a chair under it, and tried to get a few hours of sleep.

In the early hours of the morning, Sebastian knocked on the bathroom door and politely asked to be let out. He was badly hungover, with no memory of the knife fight he had lost the night before. He looked surprised that I had cleaned his wounds and given him a bed (or a tub) for the night. He was shocked that I had given a damn.

And I knew then that I'd made the right decision in saving him. He also asked if I had a "tipple," which I did not.

| 3 |

I WAS SHOPPING at Home Depot to pick out more paint, brushes, and that blue tape you use around the painting edges when it happened. I originally thought four cans would be enough to cover the nicotine-yellow walls of the tiny prep room at the back, but orangey-yellow bloodstains keep bleeding through. Sebastian had tasked me with the job of making the prep room as clean and sterile as possible for us while he dressed up the shop properly.

"A Liverpool sweet shop, witchy," he told me that morning when we woke up on cheap inflatable mattresses on the floor of the studio apartment above the shop. We dragged ourselves up. and I went to put coffee on in the galley kitchen. The studio apartment above the shop was virtually empty except for the coffee machine sitting on one lone chair and a broken-looking refrigerator gurgling worrisomely in the corner. We hadn't bought any furniture, and I wasn't sure when we would have the time (or cash) to do so. We sat on the bare wood floor and he showed me a diagram of how he wanted to set up our shop.

I was afraid he would make it look like some stodgy old Victorian shop but he had some pretty lit ideas that didn't require too many modifications. A full wall of glass jars behind sliding panes of glass, a large window display for our specials, the converted meat counter for the chocolates, fudges, and other perishables, and a number of large barrels on the floor for the honey-based "Brighton Rocks" he insisted I work on. He said they were delish.

I loved how bright and lighted and wide open his ideas were. The place was going to look practically space age. When I said as much, he touched his chest dramatically. "Oi," he said, "it ain't like I ain't been an interior designer."

"Along with the hundred other things you've done?" I pointed out, half-joking. According to Sebastian, he'd been a butcher, a baker, a cabaret singer, a street magician, and about a zillion other things. But I wasn't sure if I should take him seriously.

"What can I say? I'm one fucking talented bloke," he laughed.

"When you're not a drunken vagrant," I pointed out.

He pursed his lips. "Witchy, that was merely a blip in my otherwise spotless career history."

I loved how Sebastian could make me laugh at anything. It was like being with Josh again.

So, here I was, getting the paint and accessories he required. The white we'd bought wasn't working, so I was looking over different paint sample cards when I heard an argument break out in the next aisle over, the one with the brushes, paint thinners, and tarps.

A man with a deep, threatening voice was saying, "...don't fucking touch it. Leave it alone! I swear to Christ, Emily..."

I didn't want to get in the middle of a couple's argument, so I shifted a paint can a little to the left and peered cautiously through the rack. A pretty young black woman with a ponytail was bent over a can of paint she'd dropped. The top had come off and red deck stain had splashed across the floor, making it look like a massacre had taken place. A large, burly man—her boyfriend or husband, I presumed—was grabbing her by the arm and roughly manhandling her. "Don't touch it, for fuck's sake! What the fuck is wrong with you?"

Emily mumbled an apology, and when she stood up straight, I saw she was at least six months pregnant. Her eyes were glued to the paint she'd dropped, and she looked like she might start bawling—like the spill was the end of the whole world. Her bae jerked her around and pulled her upright as if she was some kind of puppet. I felt a sympathetic pain in my own shoulder. Not psychological; I really do feel other people's pain sometimes.

Emily didn't cry out, but she did make a low moan. I saw she was wearing an ace bandage on her arm to keep it immobile, noticeable when her sleeve rode up.

"Go fucking back to the car, you stupid cow," said the man, keeping his voice pitched low.

"Brandon, I'm so sor—"

"I said get the fuck out of here." Brandon made a motion like he was going to backhand her, which made her cringe and sent a surge of primal red rage straight into my head like someone was pounding a nail into my skull. One of the heavy paint cans on his side of the rack flew off and hit him hard in the shoulder, making him stagger to the other side and collide with the opposite rack. He made a low roar in response but Emily didn't see any of it because she was already fleeing toward the exit of the store.

The man whipped around defensively, big hands clenched into fists as if he was convinced someone assaulted him—which, I suppose, was true. But now there are no paint cans to obscure his view. He could see me through the rack.

"The fuck you looking at, bitch?" he said.

I wanted to be witty and say something like, "Not much." That was something that Nick would do. He'd probably start a fight with the guy right there in the middle of Home Depot and put his fucking lights out. But I wasn't Nick. I never react until it's too late.

I was reminded of Mitchell. I knew he was cheating on me with every girl he came across. But because I was weak and afraid of losing him, I let him do it until I couldn't endure it any longer. Then, one night, when he started in on me...well, that was it. I don't have many memories of that night. All I know is that the next morning, the Fire Department found me and the whole apartment complex buried under burned stuff.

So, yeah, I'm a disgusting little church mouse most of the time. And I was one right then as I stood there, gaping at this piece of human garbage, my heart beating so hard he could probably hear it.

"Stupid cunt," he said before walking away.

Taking a can of white paint, I checked out and walked as quickly as possible to my jeep. I was loading it in when I spotted Emily crying in a sedan two cars down. I thought it was pretty damned unfair of fate to throw her into my path again. I was being a good girl, keeping my nose clean. Closing the hatch of the jeep, I sighed and fished my cell phone out to find the name of a local woman's shelter. I took a paint sample out of my pocket and wrote the address and phone number in a blank spot. Bae didn't seem to be around, so I hurried over to the sedan and knocked two knuckles against the glass.

Emily looked up with large, nervous eyes. She didn't seem willing to roll down the window even for another woman, so I smiled and pantomimed her rolling it down.

After a few tense seconds, she relented but didn't say anything.

"I'm sorry," I tell her. "I know what you're going through. Take this." I handed Emily the card with the information for the shelter on the back.

She looked at it as if it might poison her. Her lips moved, but it took a second for her small, scratchy voice to emerge. "Brandon won't like this. He won't stand for it." She tried to give me back the card.

I look at the paint sample. It was a bright mustardy-yellow color I'd picked out called, rather ironically, *Giallo*. For one second I had a flash—yellow wallpaper in a tiny bathroom with Emily on the floor, her body pouring out gouts of blood while she cried out to no one for help. "Please take it," I begged her. "Something bad is going to happen." I nodded at her pregnant belly. "It's going to happen to you *and* to him if you don't do something."

Looking pale and terrified, Emily laid a hand protectively over her baby bump.

I didn't wait for her to take the card. I simply dropped it in her lap and stood back as she rolled the window back up.

I never learned what happened to Emily and her baby, but I also never saw anything in the local papers or on TV to suggest she was hurt as in my briefest of visions. That meant I had done a good thing. Right?

| 4 |

I DIDN'T TELL Sebastian about the incident. Mostly because I was afraid he'd scold me for stepping into a situation I knew nothing about—even though I'd done the same for *him*.

But another reason had to do with Sebastian himself. Aside from Josh, I'd never had a best friend, and even though I enjoy the occasional sexual encounter, I don't like to become romantically involved with any of my partners. Nick was the exception that proved the rule. I'd loved Nick—or thought I did—and I *still* didn't tell him even half of the things I'd experienced. Some people like to overshare. I don't share at all. Never have. Maybe that's why my relationships never work out.

But Sebastian knew something was bothering me, because the following day, while we were installing the shelves of the display rack, he stayed unnaturally quiet. Around noon, I finally caved—mostly due to being hangry and having had no breakfast—and said, "So, yeah. I almost got into a fight at the Home Depot yesterday."

"I didn't say a bloody word."

"But you thought it."

"I thought no such thing," he insisted as he picked up the hammer and looked at one of the supports. Then he turned and pointed the tool at me. "You can't save the world, you know."

His ability to pick up on certain things is uncanny.

"I saved you!" I perched on the lone stool in the whole place and grabbed a bottle of water from off a counter. Maybe if I stayed better hydrated, I'd learn to keep my mouth shut. "I should have left you a rat!"

"Oi! I was never a rat!" He shook the hammer. "And you are changing the subject!"

"We got any petty cash?" I said, deliberately changing the subject. "I need food."

"You're the money witch," he told me, going back to the shelves. "How much do we have?"

I dug out enough for some Tai from the dump around the corner. Petty cash was running perilously low these days. When I started this venture, I sank everything I'd gotten from the club into it. I had this vision that it would all work out. That it really couldn't *not* work out. I deserved for it to work out. But now I wasn't so sure.

Another thing I couldn't discuss with Sebastian. He was counting on me to make the shop work so we both didn't wind up on the street. He'd probably survive it, but, for me, it would be the end of my Hobbit adventure. I'd have to crawl back to Blackwater and my old job slinging hash at Molly's Steakhouse, and I just couldn't do that.

So, I spend the evening and part of the night going over the finances and my business plan. I ran the numbers over and over. Five hundred grand wasn't that much money in the greater scheme of things—not when it came to leases, insurance, property taxes, repairs, and supplies. I didn't think we'd have enough to do all of the modifications we wanted. We might have to open early just to turn a profit before the money ran out.

Maybe I'd made a terrible mistake. Wouldn't be the first time.

| 5 |

I JERKED AWAKE at the sound of loud voices.

It was still dark out, but there were flashing lights in the windows overlooking the delivery alley and I heard the staticky sounds of a police ban radio. As the red and blue lights strobed through the tiny, empty studio, I caught a glimpse of Sebastian in rumpled clothing and fallen suspenders standing to one side of a window, peering out.

I sat up and he turned and put a finger to his lips.

Dragging my warm blanket along, I stumbled to the window and looked down.

The place was crawling with police. Several vehicles were parked at both ends of the alley. I saw black and whites, an ambulance, and—I think—a black coroner's van, though it was hard to tell in the dark. On the other side of the privacy fence, I spotted people on the street trying to get a glimpse of what was going on.

"Holy shit," I whispered. My first thought was that some bum got rolled in the alley behind our place. But the police presence seemed a bit heavy for that.

Together, we sank to the floor on either side of the window and just looked at each other.

"Some gang hit?" Sebastian suggested. We both knew how rough this part of town was.

"I don't know. Are there any gangs in a war?"

Sebastian opened his mouth to answer when we both heard banging on the back door downstairs. We jumped at the sound, but the man politely announced himself as Sergeant Detective Something Something and asked us to open up. When we didn't immediately answer, he kept banging.

"You should answer that," he said.

"Why do I have to answer it? You're the guy."

"I'm suspicious looking."

"You don't have any warrants, do you?"

He shrugged.

"Oh, for fuck's sake!" I didn't want to do this. I'd had a few run-ins with the law, none of them good. The first time was when the apartment complex I was living in with Mitchell burned to the ground, but the authorities were more interested in knowing what started the fire and frustrated when the arson team couldn't pinpoint it. The second time was when one of the Arcana, the ancient order of angel-eaters, set me up for my roommate Tiffany's murder. That time, I wound up in the Carbon County lockup for almost three days, until Nick unraveled the whole mess and got me out. I'd never been mistreated by the police—I mean, I was a very white-looking girl and aware of the privilege that offered—but I had no fond memories of dealing with the fuzz.

Dropping the blanket, I grabbed a thick, insulated sweatshirt and shrugged it on over my T-shirt and boy shorts. Then I took the backstairs to the prep room, which connected to the delivery alley. When I opened the back door, a cold draft of air hit me and swirled around my ankles, reminding me that my legs and feet were bare.

The officer on the other side was a large, powerful-looking black man in plain clothes. Early forties, with just a touch of virile grey in his beard and at his temples. Handsome like Idris Elba. Intense dark eyes and a no-nonsense posture. His grey suit clung to his athletic build, and his afro looked regulation-perfect. He wore the kind of expression that suggested he'd seen a lot of shit but could properly compartmentalize it.

"Ms…Summers?" the officer said, briefly consulting the flip pad in his hand. "I'm Detective Miles McCall with the PPD." He showed me the gold badge around his neck as if I couldn't already see it. I noted the wedding ring on his finger. "Mind if we speak for a moment?"

I had a strong feeling about Detective McCall in that moment. I trusted him…and I had the impression he'd be important to me in some way.

Feeling a bit more relaxed about the situation, I pulled the door fully open and motioned him inside. "Sorry about the mess," I said even though it wasn't messy. A couple of ladders were set up, and some paint cans and their accessories were sitting on the workbench. But you have to say things like that to break the ice.

The detective glanced around, noting everything. "You bought the Pig Palace."

"Excuse me?"

McCall indicated the room with his pen. "This place had a real name—Bob's Place, I think—but everyone local called it the Pig Palace. Bob cut the best damned spare ribs."

I glanced at the old butcher stains I was still trying to cover on the walls. "Did you know…Bob?"

"No," he laughed, consulting the pad once more. He had a deep, warm laugh that felt like honey sliding over my body. "Vivian Summers, correct?"

"Yes." I managed to suppress a shudder that he should already know that.

Detective McCall directed those dark, penetrating eyes of his at me. Not predatory, but they could be, under the right circumstances.

I wondered if he knew about my record. I was suddenly very worried about that.

"Are you all right?" he asked, and his concern surprised me.

"Yes." I was suddenly aware that I was leaning against the workbench slightly, my posture a bit too inviting to rightfully call "decent."

But McCall seemed to enjoy the view. The coldness in the room had hardened my nipples, and they hurt as they rubbed against the material of my sweatshirt. Long ago, someone once called me a whore, and maybe they were right. I enjoy men. I enjoy having them look at me. But I don't mean to invite their perusal.

I stood up straighter. "How can I help you?"

He shook himself as if he was waking up from a spell. "We're canvassing the neighborhood and wondered if you'd seen or heard anything suspicious. Sometime around two in the morning, a crime was committed outside your establishment." He raised the notepad to show how all business he was, but it was too late. I knew he wanted me, and it gave me a little thrill to know that. Desire is a powerful tool. It makes people work against their best interest.

"Here?" I raised a hand to the edge of my T-shirt and gave it a little tug. He followed the motion. "We were asleep."

"'We?'"

I tried to determine if I heard any disappointment in his voice. "My partner and I."

I waited to see what response I'd get from that, but Sebastian interrupted us by stepping into the room. He pulled up his suspenders and gave them a loud snap to get the detective's attention.

"Help you, Officer?" he asked, and McCall narrowed his eyes and flared his nostrils slightly. It was a primitive, wolf-like response. Walking over to talk to my partner, McCall left me to glance out the door.

The alley had been taped up with yellow crime scene tape, and uniformed officers were stalking back and forth, speaking low into their radios. McCall still hadn't told me what happened, so I discreetly slipped out the door and into the narrow alley space. Barefoot and cold, I headed to where several men were standing around something crumpled on the ground in front of the generator unit. They were wearing jackets with POLICE and CORONER on them in big, contrasting letters. It made me walk a little bit faster.

I noticed the heap on the ground was wearing clothes like a man might wear, jeans and a T-shirt and some kind of leather jacket with patches on it. But what was inside didn't look human any longer, more like one of those anatomical dummies you see in science classes in college or at a doctor's clinic.

Then I spotted the very real human eyes—wide open and staring up at me—and the mouth stretched wide open in a scream of perfect agony. After that, I noted the fleshless face and arms sticking out of the jacket sleeves, and the oily substance around the body that looked like spilled cover-up makeup. In fact, I was standing in a sticky pool of it, but it was not makeup.

It was human skin. Liquefied human skin.

Not fair! I thought as the officers dragged me back. *Things like this are only supposed to happen in fucking Blackwater!*

| 6 |

"I WISH YOU'D stop thinking about it," Sebastian said as we rolled the last of the wooden barrels into place on the shop floor. "It's not as if you can do anything about it anyway."

He might have been right, but that didn't mean I could just eject the image of the dead man's raw, red-meat face and hands from my brain. I rubbed my hands on my jeans as I stood up. "I wish you'd stop crawling around inside my head, but that's not going to happen anytime soon, either."

"You know you are lovely when you are sarcastic," he remarked.

"Do tell." I left the main floor to step into the prep room and check on my honeycomb molds, pulling on an apron as I went. It was a heavy-duty apron for candy making, with a thick lining and sleeves. It went on sort of like a surgeon's jacket and tied in the back because the last thing you want is to get bubbly, boiling hot candy on your skin.

Sebastian and I had decided to take out most of the wall separating the prep room from the rest of the shop and replace it with a long sliding pocket door. It opened up the limited space, making it seem much larger, which I liked. Why not allow customers to watch us make our confections in the back? It was like combining a sweet shop with performance art. The Hibachi grill down the street did something similar. Sebastian thought it was a great idea.

I pulled open the cooling drawers containing my honeycomb stick candy—one of my personal creations, and one Sebastian said he couldn't stop eating. Crystallized honey swirled in a rock-candy pattern around long, thin sticks that were themselves made of edible sugar. He called them "sweet wands," which I'd thought was a pretty fly name for them until I realized he was making a raunchy double entendre at my expense. ("Witchy, I just love to lick your sweet wands." It made me roll my eyes big time.)

Sebastian stepped into the room behind me—then stopped short when he spotted the beehive built into one wall. It was literally crawling with activity. "Did we really, really need that?" he asked.

"Yes," I answered for the hundredth time. "We really, really need it."

I'd invested in a "beecosystem," an indoor beehive—a bee cabinet fitted into one corner of the room. The outside was made of durable oak with a display window fitted into the front, making it look like some weird Victorian curio cabinet. Inside, there were thousands of worker bees frantically building honeycombs, making nursing cups, raising little bees, and producing the honey I needed for my hard candy. I could easily slide the racks of honeycomb out of the cabinet and back in again, and, since bees are my familiars, I never needed to fog them or wear protective gear.

Occasionally, an errant bee would find its way into the shop, but since they were my animals to call, they never created any kind of havoc. Instead, they just landed somewhere in the prep room and waited for me to collect them and return them to the hive.

My bees had never stung anyone. They weren't aggressive honeybees. But that didn't mean they didn't freak Sebastian out—which was funny. He couldn't die in any traditional sense, but he wouldn't go anywhere near the hive.

"Wands!" he gasped when he spied the set candy.

He tried to grab one, but I slapped his hand away. "Stop eating our profits!"

Sebastian pouted, looking cartoonishly crestfallen.

"Go check your fudge!"

Sauntering off to the fridge like some wounded animal, he dutifully checked on his latest batch. While he was in there, he said, "It won't affect our grand opening. People die in this city all the time. I'm sure more than a few have died in our alleyway."

I winced internally at his tactless comment. The idea that our alley was a popular dying-off spot did not alleviate my concerns about our grand opening. Sebastian rightfully believed I was worried the incident would drive traffic away, but that wasn't my primary concern. The incident had already been pushed to the back pages, and I was confident no one would even remember it happened—certainly not the ones walking past our store every day and sometimes trying to peer under the edges of the white paper we'd taped over the display window.

Trouble followed me. Even as a girl, it trailed after me like a pet that wouldn't leave me alone. Ever since the incident, I'd become afraid that this was just the precursor to something bigger—and darker. I thought about the hex on the wall, and I wondered if it would be enough.

The little bell above the door tinkled, startling us both.

Sebastian smacked the back of his head on the roof of the fridge and muttered a curse before ducking out.

"Who the hell is that?" I asked, fiddling with the knot in my apron. "Did you leave the door unlocked again?"

"I don't know," he muttered. "Maybe."

Beyond the thin pocket door, I spotted a tall, thin shadow moving swiftly across the newly painted walls.

"Right, then. Let me sort the fella out."

While he was gone, I reached across the workbench and grabbed a French rolling pin from out of a nearby canister—just in case. I could use it to break the glass on the beecosystem if need be. And then...well, my familiars would do anything for me.

The bell tinkled again...and Sebastian was back, sliding the pocket door closed. He wore an apologetic little smile on his face as he plucked at his apron strings. "Left the bloody door open, I did. But the bloke was cool about it. Said he wished us luck." He paused for dramatics. "He knew your name."

I stared at him wordlessly for several seconds, wondering who in Philly it could be. I didn't have any friends here. "What did he look like?"

Sebastian raised his hand a couple of inches above his own head. Sebastian is tall, so he was indicating the guy was a real monster. "Blond and youngish. Hot." He grinned. "Real heartbreaker."

My heart thudded quickly. Dropping the rolling pin, I dashed out into the shop and fiddled with the front door lock until I got it open. It was old-fashioned and tended to stick—something else that needed updating. Stepping out onto the cracked pavement, I searched around, but I didn't spot anyone even approaching that description.

"Nick!" I called for the hell of it. But no one answered. I did get an odd look from the woman who ran the Laundromat next door. She was a thin, widowed Muslim woman with three children, and she was sweeping leaves out of the doorway and staring at me as though I might be a little touched in the head.

But then she smiled brightly and walked over to extend her hand. "Hi! I'm Safa," she said brightly, looking over my shop. "Oh, wow! You bought the Pig Palace!"

| 7 |

IT WAS TWO days before our Grand Opening. According to Sebastian, the shop was "sorted" exactly as he wanted it to be. And it was beautiful.

It felt miles wide even though it was only a tiny space and lit up like a mother ship with dozens of string lights. Hard candy in wrappers filled the barrels on the floor, and honey wands, swirly sticks, lollipops, and other gourmet confections bloomed in the jars along the lighted display wall. The confection counter housed the perishables that Sebastian was personally responsible for—cordials and fondant fancies and fudge and chocolate pops. We had dedicated half a wall to a contents menu and special order list. Chocolate boxes with the Confessions logo filled the display window. I'd even ordered cute little white bears in shirts that had our business name and website on them. I could stick a small lollipop into the velcroed paws and give them out as freebies.

I'd personally taken care of the newspaper and online announcements, and the *Philadelphia Tribune* promised it would be here to cover the event. We'd be giving away free samples all day. Of course, the local neighborhood seemed particularly keen on that. I was *so* broke, it wasn't even funny. Not for the first time, I was concerned about this little endeavor of mine. As a result, I kept second-guessing myself. I was exhausted. If this failed...well, I was trying not to think about that. I had no backup plan for my life, and it was no joke to say I would rather die than go back to Blackwater.

I sat down on a high stool near my beecosystem and watched my bees work. The low hum of the hive always soothed me like some long-forgotten lullaby. But then I suddenly started to cry.

Sebastian stepped into the room. I could see the toll this had taken on him. His shoulders were more hunched and there were dark, sleepless rings under his eyes. He looked…older. It reminds me that he was likely ancient. Still, he'd put so much faith in me—in *this*—and I couldn't even imagine why.

His dark brows knitted together and he moved forward to put a hand on my shoulder. "Oi, what's the matter, witchy?" he said in a soft, almost fatherly, voice.

I touched his hand touching my shoulder. He didn't realize how close to the hive he was. And when a honeybee appeared out of nowhere and landed on my other shoulder, he didn't even react.

"I'm just tired," I said, sucking up the tears. "Been up all night."

"Go have a lie-down. I'll finish up here."

Maybe I *was* tired. I got up and went upstairs to the loft to crash out for a few hours.

We still hadn't gotten around to getting any furniture. Frankly, I was too broke. But, hopefully, that would change soon. I threw myself down on the air mattress and lay there for a while, trying to sleep. But my mind wouldn't stop reeling with all of the possible disasters that could occur in the next few days. I also couldn't stop thinking about that mysterious man who'd gotten into the shop. Friend or foe?

What if he was connected to the murder of that man in our back alley? They say criminals always return to the scene of their crimes…

The possibilities were endless, and they haunted me. But as I lay there, I felt the little tagalong honeybee emerging from my hair where she'd been hanging out and crawling slowly across my face. A normal person would have freaked, but I felt a wave of comfort and peace as she moved along my cheek and reached my left eye. She tapped my lid as if to say *Sleep now*.

But I couldn't. I had this knot in my stomach that told me something bad was coming. Something inevitable. Something that would change me forever.

After tossing and turning for an hour, I gave up on sleep and sat up in bed. My bag was within reach. I dragged it over and took out the photo album I'd brought with me from Blackwater. I spent some time paging through it. Birthdays, anniversaries, Christmases. An occasional party I couldn't place. My parents were always big on taking pictures to memorialize every event, but the sight of them hurt me in ways I'd forgotten about.

Stan and Kathy Summers had meant well when they adopted me. They'd wanted children after Josh, but Kathy had to have an emergency hysterectomy not long after Josh was born, so that blew their plans for a large family to pieces. Adoption was the logical next step. But after I arrived in their lives, they decided it was a mistake on their part. I've never held that against them. They never should have adopted something like me. It wasn't their fault.

My parents had loved me—or, at least, they'd tried to. But we were never friends, and the older I got, the more difficult it was for us to get along. On a whim, I started picking pictures of Josh out of the album, and when I was done, I closed it and just looked at the ragged soft material cover and the *Our Family* engraved in gold leaf on it. I had never belonged with these people. They were strangers to me.

The last time I saw my parents, we were fighting. My dad called me a liar for the things I'd said. I needed therapy, my mom insisted. I needed to get my head straightened out. That was the last thing he said to me. "Vivian, go call your shrink and get your head straightened out!"

The next day, my parents were gone. Head-on collision with a drunk driver. I remembered the police officer who came to our house to tell us the bad news. He kept telling me over and over how fast it was, how they hadn't suffered at all. Like that made it better somehow.

It seemed the most natural thing in the world to get up and take the album downstairs. It was dark by that time and the shop was dim and empty. Sebastian had left a hastily scrawled note on the workbench that said he'd gone out to some local pub but that there was some cold pizza in the fridge if I wanted it.

I ignored the pizza and went out into the alley where that strange man died. *Was murdered.* I might as well be honest about it. Nobody flayed themselves alive. I was wearing pants and crocs this time, but I still felt a chill as the door clumped closed behind me.

The dumpster was maybe two hundred feet away. I could be there, dump the album, and be back inside in seconds if I hoofed it. But before I could take a single step, I recognized movement at the end of the alley, a sort of shifting darkness that brought me to an instant standstill.

A slender figure in black stood up too quickly as if I'd interrupted it. It was crouched over the place where the man had been murdered. The figure looked female, but I couldn't be certain. It was too dark and the eaves of the shop cast long shadows. But as the figure turned to stare at me, I saw her eyes. They glowed with a faint pale light in the dark.

The spit in my mouth dried up and I lurched backward, my back hitting the closed door. My mind screamed the word *witch* so loudly that I jerked from the assault of it.

The witch's glowy eyes narrowed in annoyance. I'd interrupted her private ceremony. Turning, she fled around the side of the building, her shoes tapping out a rhythm on the wet, broken asphalt.

I had a decision to make in that moment. I could let the witch go and go back inside and pretend the incident never happened. Or I could try to catch up with her. Maybe she knew something about the man who'd died here.

No. I *knew* she knew something.

Dropping the photo album, I took off after her.

| 8 |

THE WITCH WEAVED in and out of alleys and cross streets, sticking to the darker parts, making it difficult for me to keep up with her. It was obvious she knew the city like the back of her hand. I was still learning the lay of the land.

We were leaving the lighted business corridor and I saw more schools, libraries, and medical and law offices. The buildings looked older, more elaborate, made of aged brick, with elaborate turn-of-the-century iron fences around them. The library had stone lions out front. I spotted the witch disappearing down a side street that ran alongside it. She was moving in a fluid way that was unnerving to watch. As she passed under a streetlight, it popped and went dark. Others followed. I start following the darkened lamps, listening for her footfalls against the cobblestone sidewalk.

Eventually, I spotted a tall building ahead with a cross on its steeple—one of several "mini-cathedrals" that the city is famous for. The woman in black disappeared around the side of the building and down some steps to a basement door.

I slowed as I approached the looming red-brick building. It had engraved scrollwork around the doors and the windows were painted with sad-looking saints. A huge stone cross stood silent sentinel out front, lovingly draped in purple cloth. It was a beautiful building, but I could already feel the drag on my soul and I wasn't even standing in its shadow yet.

One of the most important things that Nick ever taught me was to avoid places like this. He even took me to a church in Blackwater just to show me how it felt—which was somewhere between having a bad flu and a lead weight dropped on my back while meat hooks were being sunk deep into my skin. Then there was the dry, ruthless nausea like someone stuck a cold spoon down my throat.

As I cautiously approached the building, I felt a cold sickness growing in my stomach like bad menstrual cramps. I veered around the side of the building and found the steps that led to the side door. I didn't feel *better* here, but the nausea wasn't so bad if I stayed out of the shadow of the giant cross. I spotted a pair of doors painted blue with white crosses on them. I stopped a few feet away and just looked at them, wondering if I'd burn if I touched them.

The idea was both frightening and depressing. Evil things burned at the touch of the cross. But I didn't want to be an evil thing...

I started to back up when the door swung open. A man stood there—a young priest in a black cassock and white Roman collar. He wasn't tall, but there was something subtlety virile about him. His dark, lush hair was perhaps a little too long for regulation, and it curled slightly around his ears. He had the most beautiful black Hispanic eyes. His soft, full lips and the shadow of his strong beard made my heart trip a second.

"Are you here for the group?" he asked.

I didn't know what he was talking about, but I loved the musical sound of his voice and the way he rolled his *R's*. And I did want to see inside the church. I needed to speak to the witch hiding in the Catholic cathedral, so I said, "The group? Yes."

He pushed the door open for me. "Please, come in. You haven't missed it. I'm Father Matthew Garcia. You must be new. Call me Father Matt."

"All right."

I slipped past Father Matt and onto a small landing connected to two narrow, twisting staircases going up and down. The tiny landing/foyer was at a lower level than the rest of the church. I could hear someone playing the organ above in what I assumed was the cathedral. But the other staircase curled down into the basement, and that's where the priest went.

He turned once to say to me, "I'm glad you found us."

I silently followed Father Matt down the narrow staircase. The basement smelled a little damp, but not unpleasant. It reminded me of the rec rooms in my friends' houses when I was growing up.

The staircase opened up into a large, all-purpose basement. The floor was tiled and the cinderblock walls were painted with flowery murals and words of inspiration in both English and Spanish. I wondered if Father Matt painted them. There were posters for different church activities—bingo, bazaars, charity dinners, potlucks—plus a few inspirational ones. I felt I could breathe a little better as I stepped into the room.

Near the back, a long trestle was set up for coffee and donuts. A collection of a dozen or so people sat in folding chairs in a wide circle. I suddenly realized I didn't belong here.

"You don't have to talk. You can just listen," Father Matt said invitingly. He spoke softly as if he was afraid he'd spook me.

The people in the circle were of all ages, all sexes, and all colors. I didn't see the woman in black but I discreetly moved to take an empty seat anyway. The women gave me small nods. The men cruised me, trying not to be obvious about it. Father Matt took the empty seat next to me and that makes me feel better—more protected. Though if he knew who I was—what I was—I didn't think he would be so welcoming. Thankfully, he launched into a warm but surprisingly secular welcome to everyone here tonight.

I sat there quietly and listened as a few in the circle stated their first names and announced their addiction. They talked about their week, and what they'd seen and done. Their stories weren't as sad as I expected. I could tell their daily minutia was immensely important to them.

Only one man stood out—Marcus. He talked about how he used the money his mom lent him to buy heroin instead of milk for his son. He made his son drink sugar water this week. He stopped speaking after a while and just sat staring at his untied sneaker. No one else in the circle said anything for several seconds, but the priest broke the silence by concluding the meeting and by talking about learning and coping skills and how no one was alone. He finished by reminding everyone to check in with their sponsor.

After it was over, the group folded their chairs and hung them neatly on the wall. Then they moved to the snack table. They talked in small groups of two or three. Marcus cried on his sponsor's shoulder and the man led him away.

By then, I was feeling more uncomfortable than ever. I started drifting toward the door, but Father Matt caught up with me. "Would you like some coffee? You look cold."

I let him lead me to the table. I probably look homeless. I had stepped outside the shop in just Hello Again Kitty zombie pajama bottoms, a white tank top, and an open brown plaid shirt, the stuff I'd been sleeping in before I went out to dump the photo album. He made me a cup of hot coffee and handed it to me, then suddenly took it back. "Milk and sugar?"

"Just black," I said.

While I drank the coffee, he told me what days of the week the group met. "They're good people, all of them," he explained.

I thought about Marcus. Was he a good person?

I wasn't judging. I was hardly an angel. But I was curious.

"I'm not an addict." I thought about that a moment before adding, "I don't know why I came here tonight."

Father Matt nodded sagely. "Maybe you were just lonely?"

The cross around his neck flashed, distracting me. I put the coffee down. I didn't know why I was still here. I was about to leave when the door to the stairs opened and the woman I was following walked in. She was middle-aged, Hispanic like Father Matt, and wearing a long black habit and a black and white coif on her head. She wasn't wearing the coif when I followed her. But now, at last, I knew why she was wearing all black.

The sight of her froze me on the spot, but if she recognized me, she didn't react at all. Father Matt excused himself and turned to her. They passed a few words about a spaghetti supper on Sunday. He called her Sister Marie and asked if she'd found the plastic tablecloths that had gone missing.

"Yes, Father," Sister Marie said, her eyes on him—not me. But now I could feel her need to shift her attention to me, however briefly.

When Father Matt finally walked away, Sister Marie gave me her full attention for one whole moment before turning on her heel and leaving the room via the stairs. I glanced at Father Matt. He was speaking to someone else. So, I followed Sister Marie up the stairs to the church.

The cathedral had an arching, ribbed ceiling, but its size was relatively small compared to the gigantic ones I remembered from when I was a child in Catholic School. Sister Marie walked down the central aisle between the pews, genuflected and crossed herself, and then continued on her way to the votive candles set up to one side of the altar.

I followed. The altar sported a large wooden cross with another silky white and purple cloth draped over it. The closer I got to it, the weaker I felt. I finally stopped about ten feet from Sister Marie, who was lighting a votive with a long matchstick.

"You're his daughter," she said without glancing up. She didn't even pretend to not know. "I didn't know one of your kind could enter a house of God."

"I don't know what you're talking about."

"Very well. We won't speak of it."

I took a step toward her, then stopped as a wave of dizziness nearly overwhelmed me. "How do you know?"

Sister Marie finally looked up. She was pretty but there were lines around her eyes and mouth. I could tell she'd been around the block a few times. "We all know."

"'We?'"

"We who serve the craft. We know *you*, Princess."

I laughed. "You're a nun *and* a witch?"

Sister Marie scowled as if she couldn't understand how the two could be mutually exclusive. "I am whatever is required of me." Setting down the matchstick, she gave me a critical look. "What are you doing with that sad, drunken little necromancer? Seems a bit beneath you, Princess."

"Sebastian?"

"Is that what the pathetic creature calls himself now?"

That irked me. "He's a good man."

"He's not a *man*, but, yes, Princess, whatever you say."

Her tone pisses me off. "Don't call me that." I took another step toward her, my fists clenching. I didn't feel the pain of the cross as much.

Sister Marie looked surprised that I'd made it this close to the altar—and her. She glanced around the cathedral, but we were alone. There was no one here to rescue her.

"Why were you in the alley behind my shop?"

Her mouth moved but nothing came out for a second. Then she cleared her throat. "I wanted to see the place where he was found."

"Who? The man who died?"

"He wasn't a man!" she spat angrily and clenched her fist against her chest. "That...*creature*...was never a man."

She spat it all out at once. "He violated and then murdered one of my girls. Sonja. Beat her to death. I barely recognized her sweet face when he finished with her." She glanced down. "God help me, but I don't care if He damns me for it. I'm glad that beast is dead. I hope he died in shrieking agony."

She said something else in Spanish that sounded like a curse, but I couldn't follow it. I don't know that much Spanish even though I took it in high school. She even spat on the floor.

I blinked at that, shocked by her anger. "The way he looked...I think you got your wish, Sister."

"Good," Sister Marie snarled. "It is the least God can do for Sonja—and for the other girls he violated." Lifting her head slightly, she announced, "You must excuse me, Princess. I have duties to perform. And Sonja's funeral to plan."

As she moved past me, I moved to stop her. "Why didn't you go to the police? Tell them about Sonja?"

"The police," Sister Marie laughed bitterly. "Sonja was from Guatemala. Illegal. Do you think they care about someone like her?"

I didn't know how to answer that.

She pushed past me and headed back down the aisle.

I turned to follow her.

She stopped and turned to face me one last time. "I'm sorry, Princess," she said, sounding sincere. Her face was clouded with rage. "I don't mean to seem disrespectful to someone of your breeding, but, please, there is nothing you can do. Forget about all of this. And forget about me." She nodded at the cathedral rearing high above us. "None of this concerns you. Return to your home and your life and your little necromancer."

"How...many of you know who I am? Do you...? I mean..."

"You have nothing to fear from us, Lady Lucifer." Her voice was soft and even reverent in tone. "But, yes, we know. The whole city knows who you are, Daughter of Darkness."

Her words filled me with a cold dread and a fear of things to come.

9

THE DAY OF our Grand Opening, I got up at the crack of dawn, went downstairs, and tied on my apron. I checked on the candy I set the night before. I looked over Sebastian's chocolates. I even ducked low to look in on my honeybees. Everything was going to plan.

I stepped into the display room and flipped on the spacey blue uplights. The jars of candy behind the glass walls shimmered, and the display window was full of perfectly boxed chocolates and teddy bears. The Confessions sign glowed faintly above the hex on the wall.

I thought about what Sister Marie called me while we were standing in the church the other day. A Princess. Yes, a Disney Princess...from Hell.

I was only twenty-eight, but a lifetime of bad things had happened to me. Now, for the first time, I was happy, even if I *was* hanging out with a drunken necromancer who was perhaps beneath my station. I realized—maybe for the first time—that life could be good.

There was a knock on the door of the shop. My heart fluttered. Our first customer!

I virtually flew to the door and unlocked it, flipping the sign to OPEN. The glass was decoratively frosted, so I couldn't see more than an outline. It looked like a man.

I threw the door open...but no one was standing there.

No one was walking by. No one standing by the curb, waiting for the bus. No vehicles of any kind. And, this early in the morning, that seemed suspect.

I felt the first twinge of concern and rushed out of the shop and looked around. No joggers. No dog walkers. No one going to work. There were several cars parked on the curb, but no one was in them. I checked the Laundromat next, but the building was completely empty, though I spied laundry churning in a dryer.

Turning back to the street, I walked to the curb and glanced up and down Broad Street. The florist, the bakery, and the restaurant across the street were all lit up. The nail salon was full of welcoming light. But I saw no one inside any of the establishments.

Something terrible had happened during the night while I was asleep.

As a knot of panic tightened my throat, I stood in the middle of the deserted street and shouted *hellos* up and down the corridor, but no one answered. The street was empty of life. Distantly—very distantly—a dog barked.

I tried to decide what to do next. Call the police, call my friends...run screaming down the street...?

But while I was busy working through my panic, I heard a low-grade thump that sent a shockwave through the street under my feet. I swung around to find the source of the noise, my eyes and mouth wide open. I spotted an enormous fiery pillar mushrooming up into the lower atmosphere like a nuclear device had gone off. The sky immediately turned blood red, and I could smell ozone and burned stuff even from here. Cracks streaked across the asphalt in front of me from the impact, making crazy patterns around my feet.

"What the hell?" I heard myself shout as I started running down the street in the direction of the fire. I knew, intellectually, that that was probably not a good idea. But I had to see. I had to know what had happened to all of the people.

I reached an intersection where the traffic light was blinking all kinds of crazy colors and turned left toward the cloud. I passed endless rows of dead, empty vehicles in the street and dozens of lighted but unoccupied shops.

Finally, I stopped dead in my tracks. The street was cracked and jacked up in places like a minefield of jagged asphalt. Broken sewer pipes spewed noxious gases. Cars lay on their sides—those knocked over by the explosion. The buildings on both sides had caved in from the impact, and black smoke poured from them and filled the air, making it difficult to see clearly.

Amidst it all was a giant bonfire in the middle of the street that reached a hundred feet into the sky. I stood two or three hundred feet away, and I could still feel the excruciating heat as it prickled my face and eyes and danced along my exposed skin. I'd never seen such total and complete destruction. Not in real life. Philly looked like the Gaza Strip or something out of a post-apocalyptic movie. I wondered if a bomb had been dropped on the city or if we were fighting a war I didn't know about.

I took a hesitant step toward the ruins, wondering if anyone had survived it...and then stopped when my foot came down on something jagged and hard that crumbled. I looked down and saw I'd stepped on what looked like the burned remains of a human rib cage. The sight made me jump back. But, as the black smoke slowly swirled away on a rising gale of wind, I saw how much worse it was.

Bones litter the ground at my feet. At first, I thought there were only a few, but as I looked more closely, I realized the bones numbered in the thousands and formed a path leading toward the pillar of fire. And all of them were singed and blackened as if they had been through a crematorium.

The smoke finally lifted and I saw that just beneath the fire, feeding its greedy need to burn, were more skeletons. So many more. What looked like millions of human bones were piled up as high as a small building. The bones of every person in this city. Maybe in the world.

I stood there, gaping at this impossibly huge altar of burning human remains, thinking I'd gone mad. I shook my head to clear the image. This must be a waking nightmare. But the image didn't disappear. I could feel that this was real, and, suddenly, the panic was clawing its way up my throat as it tried to escape my mouth in a primal scream.

It all grew even worse when the woman appeared, stepping right out of the fire but remaining untouched by it. Maybe I'd died and gone to hell. That was the only explanation. There was no way this was real. And, yet, it felt painfully—horrifically—real.

The woman stood proudly upon that enormous, burning Golgotha. She was supernaturally beautiful, standing at least eight feet tall. Her skin was brown like calfskin, and her hair was a blue-black skein of what looked like frayed silk that fell to her waist. Her body was encased in a tight white gown with bell sleeves and a slit up the side that went all the way to her waist. I could see she was unashamedly naked beneath the dress. On her head, she wore a giant golden headdress engraved to look like the rising sun and the long red feathers of some exotic bird stood up from it in a fan-like pattern. Her lips and the areas around her eyes were blackened with kohl, making them look endlessly deep and dark, like tarns into an unknowable future. But her eyes...oh my god. Her eyes were as huge and blind white as peeled eggs, and blood ran continuously from the corners like alien tears.

I couldn't help but be mesmerized by her awfulness, and, as she descended the mountain of bones—the skulls of which were acting as steps in a long, jagged staircase—I saw that where her bare feet touched them, they cracked open and small fires emerge.

Sister, she said in my head.

It was stupid, but I waited for her to come to me. A huge part of my brain screamed at me to run because I knew she was the one who had done this terrible thing, but my feet wouldn't move, and I couldn't seem to take my eyes off her.

I felt like my entire life had led up to this moment. I had always been destined to meet her.

She spread her arms as she reached me—a distinctly queenly gesture—and I saw she was wearing thick gold bracers on her forearms engraved with primitive and intricate flowers and birds. Some looked familiar like things I might have seen in a museum exhibit. Some might even have been wards and sigils.

The Aztec Queen stood there, towering over me. I could smell her—like rotting flowers, overly sweet, with an undercurrent of decay, and under that…fire and smoke. "Oh, my flower," she said, but her lips didn't move at all. I was only hearing the echo of her voice in my head. "It is done."

"Yes," I agreed even though I had no idea what I was agreeing to.

"And now we can be one."

She smiled down at me, her mouth stretching unnaturally wide, and more of those bloody tears fell down her cheeks and speckled her beautiful white linen gown. I saw something in her mouth that looked like long black petals spreading outward at both corners of her lips. She had no teeth, just black petal things. From down in her throat, I heard the cry of birds as if she had one stuck down there somewhere. She was beyond horrifying. And yet, I felt a strange peace overwhelm me when she looked upon me.

She loved me. She desired me. We could be one.

I wanted that. I'd never wanted anything like I'd wanted that. Not the shop. Not Nick. Not even the freedom to choose my own path. All of that was worth sacrificing just so I could be with her.

"You understand at last, Daughter of Darkness."

Reaching out, she touched my face with just her fingertips. Her long nails, painted a burnished gold, burned coolly against my skin. The sensation was incredibly soothing, and yet, her touch also excited me. She gave me her black lotus smile and nodded as if she enjoyed this power she had over me.

"You are so beautiful, little flower. So pure."

No one had ever called me that before. I'd been called a bitch, a slut. A man once called me the Whore of Babylon. But no one had ever called me pure. It wasn't something I was used to. It wasn't something I believed.

"One day you will see," she said as her hand dropped to the front of my shirt.

She undid the buttons and I felt the superheated air touch my skin as she pushed the shirt off my shoulders. I wasn't wearing any underwear, so my breasts were bare to her touch. She seemed to take great delight in them, tracing her long fingernails around one pebbled nipple until a low moan escaped my lips. Her touch was gentle but teasing. It immediately made me wet, and I could tell she knew what effect she was having on me.

It was odd, though, because I'd never been attracted to women. But with her, it seemed right. Everything seemed perfect.

"My dear little fire flower," she said, those silky black petals licking at the corners of her hungry mouth. "Will you be my bride?"

Her voice was musical in my head. I felt a dizzy combination of euphoria and desire. Yes, I wanted to be her bride. I wanted that more than anything.

I would do anything for her. My queen.

"Say it. Say the words, little flower."

"I…" Behind her, the city was burning. The bones we stood upon were burning. I was certain we were burning. I thought how this thing must have a terrible price. To be her bride. To be hers. What else must burn?

I had hesitated too long.

The Aztec Queen narrowed her bleeding eyes. "Say it!" Her voice was harsh now, scaring me.

I tried to retreat a step, but I found I couldn't seem to move my feet. I moaned in distress.

The blood started to flow more rapidly from her eyes. The petals around her mouth writhed in agitation. "Traitor," she said and closed her hand on my chest so it was a hard, rocklike fist.

Suddenly, I couldn't breathe. I gasped for air, but my lungs felt like they were full of concrete.

She gestured as though she was jerking something out of me.

I felt my flesh tear. The pain was sudden and unendurable. I screamed, but she kept plowing my chest open with that relentless gesture of hers, unzipping me from top to bottom. My blood splattered her face and dress, and the black petals licked at the crimson fluid hungrily. The bird trapped in her throat screamed with me as I slowly lost all strength and collapsed to my knees at her feet.

I could feel myself dying. With my last strength, I struggled to look up.

The disappointed Aztec goddess-queen was standing over me, holding my bleeding heart in her hand. Seeing it made me sad.

"Little flower, you could have had the world." And she squeezed my heart until it crumbled to dust in her hand.

My head dropped so I was looking at the cracked and burning asphalt beneath me. I started to choke. I gagged…and, suddenly, I heard that same bird twittering in my own throat. I could feel it fluttering in its panic. I couldn't remember how it got there, but I felt the wrenching pain of its horror at being trapped inside of me. I started clawing at my throat, trying to free it.

I'd never felt such horror.

Wicked witch, I thought. *I'm such a wicked, evil witch...*

Finally, after much struggling, I threw up the poor little bird, but it was all in bloody pieces as it flopped out of my mouth and onto the burning street...

| 10 |

"OI! WITCHY, WAKE up!"

I jerked awake, nearly swatting at the figure bending over me—then I realized it was Sebastian. My hand was up, poised to swipe at him, but he gently caught it and held my wrist before my nails could go for his face.

"Easy, there. You're having a nightmare," he explained.

"Oh." I lay there, staring up at him. "Jesus. Sorry."

"No need to be sorry," he said, letting go of my hand. "And I'm not Jesus."

I laughed at that, which sounded funny in the dark after such a violent nightmare. I sat up and saw I was sweating like a pig. Little droplets were even running down my cleavage.

He noticed, too. "Need a new shirt?"

"Please."

He walked to the basket of our clothes, which he'd brought in from the Laundromat earlier that day. They were a messy tangle and he couldn't seem to decide what was mine and what was his. Finally, he grabbed a random clean white T-shirt and threw it at me.

I thought it was likely his, but I didn't care. I peeled off the drenched one I was wearing and slid his on even though he was watching. I was not exactly concerned about Sebastian losing his mind over a pair of girl boobs. I instantly felt better for having clean clothes on. I noticed Sebastian sitting on the edge of his air mattress, watching me intently.

"What's the matter?" I asked. "Never seen tits before?"

He was quiet a long moment, and then he stated with a frown, "Pretty sure I had tits at least once."

"You don't remember?"

The little thought dimple between his eyebrows deepened. I'd only ever seen that once or twice when he was in deep thought—not a place he preferred to be. "Not really. I don't have a good long-term memory."

"Seriously?" I sat up and crossed my legs. "You don't remember?"

He made a vague gesture with one hand. "It's the witchery. It takes a toll on the selfie."

I felt sorry for him. He never talked much about his past. I used to think it was because he wanted to forget certain things, but maybe it was because there were things he couldn't remember. I'd also noticed that his accent wavered. Usually, he sounded like he had tripped out of BBC One, but sometimes he sounded Australian, and I'd also noticed he rolled his "R"s the way Russian and Slavic people did.

"And you," he said, pointing. "What did the witchery show you?"

I recoiled in my covers. "It was just a bad dream."

"I think not." He swirled a finger. "You were all glowy."

"Glowy?"

"Like a bleedin' nightlight."

I sighed. I didn't think I'd win this argument.

He got up. "Right, then. Putting the kettle on."

I waited while he brewed tea on the little propane burners on the kitchen counters. This place didn't even have a working stove, and if we didn't slide into the black after Opening Day, we'd never be able to afford one.

He brought two mugs of chamomile tea over and sat down on the bed beside me. "Spill."

I sipped the tea and licked my parched lips. Even though I'd only just woken up, parts of the dreams were already falling away from me and I had to struggle to remember anything. The bird in my throat stuck with me the most. I must have sounded like a madwoman as I explained the dream to him—what I could recall of it.

He was silent for several long moments after I finished. He sank his lower face into the mug a moment before mumbling, "Doesn't sound like a dream to me. More like a scry."

"You mean a prophetic dream."

Sebastian shrugged. "If you like."

God, I hoped not. Maybe I was just stressing over Opening Day.

"But..." It took me a moment to breathe through my sudden spike of fear. "...I died in it, Sebastian." I swallowed hard. That lump was back in my throat as it was in my dream. "We all did. And that strange woman was the one who killed us all."

| 11 |

I KNEW IT was just a dream. I knew I shouldn't listen to Sebastian about it being a scry. But, of course, I couldn't stop thinking about it.

As I finished the final touches on the shop—attaching the blue and white balloons to the display window and studying our welcome pamphlets/menu, searching frantically for any typos—I couldn't stop thinking about the burning street, the terrifying woman, and the way she made me feel. I couldn't help cringing inside when I remembered how she looked at me with such appetite...and disappointment. In my dream, I was her servant, her chosen. But I'd rejected her, failed her, and she'd killed me.

It was just a dream. Probably the result of too many post-apocalyptic horror movies on Netflix and too much stress in getting the shop ready. But it felt so real. It felt like something that had happened to me already. Or something that would soon.

That was what frightened me the most. The idea that we really didn't have that much control over our fate. That no matter what we did, what good life decisions we made, crappy things were going to happen to us no matter what. The idea was fatally depressing.

"Chocolate crosses," Sebastian said when I stepped into the prep room. He swiveled around on his stool and offered me a keen look. "It's almost Easter. We should do them. That and chocolate lambs."

As I tied my apron on, I stated firmly, "You can do chocolate bunnies or lambs or whatever. But no crosses." I drew the line at confections that could burn the skin off my fingers if I accidentally touched them.

Putting his hands on his knees, he straightened up. "Did you get *any* sleep, witchy?"

I turned and gave him a smile to make up for my snippy tone of voice. "I'm fine, Sebastian. Just not fond of crosses."

"Bad childhood experience with priests?"

"Something like that."

Later that day, a food critic for the *Metro* newspaper dropped by unexpectedly. I expected her to be super bitchy like you see in rom-coms, but she was surprisingly nice. After taste-testing a number of Sebastian's chocolate creams, she moved on to my hard candy. She loved the Sweet Stix—formerly the honey wands. I had changed the name at the last moment because I was afraid it would lead to unpleasant double entendres.

"These are gorgeous," she told me, and went on to use words like "rustic," "malty," and "crunchy-natural." I showed her the beecosystem. She was on cloud nine and started writing frantic notes in her little notebook.

Sebastian and I high-fived each other after she left. We would be getting an important review on the day of our Grand Opening. Things finally seemed to be coming together, and, for a little while at least, I forgot all about the nightmare.

But then, around ten o'clock, as we were plodding upstairs to get some much-needed rest, I started thinking about the dream again. And the woman. I was afraid to sleep. Afraid I'd see her again.

Sebastian, the bum, dropped right off to sleep and, within the hour, I heard him snoring away. But I remained awake, staring up at the ceiling and wondering what I could do to stop what might or might not be happening.

When I looked over, I saw the time on my cell phone read 11:38. I didn't think I was getting any sleep tonight, so I got back up, dressed in some loose sweats, and threw on a heavy down jacket against the April night chill. Then I went downstairs and let myself out the back door.

For a while, I stood over the spot where the man died, skinned alive while still in his clothes. I kept thinking I'd get some kind of psychic vibration, or maybe a picture in my head of what happened, but tonight, like every other night I'd tried this, I just felt empty. The asphalt was a little stain-darkened, but there was no psychic "residue" to read. Or, I was just not powerful enough to tap into it, which was possible.

I walked down the alley that connected to the main avenue. From there, I kept walking. Even though it was a Thursday, the street was jumping with people. Some were walking to or from the restaurants and bistros that line this part of the street. Others were ducking into the theater where they were playing a romantic comedy starring Sandra Bullock. I smelled popcorn as I passed. Ahead, some tough-looking kids were muscling up the street. They made a rude comment as I passed them, but I ignored them. They were stupid kids. Hopefully, they would grow out of their moronic behavior.

The florist was next. There were pretty flowers in the windows, exotic types I couldn't even guess at. They made me think of my dream and the Aztec Goddess's words to me.

"*Say it. Say the words, little flower.*"

"*You understand at last, Daughter of Darkness.*"

I stared at some fancy Easter arrangements in the window. Sister Marie had used that same name. She, too, called me Daughter of Darkness. I couldn't help but wonder if there was a connection.

Before I even knew it, I was walking again—faster this time. Soon, I saw the cathedral looming ahead. Ignoring the drag on my soul, I descended the steps to the side entrance, but I quickly discovered the doors were locked tight tonight. There was a printed schedule on the door. The support group met three days a week—Sunday, Wednesday, and Friday. But not tonight. I growled in frustration. I hadn't realized until now how much I wanted to talk to Sister Marie again.

I went around the back of the building in the futile hopes that there was another door that was unlocked. There was a pneumatic door with a push bar, but that one was locked, too. So, I kept walking around the building until I found the narrow basement windows I noticed while I was inside. I crouched down and peered in. I thought a grown person could fit if they put some work into it.

Five minutes later, I was inside the church basement with its colorful motivational posters. It was dead silent.

Now what?

I took the steps up to the cathedral, which was similarly dark and empty. I didn't know what I expected. Sister Marie hanging around after hours, lighting votive candles and casting witchy spells? Feeling defeated, I retraced my steps and went back downstairs. Not liking the dark, I flipped on the overhead fluorescent lights, which buzzed as they flickered alive. The snack table was empty except for a runner and some fill-out forms for a raffle. The folding chairs were neatly stacked on the walls.

Then I spied a door I hadn't noticed the first time I was here. I expected it to be a utility closet or a bathroom, but I could feel cold air swirling around my ankles. I tried it and found it was locked with an old-fashioned lock plate with a keyhole, the kind that needs an actual key.

I knelt and looked at it. Retrieving a paperclip from the stack of forms, I returned to the door. I didn't expect the tumblers to actually move when I jiggled the straightened-out clip—I always thought it looked too easy on TV—but they did. Probably because it was an old door with a simple lock.

Seconds later, I was standing in a dark, dungeon-like basement of some kind. Naked light bulbs hung down overhead, but they were all dark. I searched the wall beside the door and found a switch that lit up a red brick tunnel with pipes in the ceiling. I spent a few moments trying to decide why an old brick tunnel would exist under a church. Then I recalled that the Underground Railroad ran like a labyrinth under many of the major cities in this part of the state.

The place smelled moldy, and the walls were damp and cobwebby, but I saw the dust on the floor was disturbed. Someone had been through here recently. A broken copper pipe lay against one wall. I hefted it up and weighed it in my hands before starting down the lighted tunnel. It couldn't hurt to be prepared.

I heard small things skittering around in the dark, but I wasn't worried about mice or rats. I'd seen so many worse things in my life.

A few turns later, I found a dead end, which was disappointing. But when I retraced my steps, I spotted several little alcoves off the main tunnel. The first one had tall, empty racks and several barrels set along the walls. I started to rethink my earlier assumption. These tunnels were probably used to store bathtub gin during Prohibition. My suspicions were confirmed when I noticed a stack of moldy newspapers and some pulp magazines from the 1930s being used to fill in cracks in the aging walls.

Checking the other alcoves produced the same results. Racks, barrels, crates. A lot of empty bottles lying around as though someone left in a hurry. Rats had chewed everything to bits, and silverfish darted in and out of the light cast by the bulbs.

Finally, I came upon an alcove that didn't have a door. Someone had placed a few heavy planks of wood across it to deter people from entering. I was hesitant at first, but then figured fuck it and moved the planks aside and crept into the room.

It was smaller and darker than the other alcoves. There were no windows or lights, just dirty cement walls. The only light came from the weak bulb in the corridor outside. It hardly touched the room, but I could still see what was in there.

A huge iron sarcophagus lay on the floor, taking up almost the whole space. I figured it must have weighed tons, at least. It was intricately engraved with hundreds of birds and flowers as if the artisan had taken great pains to honor the occupant. The lid was carved with a human face and what was supposed to look like translucent cloth flowing over a handsome female body. The beautiful features and rounded breasts made me suck in a quick breath. The attention to detail was mesmerizing. It looked like something you'd expect to find in a museum.

The sight of it gave me goose pimples. I recognized the death mask carved into the lid.

Jolting, I dropped the pipe at my feet with a clang. I felt sick to my stomach as that horrid dream came swirling back to me in full Technicolor. It was real. It was all real. And I suddenly remembered a lot of the little details I'd forgotten, like the Aztec queen touching me so intimately while she called me her flower...

"Shit."

I shouldn't be here. I never should have come.

It felt like it would be a very good idea to get the hell out of Dodge. I didn't even question my motivation when I turned and bolted into the corridor.

But then I stopped. If the sarcophagus was real, then *she* was real. And that meant my waking dream was also real. It meant it was all going to happen.

Reluctantly, I turned back to the alcove and took in the sight of the sarcophagus again even though it made me sick and made the hairs on my arms and the back of my neck stand on end as if I was conducting a current of electricity. I swallowed so hard I thought I was going to choke.

If she was real, then she was in there. Sleeping.

And if she was, that meant she was required to rest like some second-rate Aztec vampire. She could be asleep and vulnerable right now like in all of the horror movies. Maybe I should open the sarcophagus. Maybe I should try to stop her. I had a pipe. Not the greatest weapon, granted, but still...

"What's a pipe going to do against something like *her*?" I asked myself, my voice dry and croaking in the silence. I wanted to retreat, but by doing so, I was condemning this whole city to whatever fate she had in store for it. Maybe Sebastian was right. Maybe the dream was a scry. Maybe the dream was meant to motivate me to do something...

So, I turned back to the sarcophagus and stood there, looking at it with total and absolute dread. I could feel my heart ticking in my throat and the blood pounding in my ears. I wanted to run more than anything right now—but this might be a way to make up for some of the shitty things I'd done in my life.

This could be my salvation.

I picked up the pipe and took a step toward the sarcophagus. After another shuddering breath, I put my hands on the lid. I expected a supernatural spark of some kind, or maybe for the sarcophagus to crack in half like a rotten egg, but nothing so dramatic happened. It did feel incredibly cold under my fingertips. I wondered how old it was. I wondered *what* she was. Setting the pipe down, I ran my fingertips over the engravings along the side, searching for a seam.

I felt something. But my efforts were useless in the end. When I tried to move the lid, I found it was too heavy. Pushing all of my weight against it didn't make it budge even an inch. It must weigh a ton. It was stupid to try, to even think I could do something.

Picking up my handy-dandy pipe and clutching it close like a magic talisman, I turned and hurried into the tunnel.

That was when I heard the lid screek—metal against metal—and then drop like an anvil to the floor behind me.

| 12 |

THE SOUND OF the sarcophagus's lid hitting the cement floor sent a spear of primitive terror up my spine. I didn't want to turn around, but I knew I had to. I had no choice. Whatever happened, I had to face it head on.

Something whispered along the back of my neck, making me shiver as I spun around. I expected to see her right behind me, breathing on my neck, but she was standing beside the sarcophagus a good ten feet away.

She wasn't as tall as she was in my dream—not quite nine feet—but she was wearing the same long, tight-fitting white dress with the slit up the side, but not the gold headdress. Her black hair hung down behind her to her elbows, and her eyes were fiery bright but dark. More human. No blood leaked from them. She looked younger than in my dream, closer to my own age. Honestly, she was probably the most beautiful woman I had ever laid eyes on.

Her fire-red lips curled up in a smile and her eyes squinted in welcome. She held out her large brown hands to me, the same as in my dream. Strangely, I felt safe and warm and loved in her presence. I felt like she would never hurt me.

Little flower, she said, and this time I knew she was saying it only in my head.

I wanted to go to her. I wanted that so much. I felt like we could be sisters. But something held me back. I remembered the fire and the bones. The city burning around us. I remembered her look of disappointment when I rejected her.

I felt paralyzed by my fears. Suddenly, I could feel her going through my head. It was as if someone was in the library of my mind and grabbing books off a shelf, flipping them open and then discarding them on the floor before moving to the next. She did this very quickly, flying through my mind's library in a matter of seconds as she searched for something of interest to her. Some of my book-memories she found interesting. Most she did not. She liked the ones where I punished someone.

She saw it all—all my dirty little secrets. Mr. Greeley falling down a long flight of steps after yelling *whore* at me; a girl who was gossiping about me at school slipping and falling in the girl's bathroom; Mitchell burning to death in the apartment building after calling me a bitch; Nick trying to grab me, only to jerked his away when he saw my arm was on fire...

She liked the fear in the men's eyes, and she enjoyed their pain. She liked that people were afraid of me.

I jerked backward, almost falling against the wall as I forcefully unhooked myself from her psychic claws. It hurt, but I was able to slam the door of the library of my life in her fucking face.

That made her angry, and I saw a drop of blood race from the corner of her eye and down her cheek like a fiery tear. She bared her teeth, perfect white ivory bits capped with gold points, but it was more of a smile than a sneer.

Little flower of pain, you belong to me, I heard her say as she reached for me.

I didn't wait to see what would happen next. I spun around on my heels and raced blindly through the door and down the long corridor. I ran as fast as I could around the bendy corners of the Prohibition tunnel, the fear of her—the horror of her—breathing down the back of my neck. I could feel her light touch in my scalp and in the shivery small of my back.

I could still hear her words echoing in my head as if from a great distance. The light bulbs popped out as I passed beneath them, stealing the warmth of the light away. The sudden, swirling shadows only pushed me on. I ran faster and faster, gasping and almost crying out when I spied the door only a hundred feet away...

I sprinted toward my escape as the last light bulb popped out, casting the whole tunnel in total darkness. But I could still feel her on me like a dirty film. I felt she was right behind me. And yet, I spotted a dark figure waiting for me up ahead. I though that, somehow, she had gotten ahead of me.

I raised the pipe over my head—it was my only defense—but as I passed through the door, ready to stave in her beautiful face, I saw it wasn't her waiting for me.

It was Detective McCall.

But the pipe was still falling toward his surprised face.

| 13 |

"MS. SUMMERS!"

Detective McCall caught my wrists in both hands, halting the pipe before it could crash into his face. His hands were large and strong and heavily corded. With a cop's training and instincts, he twisted my hands to one side, forcing me to drop the pipe, but not so roughly that he actually hurt me.

"Detective McCall," I said, ashamed of the fact that I almost bashed his handsome face in.

I expected him to be irate, but he surprised me. "Are you all right?" he asked, glancing past me.

I felt a chill and it took me a moment to wind up the courage to look down the tunnel behind me. Empty. *She* had not followed me.

"I...I..."

I could still feel her inside my head, running her fingers through my memories. She'd been doing it this whole time.

Turning back, I saw McCall's face. He looked even more concerned now than when I first ran into him. "Ms. Summers, were you...?"

That was all I heard before the whole room tilted sideways and faded to black.

| 14 |

I WOKE UP in the backseat of an unfamiliar car, lying under a men's jacket. I sat up, dislodging the jacket, and saw the car was parked in the lot outside the church. Detective McCall was talking to Sister Marie on the steps of the church. She nodded, looked over at me with pity, then turned back to him and said something I couldn't hear.

The car was hot. The windows were rolled up, and when I tried to open the door, I found it was locked from the outside.

McCall nodded to Sister Marie and started down the steps.

I shrank back in my seat as he approached the back door and opened it. "Awake?" His voice was firm, the way I'd anticipated.

"Yeah." I rubbed my head. My hair was all crazy curls. It had come out of its ponytail.

"Want to come around to the front?"

I slid cautiously out of the car, still wearing his jacket, and made my way around to the passenger side door. McCall appeared beside me and opened the door for me. With a soft sigh of resignation, I slid into the bucket set.

He slammed the door and went around to the other side to get in. He didn't start it, though. Instead, he picked up his police radio and called in, telling dispatch he'd taken care of the disturbance.

After he hung up the radio, I said, "How did you know?"

He pointed to a small sign I missed on the front lawn that had the name of a surveillance company on it. "We had you breaking in on video. Want to see the footage?"

So much for me being a brilliant investigator. "No," I groaned, snuggling down into his jacket, which smelled of his cologne—a light vanilla fragrance. My hands were flexing and my nails cutting into my palms. I was such an idiot!

"So, you're a chocolatier by day and a safecracker by night?"

"Confectioner. My partner is the chocolatier," I corrected him.

He gave me a serious look. "Well, then. I'll have to tell Sister Marie to take better care with her security with all of these safe-cracking confectioners around."

I didn't laugh at that. I did finally look up at him. "Am I under arrest?"

"That depends." His deep voice reverberated around the car. "Was there something you wanted from the church?"

"I..." I looked down again and picked at the polish on my nails. "I just wanted to go inside."

"Crisis of faith, huh?"

"Something like that."

He started the car and pulled out onto the street. I started running names through my head, trying to decide who I could call from the station to bail my sorry ass out. Josh would definitely want to help me out, but he was back in Blackwater. Nick too, but his wisecracking would just make the situation worse. I'd need to call Sebastian and hope to hell he wasn't passed out in an alley somewhere.

After a short, silent drive, McCall pulled onto Broad Street and then into the delivery alley behind the shop. He parked near the rear entrance, shut the car off, and got out. I stared at him mutely through the windshield as he came around to my side and opened the door.

I followed him meekly to the back entrance. "No handcuffs?" I said only in half-jest. I was still in shock that he was letting me go.

"Why? Do you like handcuffs?" he asked, and I suddenly sensed a change in the mood between us.

I smiled as I got my key out and unlocked the door. I was elated to not be under arrest. I'd had my share of cops and cells, thank you very much. Seconds later, I was standing inside, holding the door open and looking up at him. I knew he wanted to come inside.

Tell him goodnight. Tell him to go home to his wife.

Sound advice.

I wanted to be a good person. A good girl.

But I was not a girl. I was the devil's only begotten daughter, and I was not sure if that qualified me as a person.

| 15 |

I OFFERED TO make Detective McCall tea.

The prep room was dim and luminescent with humming appliances. We made some coy small talk while I brewed the tea. He was brave enough to approach the hive and study my bees before turning his full attention on me.

"You're not afraid?"

"No," I told him. "They're my bees."

"*Your* bees?" he said as he approached me. "How are they *your* bees?"

"They listen to me. They belong to me. I'm their mistress."

He looked at me hard for one moment, then pushed me back so hard my ass hit the edge of a prep table. I gasped at his enthusiasm. He then picked me up with no effort at all and set me down atop it. I was small, so that put us at eye level. He stroked the sides of my face with his thumbs like he was calming me. His warmth and the sweetness of his cologne made me melt against the hard, muscular wall of his body. He said things, then, asking me if I wanted him the way he wanted me.

I nodded but said nothing. My heart was thudding so hard that I wondered if he could hear it. I clenched my hands on the edge of the stainless steel table until it felt like my nails were going to snap off to keep from reaching for him. I could smell my own excitement, my body betraying me at every turn, and I thought he could, too.

He grabbed my hair, hard, and dragged me forward to kiss me. He was harsh and possessive. In another life, I might have been afraid, but the bees were singing to me in my head, telling me to trust him. The press of his chest against the tips of my oversensitive breasts made me shiver, and my entire body felt like it was burning from the inside out.

He licked my lips before saying, "You are so fucking beautiful." His eyes raked over me before narrowing. "I've dreamed of you. Fucking waited for you."

His hand slid down my body, his wedding ring flashing on his hand.

"Detective McCall..."

"Mac...called me Mac."

I wanted to say, *We shouldn't,* but the truth was, I wanted him. To claim anything else was a bald-faced lie. I didn't care that he had a wife and a family. I didn't care that I was invading his marriage bed. And I knew that made me a bad person. I just wished I cared that I didn't care.

"Mistress," he whispered sweetly in my ear. I could tell he was enjoying this. That his mind and body craved it. He said the word again. His voice was deep and chocolaty and incredibly sexy. "Tell me what you want, Mistress. Tell me how to pleasure you."

I whispered it in his ear.

He groaned in response as he spread my legs and leaned forward to lick over the places where his fingers had just touched me. Dipping his head, he closed his mouth over the hard tip of my breast through the fabric of my T-shirt, giving it a firm little tug like a dog playing with a toy. The sensation made me arch against him. He moaned in response. He increased his play and that dragged a cry of pleasure from my throat. He issued a low growl of pleasure as he wet first one nipple and then the other.

"Anything you want, Mistress." His voice was now sly and whispery.

He pressed his fingers against the seam of my jeans, making me whimper with unspeakable need. We started working on the clothing barriers between us. It took seconds, if that. Then he was slowly and forcibly pushing his way inside my body. I was pretty tight, but he was strong and relentless and eager. He hit me in just the right places. I whimpered and thrashed, but he held me down on the prep table and drove those inarticulate spikes of pleasure deep inside me until I felt my eyes rolling up into the back of my head.

A sudden burst of shuddering pleasure rocketed through my body, making me cry out so loudly I was terrified Sebastian might come down from upstairs to find out what was going on. Then that fear dissolved as my body arched up as far as it could go for him. I was thankful his face was buried in the side of my neck as he rutted with me because I could feel that my hair was on fire and my hands, clutching his ass, looked like they had wisps of smoke pouring off them.

I quickly shut my eyes. *Stop...please stop...no more!*

Mac groaned as we finished together. When I dared to open my eyes, I saw the ripple of a cool blue flame dancing across my exposed skin. I fell back on the table, panting and trembling in the aftershocks of our fucking. I could feel the heat in my face. I felt it racing down over my quivering breasts.

His eyes were wide and dark. He sucked in a deep breath at the sight of me burning beneath him. "What...what are you?" he asked, his voice hoarse from effort.

I slowly sat up on the prep bench, closing my legs demurely for him. I lifted my hands, watching the blue flames dance over my fingertips like sprites. Our eyes met and it took me a long moment to find my voice.

I meant to be honest and say, "*a witch.*" But I couldn't find it in me and, coward that I was, it came out, "A psychic."

It took him a moment to digest that. "A real psychic."

"Yes." The fire dimmed and finally went out, leaving a swirl of smoke twisting around us.

Mac stepped back and then realized his pants were open. He quickly fixed himself before looking back up. He looked dazed and confused, but not afraid. I considered that a small victory.

I didn't know what to say, so I put words to the first thing that came to mind, "More things in heaven and earth...you know." I shrugged.

He laughed nervously at that. It took him a moment more to compose himself, but then he said, "A real psychic."

"The police use them all the time. I could even help you find that man's murderer if you want." I was babbling. I just needed to say something to help cut the tension between us.

"That would be useful, considering what the perp is doing."

I leaned forward and tried to arrange my clothing properly. "What do you mean?"

He looked sorry that he said it, so I pressed, "Tell me. Maybe I can help."

Mac thought about that for a long moment. Then he seemed to make up his mind and started telling me about the murders. There'd been more than one, all of them similar. The bodies of known criminals flayed of their skin and redressed in their clothes and left in dark corners throughout the city. Mac thought it might be a ritual killer, someone trying to send a message.

"All of them had criminal records," he concluded. "Assault...rape...men nobody the city would miss. Frankly, I'm glad the bastards got what they deserve, but the law doesn't see it that way..."

That explained why I was hearing about this for the first time. There'd been little to no coverage in the media because it was all underworld thugs being hit. The cops didn't know what to make of it all and were burying the cases.

Don't get involved, a small voice whispered in my head. *This is connected to her somehow...*

But that was exactly *why* I needed to learn more. If these murders were connected to Sister Marie and the mysterious Aztec woman, I needed to know what part I was being asked to play in them.

I got down off the prep table and asked for Mac's phone, programming my number in when he handed it to me. "If there's anything I can do psychic-wise, just call."

"'Psychic-wise.'" He looked at the number before slipping his phone under his coat. He never took his eyes off me. I knew he wanted me. I knew we could do this all night long. But he only smoothed my hair with his hands and pinched my chin in his fingers, laying a maddeningly chaste kiss upon my lips.

"You shouldn't have given me your number, Mistress. I might abuse it."

I smiled against his lips.

As he turned to the door, I said, "Yes."

He looked back. "Yes, what?"

"Yes. I like handcuffs."

| 16 |

I WOKE UP exhausted the day of our Grand Opening. Much of it was the frenetic pace Sebastian and I had been keeping to get things ready. But some of it was worry and poor sleep. I hadn't dreamed of the woman since our encounter, but every time I fell asleep, I felt a strange sensation like someone was standing over me, and it kept waking me up. My sleep was fitful and broken up, and I felt far from rested.

When one of Sebastian's chocolate sculptures didn't turn out, I ragged him out. The store was opening in just under an hour, so I took myself out into the alley, sank down on the stoop in the doorway, and lit a cigarette from the pack I'd bought at the CVS on the corner.

I hadn't smoked in years.

I stared at the spot where the man died.

Moments later, Sebastian joined me on the stoop, his apron an ugly ruin of smeary chocolate fingerprints.

I passed him the smoke. "Sorry. I'm being a bitch."

He shrugged. "You are a bitch. But that's fine. I shouldn't have been so ambitious with the elephant," he said, referring to the sculpture that didn't survive the night in the deep freeze.

He had made several sculptures for the Grand Opening and set them out on fancy pedestals, all circus animals. Only the elephant didn't survive.

I shook my head. "Your work is amazing. Hell, you're a better chocolatier drunk than I'm a candymaker sober."

He grinned ear to ear, wisps of smoke rising from the cigarette in the corner of his mouth.

"And you have no idea where you get your skills?"

"None." He scowled up at the sky as he thought a long, hard moment. "I think I worked in a circus once."

I found that amusing and laughed. "I suck. I've had no sleep and I'm pretty sure it's my time of the month." I shrugged. "It's a girl thing."

"I was a girl once," he said, and then he stared hard at the ground as if the answers were somehow there. "At least...I think so."

I reminded myself of how amazing Sebastian was, and how many wild skills he had accumulated. I wondered how many lifetimes he had lived. But I'd never know—and neither would he, apparently.

We went back inside and Sebastian handed me a shot of bottom-shelf gin from his secret stash. The stuff was terrible and tasted like turpentine, but it warmed me up and tamed my sour mood so that, by the time we were ready to throw open the doors for the first time, I was smiling like an idiot.

The turnout was impressive. Within an hour, we had what felt like a hundred people squeezed into the tiny shop, perusing the barrels of candy, admiring Sebastian's chocolate circus (minus the elephant), and gobbling down free samples. It was Saturday, and there were couples, families, and a *lot* of kids.

One sugared-up little boy knocked over Sebastian's chocolate tent and broke the head off a chocolate horse. He started to cry. The parents were all shame-faced but Sebastian swept in and reassured them it was all right. He scooted down and talked to the boy, then "magically" produced one of my homemade lollipops from his sleeve like he was a magician. I knew he carried those around.

The boy's eyes lit up, and the couple, as well as the whole store, was suddenly happy again. After cleaning up the broken chocolate horse, we decided to move the chocolate circus off to one side so there would be no further incidents.

Sebastian was happy and smiling.

"Not upset?" I asked after we rearranged things to accommodate the increased foot traffic.

"Nah. Poor lad. He meant well. He wanted to touch the horse, was all."

I marveled at Sebastian's patience with the child—something I've never possessed myself. And not something I expected of him. "You're amazing," I told him unexpectedly.

"Yes, darling. I am," he agreed, touching his heart.

I laughed. "Humble, too."

"I like children," he said, watching the little boy walk away happy with the lollipop in his mouth.

It hit me that, considering Sebastian's multiple lifetimes, he was probably a parent at least once—maybe even more than once. Not that he would remember. Maybe he had family out there somewhere that he didn't even remember existed. I found that idea sad.

We sold out on the chocolate boxes and about half of the hard candy, including all of the honey-flavored Sweet Stix. The crunchy-natural hipsters seemed to like those. The kids, of course, were fascinated by the beecosystem, though some of the parents were horrified by the sight of it until I showed them there was no way for the bees to escape.

Around noon, Sebastian and I donned our aprons and did a chocolate sculpture and candy-making demonstration. While we were working, an older, well-dressed woman with grey hair interrupted and asked us about the hex symbol on the wall behind our workstation.

She looked ultra-conservative and I stumbled on a response.

"It's for good luck," Sebastian piped up. "Like the Pennsylvania Dutch hexes you see on barns?"

That satisfied her. Suddenly, it was not odd at all. Barns out in the country had them all the time.

A news crew arrived soon after, wanting to interview us for the evening edition. I left Sebastian to do most of the talking. He was already a big hit with the ladies and was eating up the attention. I retreated to where the grey-haired woman from earlier was standing alone, still studying the hex.

I touched her shoulder gently and she jumped. There were deep concern lines cut into her face. "Maybe I can help you find something?" I offered. Her interest in the hex was starting to worry me.

"No, dear, I'm fine," she said kindly and reached out to touch my arm. I felt a slight spark. I didn't *think* she was a witch, but she had a touch of the Otherkind in her. She nodded at the mural. "The glyphs in this symbol are so interesting. Did you paint them?"

I was hesitant to respond. I didn't know why she was so interested in the sign of my father's house, but after a few seconds of awkward silence, I said, "You know what they are, don't you?"

She shook her head. "Not really. My grandmother had books with similar glyphs. She was touched by the craft. Me..." She laughed sadly. "I'm just a retired schoolteacher and mother and wife."

We stood side by side for a long moment. I had a feeling I could trust her, so I said, "All women have a touch of the craft in them, you knew."

"Including you, dear?"

"Yeah. I'm a witch."

She didn't even blink. "I thought as much. Do you make talismans?"

I didn't know what she meant, so I said, "Like…a charm for good luck and love and such?"

"Something like that. My grandma could make them. I wish she was here."

I felt nervous asking it, but I did anyway. "Is there something I could make for you?"

She was not as old as I first thought; her face was simply ravaged by pain and years. "Not me. My son." She reached into her purse and withdrew the picture of a young man in Army fatigues. She showed it to me. "His name is Connor. My only child. He's served two tours of duty in the Ukraine."

I took the picture. Connor was in full urban combat gear, kneeling with his platoon beside a military jeep. I recognized that guarded smile. Josh had worn the same expression when he sent me pictures from his outposts.

"After Connor was discharged, he came home to live with me. But he hasn't left the house in months." The woman swallowed so hard I heard a click. "Most days, he stays in his room. Doesn't even get out of bed."

I looked up. "Have you tried talking to a doctor about him?"

She nodded. "He was seen by a doctor. A therapist, too. But they can't seem to get through to him." I saw her swallow against breaking out in tears. "I think he's given up. I'm afraid…" She looked to the floor and took a moment to compose herself before looking up again. Her eyes were wet. "I'm afraid he's going to hurt himself one night. I don't know what to do. I don't know who to turn to anymore."

Her story tore at me—and not for the obvious reason that Josh went through something similar. She looked desperate and lonely and beyond frustrated. A mother who couldn't protect her only child. I knew what it felt like to be at your wit's end with no one to turn to who could help you—who could even understand."

I looked down at the picture again, then up at Connor's mother. They looked a lot alike. "Can I keep this picture?"

"Of course!"

I let out a shaky breath. "I can't promise it will work. I haven't been doing this very long."

"But you will try?" She took the picture back and quickly scribbled her phone number on the back. "Please try." She pressed the picture back into my hand. "I'll pay any price you ask."

After that unusual encounter, I spent some time talking to a stringer from the paper about the shop while a cameraman filmed the interview. I awkwardly went on about why I was launching the business, stumbling all over myself. After a few seconds, Sebastian, a true showman, stepped in and diverted the attention to himself, which I appreciated.

A man had just entered the shop.

I pushed through the crowd toward him. "Josh!" I called and saw him turn toward the sound of my voice. His sad, familiar grin filled me with a bolt of giddy happiness as I jumped into his arms.

"You made it!"

"Of course! Did you think I wouldn't be here to see my little sis conquer the world?"

I laughed and kissed his scruffy cheek. "I knew you would. I looked into my crystal ball, you know."

He laughed.

Josh hung out in the shop until closing time, which was pretty late—around one in the morning, which was how long it took for us to clean up. Upstairs, I collapsed into a chair around the cheap Walmart dinette set we'd sprung for a few days ago, and Sebastian picked up the old rotary phone on the floor to call for a pizza from the shop down the street.

"How is everyone?" I asked Josh while we cracked open some celebratory beers.

He waggled his hand. "It's Blackwater. It's either super quiet or super fucked up. At the moment, it's super quiet, which is either cool or boring, depending on your disposition."

Our conversation segued into the school shooting that occurred last summer. The town was still recovering from that.

Sebastian perched on a stool and kept making low-key lascivious comments toward my big bro, so I made a shooing motion. He rolled his eyes. Moments later, there was a knock on the door downstairs and he jumped up.

"Pizza!" he proclaimed. "One of the few American specialties I can abide!"

After he was gone, I asked Josh about Nick.

"I only ran into him once while I was in Dollar General. He was behind me, eating something. Swedish Fish, I think. But we didn't talk."

I rolled my eyes. "He evaded you?"

"I think he was preoccupied." He stopped and thought a moment. "He's been hanging out with this fancy coven that has a big house up on Lake Ariel."

I knew enough about my ex to know he had fallen into a little coven of Satanists who just loved the hell out of him. He was like their very own personal Elvis. These days, they were all cozy up in their painted Victorian, engaging in rituals and orgies or whatever it was modern-day Satanists did.

"I didn't tell him about anything you're doing," Josh assured me, sipping from his Yuengling bottle. "I don't gossip about you, sis."

I took a sip of my own and swallowed hard. "Don't care. You can tell him anything you want about me."

"Don't be bitter."

"Nick doesn't care about me or the shop," I said, knowing that wasn't strictly true. "And, anyway, he's pissed me off."

"What did he do this time?"

"Never gave me back my athame after he borrowed it from me forever."

Josh laughed. "Good ol' Saint Nick," he said, saluting him.

In truth, I wasn't actually angry with Nick any longer about the athame or anything, really. I'd since accepted that this was just who he was. A walking disaster with a nice smile. I was not judging, mind you. He'd say the same thing about me and he'd be right.

Josh said nothing about my outburst, and as soon as Sebastian returned with the pizzas, the whole mood of the place changed and became much lighter.

"Took you long enough!" I scolded.

Sebastian grinned evilly. "Pizza delivery boy was pretty as fuck."

"Dear god. You didn't?"

Sebastian laughed like a banshee.

"Wash your hands!"

We all laughed. We ate and drank and chatted, and even though we offered Josh a place to crash, he told us he had to get an Uber back to Blackwater and pack his things. He was talking to a record producer in L.A. and he'd be gone for a couple of weeks.

I hugged him and cried all over his shoulder. "You'll call?" I knew how bad he could be about staying in touch. Sometimes, he went weeks without calling me, and then I worried he was back in his dark place.

I thought about the young soldier, Connor.

"I'll call. Promise." He kissed my forehead before slipping out the door and back into the night.

I walked to the end of the alley to wave to the Uber whisking him away.

It was after three in the morning before I crashed out. I could still smell the pizza and chocolate on my clothes—and Josh's scent, his cologne. I should have been really happy. In less than six months, I had rebuilt my life. I had Josh. And Sebastian.

But I couldn't stop thinking about the woman who was going to kill me.

| 17 |

THE REVIEW WE got in the Sunday edition of the paper wasn't what we expected. The critic had a long list of complaints we never saw coming. The shop was too small, the chocolate sub-par, and she was stupidly freaked out about the bees.

Sebastian was enraged—and he almost never got angry. The kitchen table literally started to vibrate until I put a hand over his and told him to calm down.

I read over the review a second time, telling myself the critic was an idiot, but I knew some of it was at least partly true. We did an okay job, but there was probably more we could have done. More prizes, more giveaways, more fanfare. It stuck in my craw, but I couldn't just crawl back into bed and cry over my butthurt feelings. So, I showered and changed, put my hair up in a bun, and tied on my apron as I stepped into the prep room. We had things to do.

We prepped from five to eight and then opened Confessions for its first official day as a working store. Traffic was light at first but picked up significantly around noon. Late afternoon there was a small rush. We didn't do the business we did the day before, but our take wasn't bad.

The following day, traffic was a little slower, but I chalked that up to it being a workday. But in the week that followed, there were no improvements. I didn't want to say it was the review, but I figured it probably hadn't helped much.

By Thursday, I was starting to fret and Sebastian was going out drinking every night and wasn't his best in the morning. He was hungover and perpetually grumpy. That hurt more than anything—the realization that I was letting him down.

By Saturday, we hadn't sold enough to warrant much prep and Sebastian decided to sleep in, which I translated as him wanting to run off and day drink in some godforsaken dive. I was scared he was starting to spiral. Still, I dutifully went downstairs, tied on my apron, and opened the shop.

With nothing to do and no customers, I retreated to the prep room and took the picture of Connor out of my pocket. I'd been carrying it around with me all week. I set the picture down on a prep table and looked down at it for several seconds. He was a young, handsome, sandy-haired boy with blue-grey eyes, but I could see the shadow of the sadness in the lines around his eyes and his strained smile.

I walked to the sliding partition that separated the prep room from the rest of the shop (useful when we had to carefully control the temperature of the room while making hard candy), slid it closed, and locked it. I then went to the door that led upstairs to the loft and locked that one, too.

I was now completely isolated. The room felt small, and, with no windows and only the fluorescent lights above, darker and colder. There was only the hum of the refrigeration unit and the din of the bees in their hive. I walked to it and unlocked the drop window, sliding the panel up so the bees were free to fly into the room.

There was no chaos, as you might expect. My bees were extremely well-behaved. I scooted down to address the queen while her thousands of servants—my familiars—hovered over me like a protective cloud. "Looks like I'm going to need your help, your majesty."

I didn't feel silly talking to her. I could feel their response like a low hum in the back of my brain. There was great enthusiasm among the members of the hive. They would do anything I asked.

I opened the outer and inner covers, slid out a movable frame, and broke off a square of honeycomb before returning all of the parts to their place. But I didn't close it up. Surrounded by a cloud of humming bees that would probably send a normal person screaming into the night, I took the honeycomb to the prep table, set it down, and looked at the rough square of crystallized wax and the pool of raw honey beneath in.

The only thing I knew about talismans was that they were objects of power that a witch puts a little bit of herself into. But I wasn't sure how to do that.

My bees were on that. One of them—perhaps the same bee from the other night—landed in my hair and crawled down the strands until she reached my ear. She hummed into it. I tilted my head at the moving pictures in my head.

"Okay," I said and looked down at the honeycomb and the picture of Connor beside it. I picked up the honeycomb and placed it squarely over the photo, honey and all, and then raised both hands so they were hovering over the picture. I closed my eyes and visualized the young man in trouble, what horrors he must have faced to be in such a dark place.

I reached over the bench to the magnetic strip where we kept the knives. I chose a small, very sharp one, and set the tip of the blade against the underside of my wrist. The blade flashed under the fluorescents, making this all feel very real. What if I cut a tendon? I wouldn't be able to work. So, I turned my hand and cut the back of it, instead—quickly, before I stopped to thought about what I was doing.

Dark witch's blood welled up from the tiny cut. I turned my hand and let a few drops fall to the honeycomb and picture. I wondered if I should say something—words were powerful in the craft—but I was not learned and didn't know what was appropriate. So, I just recited, "In the name of my father's house, as I will it, so mote it be."

The blood burned into the picture of the smiling soldier, slowly rendering it to black ash. I made the sign of my father's house over the honeycomb—the long line with the two prongs at the end. Suddenly, the whole mess burst into crackling flames—huge, blue, butane-like flames.

I jumped back, startled by the suddenness of it. Holy shit! I did *not* expect that!

The flames didn't last, and when they finally burned down to nothing, I saw fine white dust covering the workbench. The ritual had consumed everything—my blood, the picture, even the honeycomb. I tapped a finger against the ash, which fell away, revealing something underneath. It was cool to the touch, so I dug it out.

Only part of the honeycomb remained, a piece three or four inches in circumference. It was now in a jagged circular shape that fit in the palm of my hand like a dark gold bracelet. Although it had a honeycomb pattern, it was as hard as stone. It looked like some kind of fancy new jewelry trend.

I held it up to the light, which passed through it and made it sparkle. "Huh," I said.

| 18 |

"A CHOCOLATE FAIRY village," Sebastian mumbled. He was perched on the workbench, plowing Thai food from the little white carryout box into his mouth with chopsticks. I could barely make out what he was saying. "Chocolate toadstools and chocolate flowers and a chocolate squirrel with a saddle for the chocolate fairies to ride."

I sat on the stool next to the humming refrigerator. It was after hours and I was wondering just how fucking high he was.

"Why?" I said after gulping down some cheap red wine. "Why a fairy village?"

He shrugged. "It's past Easter so can't bloody well do bunnies and lambs. Think the kiddies would like an authentic fairy village?"

"I'm not sure if Americans will *get it*, you know? The parents might think the mushrooms are some drug-related thing."

He sighed as he stuck his chopsticks into the box. "Americans are so daft."

I smiled at that.

"Presently company excluded."

"I take no offense." I dug around my box for more noodles. They were being sadly elusive. "You ever think of going back?"

"Back...where?"

"Wherever you come from."

He shook his head and grabbed up the carryout box. "I'd consider it if I knew where the bloody hell that was."

An uncomfortable silence descended over us. Finally, I said, "I'm sorry I'm failing you."

"You are doing no such thing," Sebastian insisted. He clicked his chopsticks. "But maybe we need a new marketing strategy. I'm not giving up."

I didn't tell him about Matilda, Connor's mother, whom I talked to about a week ago. I phoned her the same day I finished the talisman, and she was at the door in five minutes, her sweet, tired face looking even more ravaged than when I last saw her. When I showed her the talisman—I put it on a long black, masculine cord so Connor could wear it like a necklace—she actually broke down in sobs and hugged me so tightly I thought she would dislocate one of my ribs.

I didn't ask for payment. I had no idea if the talisman would even work.

I didn't hear anything from Matilda for several days. But then she showed up in the shop earlier today with a tearful smile and a check that left me standing there in stunned silence, looking at all of the zeroes, thinking I was imagining this.

"Connor went out today with his friends," she gushed. "He's going to see his therapist again!"

She hugged me and started crying all over my hair. "I am going to send all of my friends to you." She leaned in to kiss my forehead. "God bless you, Vivian."

I didn't tell Sebastian about the transaction. After all, I didn't know if Matilda would follow through on her promise to send others my way. But as I sat there, I thought maybe I should. I was about to open my mouth when someone knocked harshly on the back door.

Sebastian, who was closer, scooted down the workbench and put his hand on the doorknob. He peeked out the glass panes. "It's your policeman friend." His eyebrows bounce up and down Groucho Marx-style.

I gaped at the door indecisively.

"You wanted I got rid of him?"

I shook my head. "I've got this." I climbed down off the stool.

Mac was waiting for me in the shadows near his car. All of the confusion I'd felt over the past few days alleviated a little at the sight of him. My heart thudded faster. I wished he didn't do that to me.

"Hey," he said softly. He indicated a folder he was holding. "I decided to take you up on your offer to help with the investigation. There's been yet another murder like the one in your alley. We don't have anything that even resembles a lead. Maybe you could look over these files, suss out a connection? No pressure, of course. You must be very busy..."

His deep, husky voice trailed away while he stared at me.

I didn't feel like making small talk. That was not what he was here for, anyway.

Within seconds, the file was on the ground and he had me backed against the brick wall of the building. His hands were cupped around my face and he was lunging deep inside my body, each little motion making the bricks rake over my back thrillingly. I arched my back, urging him on and on. He went faster and faster, but he never broke eye contact with me.

With a cry of release, he kissed me, called me Mistress, and we hung against the wall for several long moments, hearts ticking and blood thundering in our ears while we slowly came down from the erotic high of having done this in an alley like a pair of cats in heat.

He finally kissed the side of my face, and I breathed in his cologne. He let me down gently, and then did the most amazingly erotic thing and got down on his knees to lick all along my lower belly and between my legs, grooming me like he really was a cat. Afterward, he straightened up and smoothed my skirt and we kissed one last time, briefly, before he wordlessly returned to his cruiser.

I looked down at the file on the ground at my feet. It was lying open with scattered, bloody photographs of faceless men who had died in agony. I'd vowed to stay away from this thing. I was afraid all of this was tied to the ancient woman who haunted my dreams, and I didn't want to see her ever again. But it looked like fate had other plans for me.

| 19 |

THE NEXT DAY was slow. No surprise there. We got a couple of customers in the late morning, but only one bought anything. Then the shop was like a wasteland.

Around eleven, I told Sebastian I was knocking off for lunch. I always took it around this time with Sebastian taking his own an hour later. That way, the shop stayed open all day—a trick I learned watching Nick and Morgana trading shifts in their own shop in Blackwater.

He waved me off. "Take all the time you need, witchy."

Sometimes, I used my lunch hour to take a quick nap upstairs or, if I was too wired to sleep, I did the books or caught up on my favorite Netflix show. Today, I decided to take a walk.

About seven blocks to the south was a small, wooded park for joggers and dog walkers. I found a bench and watched some young men playing Frisbee with their pooches, though the dogs took pains to avoid me. Children and animals had been avoiding me more often of late.

Don't get a pet. It'll only run away. And don't even dream about raising a child. Nick's words of wisdom from long ago.

I tuned the dog and her owners out and looked down at the manila folder I'd brought with me. It contained the file Mac gave me. Shuffling the papers out and into my lap, I started paging through them. Lots of messy, macabre pictures and rap sheets, some of their information so redacted it was hard to follow. I wasn't sure how Mac expected me to find a connection between the dead men if I only had some of their information.

I mostly just looked at all of the terrible pictures. I had this idea that they wouldn't bother me—big, bad devil-witch that I was. But, honestly, they made me feel nauseated. They were all bad men—rapists, murderers, pimps—but their butchery was so extreme that I wondered how it was possible to have that much hate in you. I also wondered how she did it.

I knew it was the woman in the iron coffin. Somehow, she'd made this happen. But how? And why?

After shuffling through the pictures a while longer, I started seeing some patterns. Not big stuff. Just little things like the dead men were all flayed in dirty alleys. They were murdered out of the light. Some parts of the bodies looked stomped on. All of them were very staged-looking.

She was making some kind of statement. Sending a message.

Most of the dead men were wearing bandannas around their necks—different colors but knotted always to the left almost like a twisted Windsor knot.

I took a close-up picture of one of the knots with my phone and sent the pic to Sebastian with a text. *How well do you know the gangs in this city?*

He texted back: *Why were you sending me a picture of a handkerchief?*

It's a bandanna. It's for a case I'm helping Mac with. Do you know what it means? Is it a gang thing?

It took Sebastian a moment to answer. *Not a gang. Cartel. Toltecs.*

My eyebrows bounced up at that. I was no detective, but I thought this was what they called a lead.

I was about to google the cartel when Sebastian texted back, *Break's over! Shop's getting busy!*

My research would have to wait until tonight.

Right then, a kid bladed by my bench, her nostrils flared. Even though she couldn't see the gruesome files in my lap, there was a look of low-grade fear in her eyes. She quickly skated away from me.

| 20 |

"THIS IS MACY and Malcolm," Doris said, turning her phone sideways and handing it to me so I could look at the picture of her husband and their twenty-year-old daughter. They were standing together at Macy's graduation, Macy in full regalia, with a tall, rather gaunt gentleman in a nice suit standing beside her, his arm around her waist. They were both smiling for the picture, and Macy was throwing the peace sign.

Two hours earlier, the shop was jumping, but it wasn't what I expected. People were swarming and Sebastian was happily ringing up purchases, but they kept looking at me—making me uncomfortable. Eventually, I disappeared into the prep room but I could still hear them talking, asking about me.

Sebastian finally ducked into the prep room, looking confused.

"I know," I said, standing at the sink, a hand over my face while I rubbed at my tired eyes.

"What's going on, witchy?"

"It's complicated."

"'Complicated' as in something I'm going to like, or 'complicated' as in something that's going to ruin us?"

I waited for him to push for more, but he sensed I wasn't ready to spill the tea.

"Right, then." Turning on his heels, he left me alone.

None of the people in the shop sought me out or asked to speak to me in private, but one woman lingered. That was how we came to be standing in the prep room with her showing me the pic of her husband and daughter.

"Malcolm was diagnosed with end-stage pancreatic cancer six months ago. We're preparing him for in-house hospice care."

I raised my hand and stopped her right there. "I can't cure cancer, ma'am. That isn't how my powers work."

"I know that," she said with a hard swallow. "Matilda told me. I'm not looking for a *cure*."

I stared at her. She was a beautiful, middle-aged woman, posh and put-together just like Matilda. My poor friends and I used to make fun of her type of woman. But cancer doesn't care if you're filthy rich or a pauper.

Like Matilda, she looked tired, with dark rings under her eyes. "My Malcolm is dying, miss. I've accepted that. We both have. But Macy is getting married next week. She moved her wedding up six months just so her daddy could see her married."

"I'm sorry," I told her, because I was.

"Malcolm wants to walk her down the aisle. That's his last and only wish. But the cancer..." She hesitated and I saw how difficult it was for her to explain this to a stranger. "...the cancer has him in a wheelchair."

She reached out and took my hand. Her grip was desperate and surprisingly strong. "Is there anything you could do? Just for one day? So he can walk her down the aisle? Anything?"

I stared into her pale grey eyes—so full of helpless pain. I swallowed. "I...don't know."

"Matilda said you're an angel. That you can do small miracles."

"I'm not an ang—" I started to say, but then stopped myself. "Look, ma'am, I didn't know if I could help Connor or not. For all

I know, it could have been a placebo effect. Some fluke. Connor might have done it all himself."

She nodded, accepting that. "What would you say if I told you I don't care if it's real or not? If it helps Malcolm to walk, even for a few minutes, I'll pay you anything you want."

| 21 |

THE DAY'S TAKE was good, but it was not enough to keep the lights on. That was why that night, after we closed and Sebastian scuttled off to his favorite pub, I put in the time and literal magic energy necessary to create a new talisman.

It did not come out looking like the first one. Malcolm's pendant was tear-shaped.

I found my old power tools from when we were renovating the shop, drilled a tiny hole in the top of the talisman, and ran a black cord through it the way I had with Connor's.

When I held it up, it sparkled under the fluorescent lights like it was made of polished diamond.

I picked up my phone and texted Doris.

She texted me back almost immediately. *I'd be right there with a check.*

And she was.

| 22 |

I WAS TOO wired to sleep, so I built a big, soft nest of pillows and did the googling I wasn't able to do earlier in the day. After an hour and a half, I knew more about Mexican cartels than I ever wanted to. Most specialized in drugs and human trafficking—which I expected. But I also learned about drug mules: Young girls and children forced to smuggle drugs over the border by swallowing them or, sometimes—horrifically—by having them sewn into cavities in their bodies. What made it even more terrible was the fact that once these kids reached the U.S. and the drugs were extracted, they were often sold into sexual slavery to powerful white politicians and executives protecting the cartels.

The pictures of dead, beaten children were sickening, and I realized that for all I'd endured, I'd never really known horror—not like these poor kids had.

Thanks to my stupid googling, I'd never get to sleep tonight. Outside, I heard a dog howling somewhere. It was a sad and lonely sound. I felt it cut right through my bones.

Shaken, I called Mac at home. It was an impulsive decision. His number was on a card paper-clipped to the inside of the folder he'd given me.

A young girl picked up. "Wello?"

I stuttered on a response, and the moment stretched out, but I forced myself to speak. "Is...Detective McCall there?"

I heard the girl screech out, "Daaaaaddeeeee!" so loudly I jerked the phone away from my ear.

Moments later, I heard someone rush into the room. "What are you doing with Daddy's phone, baby girl?" I heard Mac say from a distance.

The girl muttered something in baby talk. Mac grunted assurances and told her to get ready for bed. A few more awkward seconds passed while I imagined him retreating to a private part of the house. A door closed.

"Mistress," he said at last.

"Stupid of me to call now," I said, looking at the late hour on the phone. "I didn't think, Mac, I'm sorry..."

"It's all good."

But I thought about what might have happened if his wife had picked up. I took a deep, shaky breath.

He relieved me of explaining myself by saying, "I've missed you."

I swallowed at that. His voice was very low. "Can we talk?"

"I'm in the study downstairs."

"Your wife won't...?"

"Brenda's upstairs with Charity."

I swallowed again. Charity must be the little girl who'd picked up his phone.

"If now's a bad time..."

"Now's perfect," he assured me. "What are you doing?"

I laughed. "Talking to you."

He laughed, too. I was frightened by how well we clicked. This was all too frighteningly easy to end well. "All right. What were you doing before you called?" he clarified.

"Looking over the file you gave me."

"Did you suss anything?"

I thought about telling him about the Toltecs and tipping him off about their hangout. I'd learned via Sebastian that it wasn't far. A dive in east Philly. Maybe it would lead him to the monster that'd been doing these things—though I wasn't sure what Mac or the police could do about a deadly Aztec goddess. But something held me back. Once I told him everything I knew, my part in his investigation would be over, and I didn't want it to be over just yet. So, I said instead, "Nothing yet. Still looking over the files. A lot of redacting."

"For your own safety."

"Terrible pictures."

"I know. I shouldn't have included them."

"I'm glad you did. It makes this feel a lot more real. These are the things you see and deal with?"

"Sometimes. Not always. Sometimes, I just wind up arresting psychics who break into churches in the middle of the night."

I giggled at that. "I was a bad cat burglar."

"I wouldn't choose it as a career path." His mood had suddenly changed. "Look, I shouldn't have involved you." He sounded genuinely remorseful about that.

"Well, I want to help. Not...help those men. You know what I mean. I don't want to see that happen to innocent people."

"Yes."

Before I could say anything else, he whispered, "I'd been thinking about you all day, Mistress. Fantasizing, you might say. It has helped me get through some seriously fucked up shit."

I swallowed so hard it felt like a walnut was stuck in my throat. "I've thought about you, too." My voice was low and breathy—what Nick used to call my sex-kitten voice.

"Tell me what you're doing now," he begged. "Or what you'd like to do."

I couldn't believe we were phone sexing, but we spent the next ten minutes talking about the things we wanted to do to each other. I didn't even feel embarrassed about it because it all felt so right with Mac. Along the way, I discovered Mac had a few highly repressed fantasies

We ended the call on a high note, but the moment I hung up, the good feeling vanished. I remembered the sound of Charity's sweet voice, and I reminded myself that Mac was married and had a child. He was telling me about the things he dreamed about while his wife was upstairs, tucking his toddler daughter into bed.

I slid down under the covers and looked at the phone. Maybe if what I was doing with Mac hurt, I'd stop. That was the worst part of this whole cruddy situation, you know? Not that I felt bad. But that I didn't.

| 23 |

I COULDN'T WAIT for Sunday, my one day off a week.

That morning, I grabbed my overnight bag and headed downstairs.

"Oi, witchy, can you cover me today?" Sebastian asked as he tied on his apron in the prep room. He always took Saturday.

"I'm not letting you off the hook so you can go out day drinking."

"Maybe I have a hot date," he argued.

"With a bottle of gin. No." I wagged my finger in his face. "I have plans."

A sly smile spread across his face. "Is your plan six-three with ebony skin and dreamy brown eyes?"

I sighed.

Sebastian stuck his finger down his throat and bent over to mime-gag.

"Stop it." I smacked him in the shoulder. "And behave yourself while I'm gone!"

Before he could protest further, I slipped out the door and hurried to my jeep, threw my bag into the backseat, and got in. I floored the accelerator as I pulled out onto the street, heading east toward the Waterfront District.

After a half hour, the neighborhoods thinned out and became poorer and shabbier and full of old projects in need of urban renewal. I spotted a dingy little open-air market and a bowling alley with the letters falling off. Old, rusting rail yards dotted the landscape, remnants of the Philadelphia and Columbia Railroad. A church was nothing but a giant pile of rubble with just the front wall with its tall, arched windows still standing. I spotted an angel with a broken face, but I drove past it too quickly to let it bother me much.

When I reached the Delaware River, I went south, following its bendy progress past a collection of sagging, turned-of-the-century row houses until my GPS told me I was there. Up ahead was a roughly paved road that led to an ancient redbrick roadhouse sitting out on a dock right over the river. It looked strangely abandoned with its mostly empty parking lot and dim windows, an even darker industrial garage situated behind it, but I saw some shadows moving in the windows. I planned to wait until after dark to make my move.

I turned the jeep around and drove back up to Delaney Street, where I spotted a 24-hour railroad-style diner with shiny chrome accents. If there was one thing I loved about Philadelphia, it was that you could find an interesting historical diner on almost any corner. After I was seated, I ordered their all-day pancakes and a chocolate milk. When my adopted dad used to take me to these places, we always ordered pancakes and chocolate milk. It was one of my few good memories of my parents. I spent a good two hours there, watching people coming and going.

Finally, as the sun began to set, I visited the ladies' room. I dropped my overnight bag and unzipped it. I changed my street clothes for vinyl pants, a strappy T-shirt with a cute red devil girl on it, a leather jacket with buckles, and motorcycle boots with silver skulls on them. I'd bought all of it for Halloween last year when I went as a biker chick, but I'd liked the outfit enough to take it with me to Philly, and now I was glad I did.

After changing, I stuffed my street clothes into my bag and stepped out of the stall. There was an older woman at the sink. She took off, leaving the faucet running.

I looked in the mirror as I dug out the cosmetics I'd brought. A little mascara and black lipstick later, I looked smoky and sinister. I shook my hair out so it was wild and shaggy. I tried a few fierce facial expressions in the mirror, but I thought they all looked silly. I could feel my heart knocking almost painfully in my chest, and my hands kept clenching and unclenching nervously at my sides.

"Fierce, not frightened...fierce, not frightened," I told the mirror. Then I leaned forward and said, "Boo!" and watched in satisfaction as a spiderweb of cracks appeared.

| 24 |

IN MY HEAD, this whole fantasy played out. I was going to walk into that dive as if I owned the place, sit down, order a beer, and get some answers. No one was going to give me lip because I was the goddamn daughter of the devil. Then I was going to take those answers to Mac and, together, we were going to take down the Toltecs.

The reality was a little different. Unlike earlier, the parking lot was packed solid with pickups and bikes, and I could hear honky-tonk music playing whenever the doors were opened. Every window was lit up with figures swarming behind the dirty glass. The rickety old doors kept opening and closing as big guys in leather vests and torn jeans passed in and out, their voices rumbling in either anger or drunkenness as they lit up a smoke or spat some chew onto the broken pavement. I could smell the stale beer and riverside mold of the place from here.

I'd parked up the road in an empty lot outside a Kwikimart. I didn't want any of the bikers noting my license plate, but now I wondered if having a getaway car closer wouldn't have been smarter.

"Jesus, remembered who you were, chick." I straightened my shoulders and was about to cross the parking lot when someone bumped my shoulder from behind—a long-haired guy of almost seven feet, his arm wrapped tightly around a tiny but tough-looking biker chick. He was wearing a leather vest with a patch on it, a jaguar feasting on a human heart and the name TOLTECS printed in an arch over the cat.

Trying not to let that rattle me, I followed them. They didn't hold the door.

Inside, the place was as hot as a steam bath. Low yellow lights gave the darkly wood-paneled walls a kind of leprosy. An old bar ran the length of the place, with a wall of bottles behind it—mostly tequila, mezcal, and the like. Leather vests and motorcycle jackets were framed and hanging on the walls, as were some celebrity photos of Mexican actors.

A raised dais near the back featured a live band playing old hair metal Mariachi-style with acoustic guitars, a guitarron, and a vihuela. A number of pool tables and a jukebox were set to one side. The other side just had tables and booths. The place was incredibly packed, with most of the occupants standing near the band, clapping, or solo dancing.

Some of the patrons eyed me suspiciously. I was, literally, the only white person in the place.

Clenching my hands into fists, I moved as inconspicuously as possible to the bar. Several big guys looked over. None of them looked friendly, so I claimed a small two-seater in the corner instead and sat down.

A thin, middle-aged Latina waitress slid up to the table. She was wearing a white strappy shirt and black Daisy Dukes. Almost her entire body was covered in colorful tattoos and calligraphy I couldn't read. Her hair was long and shaggy, and there were five hoop earrings in each ear and one in her nose. She gave me a bored look and started speaking rapid-fire in Spanish.

"Beer," I said. "Uh...*cerveza*."

She walked away, unimpressed.

I was sitting at a bad angle. I could see the employees' exit door and part of the bar, but not what was going on near the band or who was coming in the door. As I sat there, nervously rubbing at my nail polish, I started wondering if I shouldn't call it a wash and get the hell out of there.

The waitress reappeared so suddenly I nearly jumped out of my seat. She set a tumbler of amber mescal down in front of me instead of the beer I'd ordered. Frowning, I saw something swirling around the dirty glass. I leaned forward, and the biggest fucking worm I have ever seen suddenly breached the liquid like it was the damn sandworm in *Dune*, splashing my face.

This time, I did jump up in surprise, knocking the glass over.

The waitress howled in laughter.

"Stupid bitch," I growled, not expecting her to understand.

She surprised me by responding in English, "Stupid *gringo* bitch." She pointed at me.

"What is your problem?"

She laughed again, then glanced down at my hands. Her eyes widened and she choked on her laughter.

I followed her look and saw wisps of smoke wafting off my hands where they rested on the tabletop. Looking back up, I saw her cross herself and back away, her face pale and her mouth set in a thin, troubled line.

Great going, chick. Conspicuous, much?

Lifting my hands up, I noticed the burn spots my fingers had left on the chipped Formica table. It occurred to me that I had likely left my fingerprints *burned right into the table*, as if I could any stupider. I had made a major mistake coming here, but before I could decide on a new course of action, I heard a door slam shut.

A man stood at the employees' door, not tall—my height or less—but he was terrifying. He was shirtless, and, like the waitress, almost every inch of his body was covered in frightening tattoos. Some of them were of the glyph variety. Wards. He was wearing wards on his body. But his facial piercings threw me the most. I used to have an eyebrow piercing and two lip rings in high school, but this dude had practically his entire face covered in rings and studs, some intricately placed to create yet more 3-D ward across his cleanly-shaven skull. He also had a giant doorknocker, earlobe-stretchers, and subcutaneous implants under the skin of his skull to give the impression of horns. He even had a split tongue—noticeable when he looked my way and licked his lips. Feathers hung from rings attached to his earlobe stretchers, and across his bare clavicle, he wore an intricate gold collar similar to the one the goddess wore in my visions. He was just missing the feathered headdress to look like some badass *brujo* in a movie about evil Aztec high priests.

He was frightening, for sure. But it was the way he was looking at me—a combination of displeasure and primal lust—that set my teeth on edge. I'd finally decided this was a *very* bad idea and started to get up, but someone grabbed me from behind.

Heart thudding loudly in my ears, I whipped around to face one of the big bikers. "Let me go!" I tried to jerk my arm loose, but his grip was like a vice. And when a second man grabbed my other arm, I knew it was too late.

Despite my protests, they easily dragged me toward the *brujo*.

He smiled as I approached, and I saw he had filed his teeth to points. It added another layer of scary to his already nightmarish image as the two large, burly men held me kicking between them.

Cast a spell. Set them on fire. Do something, you idiot!

I tried to whip up my power, but the *brujo* raised his hand and passed it across my face. I expected to pass out, but it was so much worse than that. It felt like someone had doused my entire body in freezing cold water. Immediately, my teeth started to chatter, my body shivered, and I felt all of my joints stiffen up. My power—my fire—felt frozen inside of me.

"No more of that, *bruja roja*," said the brujo. "I put that fire out, *si?*"

"W-who are you?" I moaned between shivers, shocked when I saw the cold mist coming out of my mouth. You would think I was standing in a sub-zero snowstorm instead of a sweaty biker bar.

"They called me Tupoc. What do they call you, my red witch?"

I didn't want to give the *brujo* my real name. Names had power. And anyway, I needed something that sounded badass, so I improvised.

"Lady Lucifer."

Tupoc laughed at that. "That! Is that your superhero name?"

The other men laughed with him.

That made me angry, but I couldn't do a thing except hang between the two dumb beefcakes holding me up. I could do nothing but shiver like some fool.

Tupoc said something to the men in Spanish and pantomimed over his bare chest like he was holding a woman's breasts. What he said didn't sound good, but the men laughed and started talking back and forth, saying things that I could only assume you never said in front of your mother.

"*Si, si,*" Tupoc laughed. He licked his lips again and reached out to run a hand over my breasts. The moment he touched me, it sparked the rage deep inside of me. I totally freaked out. I couldn't use my power, but, with a cry, I kicked out at him, driving my boot into his solar plexus.

The impact knocked him back a few steps, but it didn't drive him to the floor the way I'd hoped. Instead of angry, he looked impressed, his eyes facetiously large. Then he grinned again as if this was a game. He looked at me as if he wanted to rip my clothes off right then and there.

I started to panic. I twisted and turned in the men's grip, but I just wound up hurting myself as I fought them.

Tupoc, still grinning, prowled up to me and grabbed me by the throat. The moment he did, my entire body automatically seized up. The men let go of my arms so he could raise his arm up. My feet left the floor. His strength was ridiculous. I started to choke, so I wrapped both hands around his wrist, squeezing to try and get him to release me, but it was like grabbing a stone statue. I dug my nails into his flesh, but I didn't even make a dent.

My entire world shrank down to just a need to breathe. I couldn't. I couldn't do anything but panic and claw at his hand as he held me up above his grinning, monstrous face. I couldn't even scream because I couldn't suck in enough oxygen to make even a whimper.

"Stupid *bruja roja*. You will die so easily!"

Tupoc threw me half the length of the bar. I was grateful for it because it meant his hand was off my throat and I could breathe. But when I hit the floor, the impact just knocked the much-needed air right out of me and I continued to coast across the scarred hardwood floor until I hit the bar. The impact made me gasp in pain and surprise. My head clunked back against the bar and the whole place spun around me.

The patrons of the bar—the bikers, their women, even the barkeep—started roaring with laughter. They shouted things back and forth in Spanish, all at my expense. I was in pain and too scared to move. But also too scared not to. And I was mortified. Maybe that was the worst of it.

I cowered back against the bar as if their voices were a physical force pinning me there. In high school, I'd had an accident in gym class once. I ripped my volleyball shorts in a very revealing place and didn't know it, and not one girl told me, though I heard them whispering the whole time. It wasn't until afterward that the PE teacher stepped into the locker room to tell me. I asked her why she hadn't said anything earlier, and she shrugged and said she thought I'd done it on purpose.

Because, you knew, I was the class freak and whore.

Up until that day, I'd never cried so hard as I did then.

Now, I thought about that as I sat there, hurting and confused. I was such a fucking fool to think I could investigate this case. To come here, alone and unarmed, and take these people on. I was a confectioner, not a private investigator. But, as the Whore of Babylon, I supposed I deserve this...

No, you do not.

The voice was crystal clear in my head, but I didn't recognize it. Curious, I sat up straighter, listening hard and waiting for it to return. But the voice was gone.

Tupoc stopped laughing. He looked me straight in the eye. "*Bruja roja*, are you ready to play some more?" He made a show of grabbing his crotch.

I watched in absolute horror. I was so stupid and weak. I froze up—not that I could get to my feet even if I wanted to. I was in too much pain, and I thought I might have broken my ankle in the fall.

Tupoc's snakelike tongue swept across his lips. I felt my terror edge up another notch. He started to come for me...and then everything stopped. Everything.

Freeze frame.

I sat up and looked around the bar, but all of the faces of the men and women laughing at me were frozen like a collection of ugly masks. The barkeep, laughing and pouring a beer, was also frozen, and so was the tap, with frozen beer foaming out of it and into a mug.

I didn't understand. It was like someone stopped a movie mid-play on a DVD player. This was pretty big magic, whatever it was. But it also meant I had an opportunity to get the hell out of there, so I tried to claw my way to my feet. My ankle buckled, though, and I fell back down with a cry.

"Don't get up," said that same disembodied voice from before—except it was coming from the open door and not from inside my head. "You'll only aggravate your injury."

I slid back down as a strange man entered the roadhouse.

He was tall and blond and ridiculously handsome. He was wearing a pricey Italian suit in cream and a straw Panama hat with a red band. As he approached me, he lifted his head and I spotted his face...and gaped.

"Nick!"

It was my first assumption. He looked like Nick...just not. There were subtle little differences. His eyes were a bright, Caribbean blue-green, unlike Nick's winter-storm grey eyes, and he was wearing little square, silver-framed glasses. Nick didn't wear glasses. This man's features were older and more engraved—or just wiser and more learned. And he didn't have Nick's shit-eating grin. I saw he was carrying a walking stick like someone out of a British period drama. The stick was dark mahogany, almost black, and the head was made of silver in the form of a snake.

My realization of who I was facing struck more fear in me in that moment than Tupoc ever could—than *anyone* could, even Mr. McCarty, the man who'd spent a year raping me when I was nine years old.

"Holy Christ," I whispered.

And he laughed. "I'm afraid not, daughter."

| 25 |

SO THAT WAS how I wound up meeting the Devil in a filthy roadhouse.

I found myself trying desperately to scramble to my feet—to escape.

"Stop. Be still," he said. His voice was deep and stern and vaguely menacing as he set the walking stick down on the top of the bar. I expected an accent—British or Australian or maybe a sinister German—but to my surprise, he didn't have one.

When I continued to try and get to my feet, he gave me a direct look and said, *"Stop struggling, girl."*

His voice was so commanding that I froze up on the spot. I was completely helpless as he crouched down in front of me so we were looking into each other's eyes. He quickly undid the cravat at his throat. That made my heart beat double-time in my chest. But once he got the neckcloth loose, he bent over my ankle and slid my boot off. My ankle was already swelling and ugly. When he took it in his hand, I jumped a little. He was gentle but it really hurt.

"Calm down. I'm not going to hurt you," he told me, sounding exasperated. He spent the next few moments binding my ankle with his cravat before setting my foot on the floor. Then he stood up. "Can you stand?"

"I...don't know." All of my old Catholic School training had come back to haunt me and I was terrified to speak to him.

He offered me his hand.

I looked at it.

"Do you think I want to hurt you?"

"I didn't know," I said again, looking up at his tall, kingly frame. "You're...."

"Your father," he finished. "Give me your hand, daughter."

I half-expected his hand to feel burning hot, but it was just a man's hand. A very strong hand as he pulled me to my feet. "Lean on me," he said, offering me his shoulder.

I couldn't walk, so I had no choice but to put my arm around his waist. He walked me back to the two-seater in the corner. I couldn't believe this was happening as he helped me sit down and then retrieved another chair, which he set down next to mine. "Elevate your ankle. It's not broken but it is turned well. Elevating it will help with the swelling."

I put my ankle up while he sat down across from me. He watched me expectantly, but I just kept staring at him stupidly. After a few swallows, I managed some words. "He...told me about you...naturally...but I didn't think..." My voice trailed off uselessly.

"Nicholas?" His smirk became a lopsided sneer. "I'm sure it was nothing good. You mustn't listen to him. He's rather overdramatic, our Nick, isn't he?"

Strangely, I felt at ease now that we were both sitting down. But I couldn't help but glance around the bar at all of the frozen people.

"It's a time-lock," he explained. "They're *not* frozen. You and I are merely occupying a single picosecond between one second and the next. 'Time-lock' is a misleading description of what we are experiencing. No one is actually 'locked' in time. Everything is just moving extremely slowly. Slower than you or I can even see."

When he saw I had no idea what he was talking about, he indicated the room. "A picosecond is to one second as one second is to approximately 31,689 years."

I suddenly barked a small laugh. "Oh. So...as long as we don't sit here more than 31,689 years, we'll be fine."

He nodded as he removed his hat and set it on the table. His blond hair was slicked straight back. It made him look like David Bowie playing a Prohibition-era gangster. "Exactly."

"Do you think we'll finish in time?" I said because I was freaking out and sarcasm was always my go-to mechanism. "I mean...I have some questions."

He grinned then. Not sinister. He looked genuinely amused, though his teeth looked sharper in his mouth than anything a human should have. "How about we make a deal, daughter? You may ask me anything you want. But then you must answer *my* question honestly."

"A deal with the Devil," I laughed.

He put a hand to his chest. "Retired."

"Still..." I looked down a moment, then back up. "All right."

"Ladies first." He made a flourish with his hand.

I tried to think of something. But now that I had the man I had always wanted to talk to right in front of me, ready to answer all of my questions, I couldn't think of anything that didn't sound stupid. Is Bigfoot real? Who really killed JFK?

Shaking my head, I finally thought of one. "Nick said you stole his mother away and left him behind. Did you?"

He leaned forward slightly. "Yes. My turn."

"Wait...that's it?" I hold up a hand. "Just...yes?"

"It's the truth. Now, my question." His smile slipped just a little. "Why haven't you learned to fight, my little witch?"

I stared at him mutely for several seconds. "Fight?"

He nodded.

The only logical answer I could come up with was: "I never thought I would need to fight."

He nodded, accepting that. He was annoying laconic, I decided. "Your turn."

Again, I didn't know what to say to him. How to talk to him. "Are you...I mean, is it true? Are you really retired?"

"Yes. Why haven't you learned to use your powers? Nick did teach you, after all."

It was hard to keep up with him—the way he jumped back to me as a subject of conversation. "I did learn...some." I took a deep breath before continuing. "But then we broke up and I decided I never wanted to see him again. Not after what he did to me. The way he betrayed me. I guess I just figured I was done. Though, today..." I looked around the bar. "This proves I could use more training, huh?"

He seemed satisfied with my answer.

I suddenly thought of a question. "What name do you use when you're here...on Earth, I mean?"

He didn't hesitate to answer. "Dr. John Englebrecht when I teach ethics at the University of Philadelphia. Next question."

"Wait...so what name do I use?"

"John."

I was a little disappointed by that. It seemed mundane.

"Next question...why do you keep asking questions about me or Nick but not yourself? Surely, you are curious about...her."

I licked my lips nervously. I knew who he was talking about, but it still surprised me that he should ask. "Why would I want to know anything about her? She's nothing. She didn't want me in her life. So what difference does it make who she is?"

"You're not the least bit curious?"

His persistence spiked the outrage in me and I clenched my hands on the tabletop. "Why should I be? I have nothing to say to her. I'd rather know more about *you*."

He smirked and steepled his long, thin fingers together—but I couldn't tell if he was pleased or just humoring me. Rings with large, dark gemstones crackled on his fingers. "What would you like to know about me?"

"Everything!"

"You'll have to be more specific than that."

"How old are you? What have you seen?"

He looked at me oddly. I realized I was babbling like some excited groupie. No, I needed to control myself around him. And there *was* something I'd always wanted to know. Something important.

Another deep breath. "Was I…?" I looked at my hands and then back up. "…some kind of accident? Did you mean for it to happen? For me to be born?"

His expression never changed. "You must understand something important, child. I may have sired you and your brother, but I have little interest in playing the role of teacher, mentor, or father. Any plans you are developing in your head for a 'relationship' must cease immediately."

"I wasn't…"

"There are no Chosen Ones. You had no great destiny ahead of you. You exist. There is no more to it than that."

I stared at him, dumbstruck. I could feel something in me crumpling up and dying. I sat back in my seat and rubbed my stomach like I had a stomachache. "So…so you don't love us? You had no feelings for us at all?"

"Of course not."

"How…can you say that?" My voice sounded so small. So hurt.

He smiled a little. "I am being honest. I told Nick something years ago, and I will tell you the same thing now. My gift to you both is total honesty. I will never lie to you or deceive you in any way, daughter. That is a far greater gift than you can ever appreciate."

"So...this..." I spread my hands. "Coming here...talking to me...none of this means anything to you?"

"Everything I do means *something*," he corrected me. "What you mean to say is do *you* mean anything to me. And the answer to that question is no."

"You didn't care that I exist?" I could barely get the words out. My head was spinning.

"You exist. I care about that. But I do not allow myself unnecessary emotional attachments. Understand?"

I didn't know what to say to that. I'd just met my biological father for the first time, and he was telling me directly that he didn't love me. That I mean nothing to him. That we could never have a relationship. I wished...

I struggled to keep tears from welling up in my eyes.

...wished this had never happened.

Nick was right about him. He warned me that our father was a loveless shadow of a brute, but in my heart, I didn't believe him. I thought he was being bitter. Oh, my god, I'd never felt so damned alone in my life...

He interrupted my reeling thoughts. "Love is sentimental. Human. You are not, firefly. Stop crying." He handed me a handkerchief from the sleeve of his suit coat.

I just stared at it as I sucked back the tears. After a few seconds, I wiped them from my eyes with it.

"My turn," he insisted. "Do you want to learn to use your powers properly?"

I suddenly didn't care. But then I looked over at Tupoc, still standing there, leering down at the place where I was lying minutes before. If I could fight properly, creeps like that wouldn't be hurting anyone. I looked back over at my father and said, "I...guess."

"You guess?" He sounded annoyed.

"Yes." I wiped the remaining wetness from the corners of my eyes and sat up straight. "Yes, I wanted to learn to fight."

He nodded once and reached into an inside pocket of his natty linen jacket and produced something vaguely rectangular-shaped wrapped in red silk. He set it down on the table between us.

I looked at it numbly. "Is that a present?"

"Yes."

"Is it for me?"

"It is."

"Why?" My voice was so bitter.

"Because I want you to have it."

I reached for it and slowly unwrapped the satiny cloth. Inside, I found a stack of Tarot cards forged from what felt like paper-thin sheets of steel. They were cold and intricately engraved with the images of the higher Arcana on one side and the sign of the House of Lucifer on the other. I spread them out in a shiny silver fan and looked at them. They were so thin that you could prick your finger on the edges. "What are they?"

"My Tarot cards." He got up. "Learn to use them."

I had no idea what he meant.

"What?" I looked up and suddenly grabbed his hand. "John, wait!"

He looked down at me. His face was beautifully passive. Untouched by human emotions. I realized I was likely looking into the face of a sociopath and almost let go of his hand. He didn't shake me off, though.

"How?" I begged. "How do I use them?"

"Learn. Or be taught."

I stared at him, open-mouthed. "What does that mean?"

My father glanced at my hand, so I let go of him. He put his hat on. He smiled a little. "I'm pleased I came."

I watched him go to the bar and collect his walking stick. Then he turned to Tupoc and looked the man straight in his frozen eye as if he were studying him. "*Brujo verde*. He is very powerful."

"A powerful witch," I said.

John looked over at me. "Indeed. You will need to kill him. I cannot. None of the reigning Lucifers, past or current, can kill a mortal. It's in the rules. But you are not yet on the throne. So you may still take his life." His eyebrows shifted up his icy, handsome face. "I suggest you do so, daughter."

He turned back to the *brujo verde* and passed a hand over the man's pincushion-like skull. "As I figured. You and he are bound by a red thread."

I got up and limped forward. "What does that mean?" All of this was so surreal that I didn't know what to make of it as I jumped-limped by boot back on.

John turned to look at me, amused by the little dance I was doing. He tapped his temple with the stick. "It means you and the *brujo* were bound together in a dance of death. One of you will kill the other, but I can't see which way it will go—perhaps the Fates have not yet decided whose thread should be cut."

My heart thudded once, hard, in my chest. First, the woman in the iron coffin, and now this...it was like everyone in the known universe wanted to kill me. The irony of the situation was that I was nothing. Insignificant. My father said so himself. Certainly not worth this much effort to kill.

Before I could say anything to that effect, John turned back to Tupoc, lifted his snake cane high into the air, and used it to lay into the man. I heard a crunch as the cane connected with all of those facial piercings. The impact drove Tupoc to the floor at John's feet. Blood splattered the floor, John's shoes, and even his suit pants, though he didn't seem to mind.

He leaned forward and whispered, "That is your punishment for threatening one of the royal Lucifer line with your tiny penis, *el cerdito*." He said a few more words in a language I didn't understand. I was terrified it might be Divine—angel-speak, the oldest known language in the universe.

After he finished, John spat on the man before straightening up and turning to glance at me. I saw his eyes were lit from within. He was enjoying this way too much. It was like a drug to him. "That was fun. I would like to see you again, daughter. Perhaps a 'daddy-daughter date?' Provided, of course, you don't die before we meet again."

I limped toward him, unafraid now. He couldn't hurt me any more than he already had. "Why?" If he did not love me…if he didn't care that I existed…why would he want to spend a single moment more with me?

He smiled and his icy cold eyes drifted over me. "You are a beautiful creation, firefly. I wish to look upon you again." And with those words, he sank through the floor in front of me like a ghost and was gone.

I was alone once more.

Seconds later, the time-lock began to dissolve and life returned to its normal pace in this shabby little roadhouse. The people around me, including Tupoc on the floor, begin to move in a kind of nightmarish, bionic slow motion. I didn't wait around. By the time everything had resumed its normal speed, I was already halfway to my jeep with the Devil's Tarot cards in my pocket.

| 26 |

I SPENT THE next three days turning that conversation over in my head while I work my butt off in the prep room. I don't think I've ever worked so hard, so long, or with so few breaks in my whole life.

Sebastian finally noticed and sidled up to me and put a hand on my arm. "Tell me what's going on."

I looked up at him. Even three days after that strange encounter with my father, everything felt so surreal. "I'm okay."

"You're not okay." He indicated the jars surrounding us. I'd made so many sweets that the display room was full and we'd begun moving the stuff into the prep room. "You're twitchy, witchy. You won't stop making candy. You're spiraling."

"I don't spiral!" I said irritably.

He gave me a close-lipped half-smile as if he didn't buy my bullshit. "Even though we're scarcely moving this stuff, money keeps magically appearing in the joint account. Can you tell me about that?"

I'd totally forgotten he could access the joint business account. He never checked (to my knowledge), so, naturally, I assumed he'd never notice the extra cash.

I kept stirring my honey pot, but he reached over and turned off the heat. "You're ruining my candy!" I said.

"Tell me what's going on," he insisted, sounding upset for the first time since I'd known him.

I bit my lip and looked up at him. I rubbed my sticky hands over my apron. "If I tell you, you'll get angry with me."

He looked at me as if I was insane. "Maybe let me decide? I mean, aside from you robbing banks or doing hitman stuff in your spare time, I'm pretty much okay with anything." He thought a moment before adding, "You're doing amateur cam stuff, ain'tcha, luv? Not that I'm judging, mind you. I did a little softcore back in the day—"

I held my hand up to stop him. "I'm doing…side projects."

"Side projects." He continued to stare.

I sighed. "Nothing illegal. Or shady. More like…helping people with small magical problems."

Left with no alternative, I told him about my encounter with Matilda—and then, later, Doris. Connor was getting the help he needed from his therapist, and Malcolm walked his daughter down the aisle. He couldn't do more than shuffle across the dance floor with his daughter during the daddy-daughter dance, and he died two days after the wedding, but Doris was so moved that she gave me another check a few days after her daughter's wedding. That and a lot of tears.

Those were good things, right? Still, after I told Sebastian, he looked strangely concerned.

"You're mad," I said.

"Nah," he managed after a long pause. "And you're making money this way?"

"You make it sound dirty." I sank down onto a stool and gestured wildly. "I figured if we can't make it on all this crap candy, at least I can keep the lights on with my crap craft talent."

He moved a stool beside mine and sat down. It took him a moment to respond. "I'll be honest, Vivian. I'm no fan of the craft. I'd rather you did porn."

This was serious. He never called me Vivian.

I tried for humor. "This—coming from a necromancer." I bumped his shoulder.

"I wasn't *born* a necromancer..." He paused, looking thoughtful. I knew when he got that faraway look that he was trying his damnedest to remember...something. "I mean...I don't think I was. I think I was a regular ol' witch like yerself, but the craft did something to me. It did *this* to me."

He touched his chest like he was still not at peace with the body he was in. "It has bloody fucked up my whole life, and I don't trust it. But...if you think you can handle it, I won't stop you from using it."

"Do you mean that?" I asked uncertainly.

He looked up. "No. I just like to hear myself talk, you cunt."

I shoved him and he shoved me. We both laughed.

And, for a few minutes at least, I forgot that my father didn't love me, that I was a half-ass witch who didn't know shit, and that forces were trying to kill me for their own dubious reasons.

Gasping with laughter, I said, "There's more."

"Right." He got very serious and waited.

It took me a bit to wind up the courage for this one. "On my day off, I followed up on a lead."

He blinked, taking a moment to digest that. "You mean...that case you're looking into for the sexy detective?"

"That's the one." I rattled off a concise version of the day, but I didn't mention meeting my father. I was not ready to talk about *that* yet—even with Sebastian. When I got to the part where Tupoc grabbed me, I told Sebastian I managed to wriggle free and run away. I didn't tell him anything about the metallic Tarot cards I had hidden under my mattress upstairs, but I did tell him about the

Aztec woman I saw. I didn't want to overwhelm him with all of my crazy family stuff, but I did want his take on her.

"Do you think...?" I glanced down and took a deep breath. "Should I tell Mac about Tupoc, the Toltecs, and the Aztec woman?"

He thought a moment. "The dead men...they had tattoos like what you saw on the bikers?"

"Yeah."

He tilted his head slightly. "If it's a lead, you should tell him."

"Yeah, but..." I hesitated, took a deep breath, and then told him what was really bothering me. "This is all connected to the Aztec goddess, right? Somehow?"

"All the more reason to tell him."

"I know what you're saying, but that thing is dangerous, Sebastian. Mac's not prepared to deal with something like her. Hell, *I* was not."

"You like him."

His comment surprised me. "Yeah."

"Then protect him." He reached out and pushed a lock of hair off my face that had come loose from the usually tight chignon I wear it in when I'm working. It was an almost fatherly gesture. "Witchy, did it ever occur to you that you've been given these powers to protect Mac and help put an end to whatever this thing is?"

| 27 |

WITH SEBATIAN'S BLESSING, I ripped off my apron, rushed to my jeep, and drove like a bat out of hell down to the police station, hoping I wasn't too late and Mac hadn't gone home yet.

Inside, I was surprised. I always thought an inner-city police station would look chaotic like the ones on TV. Perps being walked to the jail cells in the back while suspects were being tearfully interviewed in small, dark rooms. Maybe a smartass kid handcuffed to a desk sergeant's chair and giving him lip. But it was surprisingly orderly. A couple of cops wandered past me, sipping coffee, while a female cop stood at a vending machine, feeding quarters into it and banging on the glass until she got her Diet Coke.

I moved to the dispatch desk. A young black man sat behind it, doing a Sudoku puzzle. "I'd like to speak to Sergeant Detective Miles McCall," I told him. "It's concerning a case I'm helping him with."

The young man looked up, seemingly surprised by my statement. "Mac? He's going home."

"It's important. He asked me to check in with him."

Not exactly the truth, but I knew Mac had been waiting for something. I also knew the moment he knew I was here, he'd set everything aside to talk to me.

The young desk sergeant picked up an old-fashioned desk phone and relayed the information to someone in the back before setting the receiver down. Seconds later, I saw Mac come around the corner and motion to me. He was carrying his coat over one arm. He looked as handsome as always but also tired.

The station was mostly empty, the offices dark, and the bullpen quiet as I followed him back to an abandoned office. He closed the door but didn't put on the lights. Going to his desk, he half-sat on it. The glow of the city filled the room, outlining him like a gumshoe in a pulp story. "I didn't expect you would come here."

"I have information on that case and I didn't want to give it to you over the phone," I told him as I undid my jacket and wandered around his office. I wasn't trying to be catty or seductive, but I saw him looking me over. Under my jacket, I was still in my cook's whites and Dr. Scholl's no-slip shoes—and none of that was sexy in any way. But that didn't seem to be a deterrent for him.

Mac redirected his attention to my face. "I thought you didn't have anything for me," he said, referring to the phone call we'd had a few days ago.

"Yeah, well…things have changed."

"And here I was afraid you were just avoiding me."

I clasp my hands together coquettishly. "That, too. Talking to your little girl spooked me."

Mac smirked. "You'd like Charity. She's my little power girl. Likes all those warrior-girl shows."

"What's her favorite?"

"The blonde girl. With the cat friend."

"*She-Ra and the Princesses of Power.*"

"That's the one."

He seemed so relaxed with what we were doing, it frightened me.

He indicated the bullpen beyond the door. "Do you want some coffee? It's shit, but I can doctor it up some…"

"I won't be here long."

He looked disappointed by that.

I wandered over to a large, well-worn chesterfield situated against one wall. I imagined Mac sleeping many a night on it while working a case. I sat down and looked up at him.

He shook his head. "Just looking at you does something to me. I feel like some fool with a second-grade school crush."

"I'm sorry," I told him honestly. "I'm not trying to do that..."

"I know. It's my fault." He raised his hand to stop me from protesting. "I'm not that guy, Vivian. The one who says he had no control, that it was the woman doing it to him. I knew damned well what I'm doing. I *want* to do it. It really is me, not you."

His statement left foolish tears in my eyes. This whole thing was supposed to be selfish and about the loss of self-control and self-interest. It was supposed to be about personal gratification. He and I were supposed to be terrible people for doing it. I was not supposed to care about him and feel this connection.

Mac turned to a dry board with pictures and writing all over it. He picked up a Sharpie. "You said you have info on the case?"

I summed up my adventures over the last few days, telling him the same story I told Sebastian, just with a lot less craft information. But when he turned to look at me, I cringed.

"You went to the roadhouse where you knew the Toltecs hang out?" he said, sounding appalled.

The anger in his voice dissolved the fluttery feeling in my tummy as if someone had dumped a bucket of ice water over my libido. His glare made me shrink in my seat. "I wanted to make certain before I came to you."

"Certain about what?"

"I don't know! That they exist. That they seem like terrible people—the kind the murderer would target."

Mac threw the Sharpie across the room and went to stand by the window. In the glass, I saw his face contorted into a knot. He was breathing roughly. It frightened me.

"I'm not a child, you know," I told him defensively. "I can take care of myself just fine."

Not exactly the truth, but he'd made me angry and I needed to lash out.

He took several moments to get his temper under control. During the course of it, he put his hand on the cold black glass and spread his fingers so I could see his wedding band. The silence between us was thick. "You could have gotten hurt. Gotten killed. And it would have been my fault. Did you even think about that? You could have died because I gave you that file, and that would have been on me. I would have had to carry that for the rest of my fucking life!"

He swallowed hard. I could tell by the pain in his face that this was hard for him. I'd been hard on him. What we'd created between us was hard on him.

I got up. "Don't be angry with me."

He turned and looked at me with an emotion I couldn't translate. Lust. Fear. The light of a passing car passed across the window outside, making him look pale and ghost-like for a moment.

"God almighty," he gasped at last. "I look at you…at the languid, effortless beauty of you…and all I can think about is touching you. I can't seem to think beyond you."

His words made my heart surge. After being told by countless others that I was dirty and evil and everything that was wrong, I needed this. I needed him. I reached out and touched his cheek. He closed his eyes and seemed to revel in my mouth. Then I slowly undid the buttons of his shirt. The sight of that smooth, dark wall of muscle nearly undid me.

Mac suddenly loosened his necktie. "My place. My rules."

He grabbed me by both wrists. His hands were large and corded and capable of great violence, I thought. He twisted me around so the front of my body was pressed to the wall and held me there as if I were a dangerous criminal, his one hand spanning both of my wrists. His other went to the side of my head and turned it gently.

His mouth captured mine. His tasted hot and meaty like a hunter and, in seconds, it was all I could do to control myself. Amidst his kiss, I made these soft, kitten-like noises that drove Mac crazy. Soon enough, he was responding with a long, low, throaty growl while he produced a pair of handcuffs from his utility belt.

"Mistress, do you trust me?" he asked.

I told him the truth. "Yes."

Christ, I'd never felt so out of control—except, perhaps, with Nick.

He slid the handcuffs over my wrists and secured them snugly, but not so tightly that they chafed. I could tell he knew what he was doing. They jingled as he turned me back around, grabbed the front of my jacket, and pulled it apart and down my arms. The sleeves caught on the handcuffs and could go no farther. Then he did the same to my white cook's shirt, tearing it open so violently I started.

He looked me up and down as if he was mesmerized by the sight of me in just my boring grey, racerback sports bra. It was not a pretty, sexy bra—it was my work bra—but he didn't seem to care. Putting one big hand on my hip, he dragged me against him, the gesture rough and primal. I stumbled. He rubbed the front of his hard, lean body against me, a distinctively possessive gesture, while he dipped his head and nipped none too gently at the side of my throat.

"Ohh," I said as he kissed and tortured me.

"I'm not hurting you?"

"Maybe if you tried harder..."

"You really are something," he said, leaning back.

"Your station. Your rules."

I knew he wanted—needed—to hear those words.

"Fuck!" he roared as he dragged me to the sofa and forced me to kneel on it.

He hesitated, breathing hard through his lust. I could tell he was waiting for me to object. I had given him permission to do anything he wanted to me, but I was still the one in charge of things. Topping from the bottom, as it were. I gave Mac a demure look over one shoulder.

"God, you're so fucking beautiful I can barely control myself," he gasped.

"Don't," I commanded him. "Do what you want. *Whatever* you want."

Mac's eyes gleamed with a wild light as he moved into position behind me. "Don't move," he said. "And don't come."

He pushed me down into the cushions and shifted his body so I was pinned under his weight. The room was suddenly filled with breathy, intimate sounds and the jingle of the cuffs as he covered me. Unexpectedly, he leaned down to kiss me on the side of the face. It was a strangely sentimental gesture.

I moaned and wriggled a little beneath him.

He grunted in response, then sat back to shrug off his shirt. His body was incredibly hard, but his skin was soft and darkly lit from within. It felt like silk stretched over stone as he pressed the sizable erection in his trousers against my back. Reaching around, he grabbed my breasts and squeezed them so hard that I let out a little cry of surprise. His muscles rippled as he stroked and squeezed me, letting me feel his raw strength.

"Harder," I encouraged him. "You could hurt me a little if you like."

He squeezed my flesh even harder and I moaned and twisted in his cuffs.

Leaning down, he kissed the back of my neck.

I had pictures in my head of the things he wanted to do to me. Things he had been thinking about all week. Things he wanted to do his whole life—if only he had the right partner. "Yes," I said when he let me up a moment to breathe. "I want those things, too. Punish me, Mac. Consume me."

"Who the hell were you?" he demanded—not in confusion, but in elation. His hands, shaking with desire, undid my white cook trousers, and he pulled them and my boy shorts down my legs. He then bent his head to kiss and lick the base of my spine. I sighed at the roughness of his cheek tickling me, and when he moved to bite at the flesh of my ass, I bucked my hips a little.

I spread my legs, hoping he'd relieve me of his terrible, endless wanting, but instead of quickly taking me the way I wanted, he worked his slow way back up my spine. I shivered all over. "Mistress," he said. His sweet eyes seething with lustful need. "My sweet Mistress."

He kissed me again, hard, and I wanted to cry out with need and frustration.

Mac grunted and unexpectedly slapped my ass. The sound of flesh on flesh echoed around the room. The sting seemed to go right through me and to my nether parts, making me wetter than ever.

He immediately regretted it. "I'm s-sorry. I—"

I moaned in response. "Don't apologize. And don't hit me like a little girl." I lowered my head while arching my back. "Harder."

He did as I commanded him. This time, he put more confidence into it.

When Nick and I were together, we enjoyed a little light BDSM. Nothing too serious because, like Mac, I knew Nick didn't enjoy inflicting pain on his lovers—even to get them off. Mac was much the same way. He increased his force with each blow, but he kept asking me if that was okay—and, once, if he'd hurt me. I loved how concerned he was.

"Take me," I finally commanded. I was ready at last.

He obeyed. Within seconds, I was mewling while he entered me and tenderly kissed my neck and shoulder as if to make up for the impacts. "Christ, you're such a sweet little bitch," he said, and I was surprised by the ferocity in his voice. "I could fuck you all night."

He wrapped an arm around my waist and jerked me upright on my knees while we coupled, whispering, "Fuck, you're tight. Fuck, I love you."

"More," I moaned. "Give me more."

He started working my body in a slow, erotic rhythm. It made me groan, gasp, and almost scream. His big hand slid up my body, keeping me up on shaky knees. A delightful electricity filled us both, and our cries of pleasure made me fear someone working late would look in out of worry.

He smelled so good, like vanilla and sex. He bit the side of my neck as we shuddered and twitched and the cuffs snapped around my wrists as we finished. After he let me out of the cuffs, I turned and gripped the mantel of Mac's head, burying my face affectionately in his neck while we both snuggled down into the sofa and slowly worked on catching our breaths and coming down from our high.

I felt a flash of fear even as I touched his precious bite mark with soft, loving fingertips. Afraid...because I thought I might love this man.

| 28 |

IT WAS LATE when I got back to the shop. There were police cars from three different precincts parked outside, as well as an ambulance with flashing lights at the curb. My earlier good feelings evaporated at the sight and I hit the brakes so hard that I nearly rear-ended the SUV in front of me that had slowed down to watch the cops crawling all over my shop.

With a curse, I pulled to the opposite side of the street—it was the only place to park at the moment—and killed the engine and leaped from the jeep. I had a bad moment of déjà vu as I crossed the street. I once came home to cops crawling all over the duplex I was renting with my friend Tiffany back in Blackwater. When I walked in, I learned Tiffany had been bludgeoned to death and the cops thought I had done it.

My heart wouldn't stop vibrating inside me as I approached the shop. And yet, the closer I got, the slower I walked, so it felt like a long time before I reached the sidewalk. By then, everything was moving through a surreal curtain of syrup. A cop standing by the smashed open door of my shop turned to me and said something about not entering. But I shouldered past him and into the shop anyway.

Everything was smashed. Glass and candy were scattered across the floor in a glittering avalanche. The glass cabinets had been shattered with a blunt-force weapon of some kind—probably the aluminum baseball bat abandoned on the floor. The display window was broken. Sebastian's little chocolate circus—stale and inedible but still beautiful—was lying in broken pieces across the countertops. My shoes crunched over my life's work as I raced in slow motion toward the prep room. I passed the ward on the wall and saw someone had spray-painted a rough outline of a roaring jaguar head over it.

My brain registers that detail in particular. The paint was red but seemed to be melting away on the wall as my own ward reclaimed the space. The Toltecs had attacked the shop, and the ward had fought back.

I stopped in the doorway of the prep room and just took in the sight before me.

It was the only room that looked untouched. Someone had knocked one of the standing mixers down, and some ledgers were lying on the floor, but that was it. It might even have been an accident when one of the cops was bumbling around the small space.

The real horror was what was lying on the floor in front of me, bleeding into the cracks of the tiles.

I stared at Sebastian's bloodied, lifeless face staring up at me. His eyes were wide open and his mouth gaping in a soundless scream. His hands were wrapped tightly around the handle of a knife protruding from the center of his chest. Blood had drooled out of the corner of his mouth and made a small pool there. There was another, larger pool underneath him.

He couldn't scream. So I did it for him. I screamed loud and long even as the cops dragged me away.

| 29 |

SITTING IN THE back of an ambulance, an EMT took my blood pressure and asked me my name, the year, and who the president of the United States was.

Annoyed, I threw off the blanket they'd given me. "I'm all right!" I shouted, getting up.

The EMT, a remarkably burly, middle-aged man with a thick beard and carrot hair, didn't try to stop me. I must have looked pretty scary at the moment. The initial horror had left me all hollowed out, but now it was quickly filling up with rage.

Rage for what happened to my friend. Rage at those who did it to him.

Beaten and stabbed. That was what the police told me. They had eyewitnesses that said several Latino men broke into the shop about an hour ago—angry, tough-looking dudes—and that there was shouting and the sound of breaking glass. Safa from the Laundromat went to investigate as the suspects were charging out of the shop. She immediately called the police.

Now, Safa came over to comfort me. I tried not to choke up. While I was making love to Mac at the police station, my best friend was being beaten and stabbed to death on the floor of our shop. Intellectually, I knew it was not my fault. I knew it was the Toltecs, but that didn't mean I wasn't going to blame myself too. As Safa described what she saw, I realized Tupoc had led the charge. They hit the shop because of me. They wanted to send a message: *I was not tough. I was not invincible. I was just meat to them.*

And they were right. They knew I would blame myself.

After the EMT cleared me, I went back into the shop. I must have been putting out some seriously weird vibes because the police officers crawling over the place didn't even try to stop me as I made my way to the prep room. Sebastian was gone. His body had been loaded into the coroner's van outside. But as I stood there, staring down at the bloodstains on the floor, a housefly landed directly on my nose.

I raised my hand to swat at it when I realized it was waving one tiny leg at me.

Witchy! Witchy...you cunt...look at me!

The voice in my head was frantic. I realized, belatedly, that I'd been hearing it for the last few minutes or so. I just hadn't been able to pay any attention past the horror I'd been feeling.

"Seb—!" I stopped myself and glanced around. As soon as the officer in the room left, I held out my hand, and the fly landed in my palm. "Sebastian?"

Took you long enough! Where in bloody hell have you been?

"I thought you were dead! What happened?"

Those cockers got me good, but I got out before they could really damage me.

"Got out? You mean you jumped into...this?"

The fly waved its legs frantically. *I can't stay like this! If I don't get back to my body soon, it will die for good and I'll...* He glanced all around. *Where in the hell did they take it?*

"It's in the coroner's van," I offered helpfully.

Right. They're going to take me to the morgue. Put me in one of those refrigeration units.

"Yeah. That's what usually happens."

If I get too cold, I won't be able to get back in. Take me to the van!

His voice was so frantic that I made an about-face. The coroner's van was parked right out front, under a street lamp.

At that very moment, a new cop appeared in the room, a black woman.

I gently clenched my hand over Sebastian, ignoring his cries of protest in my head. "Officer?" I said, raising my free hand to get her attention.

She turned to look at me. Her face was stern but kind. "Sweetheart, what are you still doing in here?"

"I want to see my friend Sebastian."

She shook her head sadly and rested her hands on her gun belt. "I'm sorry. I know it's hard, but I can't allow that." Her voice dropped an octave. "No one gets into the meat wagon after it's full…" She hesitated. "No offense."

I opened my mouth, unsure how I'd convince her to let me see Sebastian's body.

Bugger this! Sebastian said in my head.

Seconds later, the lady cop staggered backward as if she had been violently pushed by an unseen force. She nearly collided with the workbench behind her before she found her balance. I instinctively reached out to help steady her. Her head was down, but when she looked up, I could tell something was wrong.

The expression on her face was completely different—less kind. And her eyes were blue. Sebastian's eyes. She looked like she was going to be sick as she clutched her head. "Never gonna get used to this shite!" the lady copy said in a distinctive Cockney accent.

"It's you."

The lady cop dropped her hands and straightened up. I could literally "see" Sebastian in her body. He was wearing it like a suit. But he was struggling with it like some puppet master who didn't quite have it right with his marionette. "Right, then. Get me to the 'meat wagon,' if you will. This is always so bloody hard in the beginning."

I didn't know what to say, so I slid an arm around Sebastian's waist and duck-walked him out the back door where there were fewer cops to notice us. Together, we made it down the delivery alley and around the corner to the street. By then, Sebastian was starting to recover and walking on his own.

"Well, now...this is not good."

"What isn't good?" I couldn't imagine how things could get any worse.

"It's getting easier to drive her."

I just looked at him. "What does that mean?"

Sebastian twitched slightly as if he was on the edge of a seizure, then recovered. "The easier it gets, the more my selfie takes over, and the more *she* slips away. And the more permanent this body becomes."

"You mean...you're killing her?" I hoped I was not right.

He made a face. "More like...becoming entrapped in her. Where the hell is that wagon?" He was starting to sound panicky again, so I steered him toward the coroner's van. By the time we reached it, he was almost "driving her" perfectly, so the officer standing next to the van didn't even blink when Sebastian said, "I need to look at the bloody body."

Unfortunately, the officer, who obviously knew the female cop, frowned in response.

Before Sebastian could screw this whole thing up, I suddenly barked, "I heard some glass breaking inside. Do you think they came back?"

Sebastian caught on and, glancing briefly at the cop's name badge, joined in with, "They need you inside, Roberts!"

Officer Roberts stiffened, took one look at Sebastian, and suddenly headed toward the shop while playing with his shoulder radio.

"Good job," Sebastian said, pawing at the coroner's van. "Get this open. I can't feel my fingers."

Even though the last thing I wanted was to see inside a meat wagon, I grabbed hold of the back hatch and yank on it. No go. Then I realized it likely unlocked from the front seat.

"Stay here," I said and raced around to the front and opened the driver's side door. Luckily, no one was in the van. I searched along the floor until I found the trunk release and pulled the lever. The back hatch hissed open. By the time I made it back around, Sebastian was standing inside the spacious van, looking down at a black body bag lying on a collapsed stretcher.

"I hope it's not too late," he said, kneeling beside his own body.

"If it is?" I said as I knelt on the opposite side.

He looked down at his hands. "My selfie takes over and I get to be a hot black chick in the city in my next life."

"And you got to kill a hot black chick—who is innocent," I reminded him.

He looked up grimly, reached for the zipper on the body bag, and then stopped. "I can't."

"Oh, for Chrissakes! You're a necromancer. Haven't you dealt with dead bodies?"

His bottom lip trembled. "It's different when it's...you. Spookier."

With a sigh of frustration, I unzipped the bag for him. I was okay until I saw Sebastian—his body, anyway—inside the bag, looking all blue-faced and cold and dead. I immediately zipped it back up. "Oh, god."

"Yeah."

We both looked down at Sebastian's body (ex-body?), and I felt my eyes fill with tears even though I knew it was stupid. He wasn't really dead. He was right here, looking at me.

Sebastian, for his own part, smiled. "Aww, you love me. You really, really love me!"

"Shut it!" I unzipped the bag again with some force and pointed at the corpse. "Get in!"

Sebastian looked terrified as he reached out and tentatively laid his hand on the corpse's chest. He grimaced. "I might not be able to do this." He looked up. "It might have been too long."

I realized he was truly terrified and reached across dead Sebastian to put my hand on living Sebastian's arm in solidarity.

"Right. Here we go." He closed his eyes and, for what felt like forever, nothing seemed to happen. Time ticked by, and I started to fear this wouldn't work, or that we'd get caught by the coroner or the other cops—who had to be on their way back.

Then, all of a sudden, I felt a surge of electricity under Sebastian's arm. It was as if electric eels were moving under his skin. I assume this was his "selfie" on the move. I got some flashes of things in the past, but only crazy, disconnected stuff: Horses and carts, gaslights, fisticuffs, filthy public houses, crowded streets that could be in London or Paris or anywhere. I saw myself in a Victorian-style nursery, holding a squalling, frightened baby up in front of me, my wrists covered in lace and ruffles—and blood. That image was particularly powerful—and disturbing. Then the images started moving too fast for my brain to follow and I heard a massive intake of breath.

Opening my eyes, I saw the female officer kneeling in front of me. She was as still as a statue, but her eyes were white like boiled eggs, seeing nothing. Ex-Sebastian was sitting up in the black body bag, having pulled the knife from his own chest, and was staring at me with absolute horror. I had never seen such terror in my life.

"Holy fucking Christ on a cracker, you're—!" he screeched, then stiffened and seemed to pass out. I waited, trying not to freak out. When he came to a few seconds later, he didn't wear the same expression.

"Witchy!" he said in greeting. He spotted the van and body bag and suddenly scrambled up. But the thick black bag prevented him from moving too fast and he wound up flopping back down.

All this surprised me so much that I let go of the officer, who slid sideways and slumped to the floor in some hypnotic state. Jumping up, I cringe away from him. "Sebastian?"

Formerly dead Sebastian collected himself and then extradited himself properly from the body bag in such a way that I wondered if he had done this in the not-too-distant past. He didn't seem to remember his earlier outburst, though he did say in a sleepy voice, "What the hell was all that? Why the hell were you on fire? Christ!"

He was touching me when he did his magic. He must have seen things in my past the same way I did his. A sort of exchange of mental baggage.

Our eyes met and I searched for that look that said he knew about me, or that I had frightened or disgusted him.

Sebastian, still weak from his little adventure, blinked with his unfocused eyes, then tottered to the edge of the meat wagon and collapsed into a sitting position. "Help me down, luv. I need a fucking drink or ten."

| 30 |

I GOT SEBASTIAN into my jeep before anyone noticed his corpse was walking around and drove until I hit the first no-tell motel I came upon—the Seaside Inn, whose name was ironic, considering the state of PA was landlocked. After tucking him into our sixty-dollar-a-night room (he looked exhausted and nodded off almost immediately) and writing a quick note so he wouldn't wake up and panic, I grabbed my keys and went back out to the jeep.

I drove. Around midnight, I stopped at a gas station to fill up. Inside the Wawa was a sleepy female clerk sitting behind the counter, yawning and texting on her phone. I paid for my gas and picked up a vitamin water. Passing the Hostess display, I suddenly decided to stock up. I mean, it seemed to work for Nick whenever he was in the middle of a crisis.

Thus armed with water and calories, I returned to the jeep and just sat in it in the dark, stuffing my face with Devil Dogs and watching the other cars pull in and out while I tried to decide what to do next. There was no way I could go back home. Confused cops and pissed-off Toltecs waited back there (and monsters and whatever other shit I'd brought down upon myself), and I was not prepared to face any of that at the moment.

I planned to just sit here all night and eat chocolate and maybe cry for a little while until I'd cleared my head. It was while I was bending over in the dark, digging napkins out from under my seat to wipe my leaky nose that the cards my father gave me fell out and into the footwell. I set the Devil Dogs aside and leaned down to pick the cards up. Undoing the cloth, I looked at the rectangles of sharp metal, wondering if I could somehow use them to help me determine what to do next. Maybe I could scry my way out of his unholy mess. I wasn't really a Tarot person, but I was willing to try anything at this point.

I set the cards in a stack on the seat beside me and carefully shuffle them. I managed to cut my fingers twice in the process, so I didn't see that as a good sign. When I finally decided to cut the deck and try a three-card draw, I drew first a Devil card...and then another Devil card...and, finally, a third Devil card.

"What the fuck?"

I tried again, but I got the same results. All Devil cards.

And again.

Than again!

"Well, fuck! What's the point of you!" I screamed like a lunatic at the cards.

A middle-aged woman in nurse's scrubs walked past my jeep on her way to her car, giving me an odd look.

Sighing, I leaned back in my seat, the cards in my lap. What did my father say? *Learn. Or be taught.*

"Thanks. That helps a lot, Dad."

I must have nodded off for a time because before I realized it, the sun was coming up over the trees at the edge of the parking lot. Sitting up straighter, I felt a terrible kink in my neck and back. I also spied a billboard across the street that I hadn't been able to read in the dark:

This October, get in touch with your inner Witch!

There were pumpkins and black cats on the board, and a woman dressed in black robes, with a big, welcoming smile and a broom, pointing directly at me. Under it was a website for the Annual Witches' Walk through Oldtown—the parade that took place in the older part of Blackwater every October. The Witches' Walk was the biggest annual celebration in Blackwater. Actually, it was only one. Tourists come from all over the country to watch self-styled witches (and regular people in costume) march through the streets to the sound of a big band and point dramatically at the onlookers.

"Get in touch with your inner witch," I said.

Hell, why not?

I started the jeep and put it in drive. Blackwater was only a hundred miles away. I could be there in two hours.

| 31 |

I WAS WORRIED about stepping into Curiosities again. Seeing Nick...encountering Morgana...the idea sent a cold, icy finger up my spine. Nick and I didn't exactly part on good terms last time, but I knew I could probably deal with him. Morgana was another story.

She'd never liked me. Can't blame her. She was this tall, cool, powerful green witch connected to the elements, to the stars and the Earth and the skies and all of the good things in the world. She was like a real-life Glinda the Good Witch. She lived in a state of peace with the universe and had complete control over her powers. She helped people and asked for little in return.

Me? I was a hot mess train wreck witch. I tried, but I knew I'd never be as good as she was. I'd never be good, period.

Parked on the curb outside the shop, I grabbed the wheel and took a few deep, rapid breaths. I didn't feel better, but gulping all that oxygen too fast did make me feel dizzy.

"Fuck it."

Getting out, I walked to the door, grabbed the old-fashioned latch, and pulled. With a tinkle of the bell, I was in the store. It was warm and stuffy and crowded with displays. Not the kind of place you took your toddler. I saw racks of books and how-to DVDs, shelves of healing crystals, small pots of tinctures, and New Age-style curios and baubles. Not all of it was "magical stuff," of course.

Blackwater was a tourist trap, so there was a whole section dedicated to souvenirs—Blackwater ball caps, T-shirts, wind chimes, and lawn art. Nick and Morgana made a lot of money off travel junk. But I knew the real magic was made in the backroom, and every townie in Blackwater knew it as well.

The funny thing about Blackwater was that if you asked any of the townies, they would act like they hated the shop and its reputation, but nearly all of them came here when they had a problem they couldn't solve on their own. While I was with Nick, I saw the full gamut of customers—people with embarrassing rashes, sexual performance issues, or even more serious issues like cancer or genetic disorders that wouldn't respond to traditional medicine. I saw old ladies buying tinctures for their rheumatoid arthritis and young girls buying pennyroyal for homemade abortions. I assumed Morgana was very good at what she did, because no one ever died, and no one ever came back angry.

I wanted to be like that. I wanted to help people.

Maybe it would make up a little for all of the shitty things I'd done.

The shop was empty except for an older woman in a flowered hat looking through some sparkly scarves. Morgana suddenly appeared from the back room and said in a cheery tone, "Here you go, Mrs. Bailey."

Lucky for me, the rack of dreamcatchers was blocking me from her view.

Mrs. Bailey, dressed in a long, lavender dress, glided to the counter and accepted a small white bag from Morgana. "Thank you, dear. This means so much."

Morgana, looking pristine in a long, flouncy white gown that made her hair glow fiercely yellow and gave her an almost angelic countenance, folded her hands together. She blinked slowly with those large, wise, crystal-blue eyes of hers. "I know Nick usually takes care of you, but he's away on business, I'm afraid."

"That's quite all right, dear! I love seeing you, too!"

The two women exchanged pleasantries and even hugged before Mrs. Bailey made a dramatic exit from the shop.

Morgana remained behind the counter, smiling. But as soon as Mrs. Bailey was gone, her smile fell, she put her hands down, and she said in a much darker tone of voice, "You can come out now, Vivian."

I swallowed hard. I hated that she had that effect on me. Stepping out from behind the rack, I approached the counter and the woman I feared almost more than any other.

Her eyes were...not cold, exactly, but certainly remote. Her hands hung loosely at her sides and her posture was relaxed—unconcerned. The thing that bothered me most about Morgana was not that she made a concentrated effort to hate me, but that I didn't register for her at all. I was merely an annoying fly in the ointment of her life, unworthy of such a strong emotion as *hate*. She made me feel insignificant.

"He's not here," she said, cutting right to the chase. "I'm sorry you made the trip."

"Away on business," I said, hating how small my voice sounded. It was like when I talked to my parents or the teachers at school who hated me. I was the Mean Girl everyone reviled. I was the pariah.

She didn't answer me. Instead, she started polishing the glass countertop with Windex. I was amused to see that the display was holding *Dark Shadows* memorabilia this week. I saw DVDs of the old series with Jonathan Frid looking particularly fierce on the covers and a few other items that probably gave the tourists mini-orgasms, including reproductions of Barnabus Collin's infamous wolf cane and signature ring.

"Are you high?" she suddenly asked me.

My head snapped up. I was exhausted and punch-drunk, so my mouth ran away with me. "Why?"

Her eyes shifted with annoyance. "I don't want you breaking anything."

Finally, I was angry. She could ignore me all she wanted, but belittling me was really roasting my chestnuts. "Don't worry, I won't break your stupid tourist shit," I spat.

I saw her perk up. I thought maybe I'd finally gotten to her, but then I realized she was staring at my hands. My fingertips were smoldering again and leaving black marks on the glass.

Morgana lifted her head and flared her nostrils. Finally, she looked a little concerned. "Lady Lucifer," she said, "You've really come into your power, hadn't you?"

"That's right," I agreed. "I'm not the stupid little girl you think I am."

"I never thought that."

Her admission unbalanced me. In retaliation, I said, "I want to talk to Nick. Not you."

"He's not—"

"A business trip. Sure, whatever. But when have you ever trusted him with something like that?"

She sighed. Digging a memo pad out from under the counter, she jotted down an address, ripped the page off, and handed it to me.

I looked at the paper and realized it was a Lake Ariel address.

"Nick's found himself a coven of Satanists to hang with. Maybe you've heard of them? The Children of Endor?"

I remembered what Josh told me.

"Their summerhouse is up on Lake Ariel. He's there now if you need to speak to him that urgently."

Fair enough. I took the paper.

"But be warned," she added, her face strained. "He's not the same man you knew."

I looked down at the paper in my hand, then back up. "What does that mean...?"

But Morgana was gone with just the beads in the doorway to the back room lightly swaying.

| 32 |

I HAD TO drive slowly past the long line of luxury cabins on the outskirts of Lake Ariel. The guy back at the gas station I stopped at said the turnoff came up fast on you, and he was not kidding. The gravel road—little more than a goat path, really—came out of nowhere and cut right into a steep switchback. I rumbled along for another five minutes, passing various Private Property notices before the road crested a hilltop.

At the top, I spied the Victorian farmhouse for the first time. It was one of those huge, rambly structures that was probably 150 years old but well cared for, with its white vinyl siding, green shutters, and a large array of solar panels on the fresh-looking metal roof. At least Nick was doing his part for the environment.

I spotted a large, unattached garage, a massive indoor greenhouse that took up an entire wing, and a large, paved pavilion. The house was incredibly secluded, and though it didn't have a black iron fence around it or any obvious barriers, I didn't doubt it had some form of either high-tech or magical surveillance. And I knew I was right when I parked on the white gravel pavilion and saw a young man come around the side of the house. He was sweaty and looked to have been gardening. He took one look in my direction, peeled off his gardening gloves, and disappeared into the house.

I got out and started toward the house. That was when I saw the front door open. I steeled myself for unpleasantness. I figured Nick wasn't going to like me harassing him at his personal hacienda, but the half dozen people who emerged didn't look particularly threatening. They were all young people—college age, I guessed—and dressed in flimsy clothing like robes, nightgowns, or just trousers, the outlines of their smooth, young, naked bodies clearly visible through the soft white material. They were barefoot and watched me for a long moment as I stood there at the foot of the porch stairs, rubbing my sneakered left foot against my right calf.

I shivered a little, recalling what Morgana said about Nick being holed up with a bunch of Satanists. They didn't look particularly threatening, but then, neither did any of the cultists in *The Wicker Man* until the final reel of the movie.

Steeling myself, I started walking toward the Wicker People, watching them carefully for any signs I was in trouble, but they didn't move at all—not until I was within a few feet of them.

Then the first one in line, a young man, bare-chested and dressed in just white, summery linen slacks, stepped forward and held out both hands as if to welcome me.

"You are she?" he asked, sounding breathless. "Lady Lucifer?"

This again.

"Y-yeah. That's me. I guess."

He nodded once. "Your presence is unexpected...but not unwelcome." He sank to his knees and the others followed suit until all of the young Wicker People were kneeling in a row in front of me. Some even began to sing some wordless dirge, their voices rising up like a choir.

"Welcome home," said the young man at my feet. "How may we serve the Princess of Perdition?"

| 33 |

INSIDE THE EXPANSIVE foyer, the young man in the white trousers—Henry—offered to take my hoodie, but I clasped my arms around myself.

A woman who looked a lot like him joined us. "Hello, Princess, I am Amber." She smiled brightly, her eyes virtually dancing with light. She wore a diaphanous white nightgown that left very little to the imagination. I looked over at Henry and noted that I could pretty much see right through his white cotton trousers. Both were pretty and delicate, with sandy blond hair and large green eyes. Their bodies were highlighted rather than hidden by their wardrobe choices. I tried not to stare, but I couldn't help myself. I kept glancing at Amber's pert nipples tenting the material of her gown.

Dragging my eyes away, I looked around at the rest of the coven. I had the impression that, for these Satanists at least, clothing was pretty optional.

"Perhaps we should give the princess some breathing room," Henry said to Amber, sensing my unease. His sister nodded and both of them grew very still but waited as if expecting orders from me.

I found I could breathe easier without them crowding me. They radiated such a strong sense of raw sexuality that it made me uncomfortable. I mean, I was hardly a prude, but I was also not into the whole "free love" thing, whether it came from Satanists or just regular hippies.

"You are welcome anywhere in the house," Henry further explained. He indicated the room and everything beyond it. "But we are here if you need guidance or are looking for something."

"Yes," I told Henry. "I need to talk to Nick."

Amber's eyebrows bounced up. "Of course, Princess."

I wished they would stop calling me that.

Amber looked at Henry, who nodded. They seemed to pass some silent communication between them. Looking back at me, she said, "We can take you to him if you wish."

"I wish."

Henry and Amber escorted me through the corridors of the house. It was spotless and tastefully and simply decorated despite the rather unusual number of young people living here. There were rooms where small classes seemed to be going on. Real-life Hogwarts, I assumed.

Amber motioned to a pair of French doors up ahead and whispered, "Nick's in the atrium. Meditating."

I'd *never* seen Nick meditate in my whole life. Maybe zone out on a Netflix show after too much weed. But meditate? No.

The twins opened the French doors for me, and I was hit with the hot, verdant air that came gusting out of the semi-attached greenhouse. Once inside, I saw it was full of small flowering trees, large, frilly flowers, and countless herbs growing in pots. I didn't doubt most of them had medicinal and ceremonial purposes. They were probably used in the classes I saw. But I couldn't identify them. I'd never been that kind of witch.

After the twins closed the doors behind me, I started picking my way down a path between some tall, potted plants that looked suspiciously like Mary Jane. As I pushed some leaves out of my way,

I almost tripped over a man lying in one of those old-timey canvas loungers that you have only ever seen in *Tom & Jerry* cartoons. He was wearing sunglasses against the glare of the sun pouring through the greenhouse and holding a phone up in front of his face. Because he was lying so low and had the phone up to block the sun, I could see he was talking to a pretty girl on Facebook, sending her heart emoticons in a PM.

"Nick?"

Nick Englebrecht almost jumped out of his skin at the sound of my voice. He dropped the phone, then scrambled to catch it before it smashed on the floor. Sitting up quickly, he pushed the sunglasses to the top of his head and looked at me. Maybe it was because I'd surprised him, but he didn't look like himself for a second. There was something...harder about him. Which seemed an oxymoron because Nick has always been all hard lines and sharp edges: Too tall, too thin, too coarse, too mouthy...far too dangerous for my own good. Somehow, though, all that seemed amplified.

Seconds after he saw it was me, his mouth softened, his eyes cleared, and he just looked like Nick. Scruffy, blond Nick who hadn't shaved in maybe two days and needed his wardrobe updated, because in the white tank top, slightly baggy jeans, and open brown flannel shirt, he looked like some throwaway grunge artist from the 1990s. One thing struck me as really odd, though. Nick used to wear his hair in a scruffy, spiky shag, but now it was long enough for him to have to tie it up in a messy man-bun.

"Viv," he said, getting up. His voice was guarded as he slipped his phone into his back pocket. He couldn't seem to pull his eyes away from me. "Sorry, I was..."

"Meditating?" I arched an eyebrow at him.

He smiled sheepishly. Wickedly.

God, that smile. It still made me weak in the knees, and I hated him for that. I hated that no matter what he did, or how much he fucked things up, you wanted to forgive him. You wanted to believe in him. If he weren't such a slacker, he would have already created a death cult or become a politician and started a full-scale war or something.

"Meditating...yeah. The kids were great." He cocked his head toward the glass doors. "But they can be a little...clingy. So I come out here to get away." Clearing his throat, he quickly changed the subject. "So, what were you doing here? Not that I mind, because I don't..."

Standing there, surrounded by all of that sunshine, I found it very hard to believe he was the Devil's heir. That he was, in fact, the reigning Devil on Earth. The scourge of church institutions and good and decent people everywhere. He didn't seem very devilish, at the moment. But, then, he never really had.

"I came to talk to you." Suddenly, I felt shy and wrapped my arms around myself despite the oppressive heat of the greenhouse. "It's important. And not something I can discuss over a phone."

He nodded. "Okay."

I noticed he was keeping some distance between us. No surprise there. I'd warned him away from me enough times. And he, unlike most people, knew what I could do when I was really upset.

I hated this. That he feared me. That I hated him as much as I loved him. What we had was so fucked up.

Gathering myself, I dug the cards out of my hoodie pocket and unwrapped them so he could see. "Our father gave these to me to protect me." I looked up. "I'm in a lot of trouble, Nick. In way over my head, in fact."

I saw the concern on his face as he first looked at the cards and then up at me. It squeezed my heart a little.

"But that's not why I'm here," I quickly added. "These are supposed to help me. Except I don't know how to use them. Hell, they don't seem to work for me at all!"

My eyes filled with burning tears—the shame of my incompetence—but I dashed them away. I didn't expect Nick to take much pity on me. During our last encounter, we'd screwed each other's brains out, and then he left angry. We'd vowed to never cross paths again. We'd both been so upset with each other.

The lust, followed by the anger. A cycle that never seemed to end...

I stared down at my feet, awaiting his judgment.

When I felt him approached, I stiffened up. But he didn't strike me down or throw me out even though I probably deserve it. Instead, he put a long arm around me, and soon enough, I found myself collapsing against his chest, smelling the light, airy scent that was just him, and felt his warmth soaking into me. I tried not to cry like a fool and failed horribly.

"Oh, Viv," he said and kissed the top of my head. "We'll figure it out."

| 34 |

WHEN WE WENT back inside the house, I saw Nick's little coven racing around with dishes and silverware. "I really don't want to put you guys out..."

"It's no problem. We're happy you're here," Amber said, breaking away from the others. Her voice was giddy with excitement. She was carrying a lighted candle that made her eyes, bright and adoring, look like they were full of stars.

This was weird. I'd never had a "fan" before, but I guess it felt like this.

"Nick, the caterer is arriving in ten minutes with dinner," she told my brother before turning to me. In a conspiratorial whisper, she added, "It'd just Domino's, but we like to call it that."

I tried not to laugh at that. "You shouldn't have gone to such trouble."

"It's extremely rare to have both young Lucifers here at the same time. We want to celebrate it tonight with a spontaneous esbat. I mean..." Amber's eyes darted back to Nick. "If that's okay with you, Nick."

The deference she was showing him was astonishing. I realized these guys were deadly serious about their order.

"Sure," Nick said with a shrug. He looked at me. "I'm always up for a party."

Amber shook her head good-naturedly before racing off to finish lighting the candles.

We ate pizza and hot wings on the large attached deck. That, at least, felt normal, though the coven watched me intently, hanging on every word I said even though they were mostly just single-syllable responses to Nick's questions about what I'd been up to lately. I didn't reveal too much. Mostly because I didn't want the young people here being caught in the wake of...whatever fucked up situation I was presently in the midst of. They seemed nice for Satanists—and Amber and Henry were particularly friendly. I had the feeling they would do almost anything for Nick—and for me.

While the coven happily cleaned up the dirty dishes, I followed Nick down a flight of stairs to the basement, which had been converted into a cozy, English-style study. The room was expansive and paneled, and the walls had bookcases full of arcane texts. One whole wall was dedicated to athames, wands, and other popular tools of the craft. More ideograms were carved into the floor—for ceremonial purposes, I assume. But it didn't feel scary down here. There were brown leather chesterfields and soft lamplight set up for relaxation. We stopped at a large desk covered in books, many of them lying open.

Nick picked one up and showed me a text on conjuring—not the kind of book I expected Nick to have much interest in. He had always played fast and loose with the craft, and I knew he winged his spells most of the time. Sometimes, that worked. Other times—not.

"I've been studying my ass off," he explained, and I could tell he was immensely proud of his accomplishments. "Conjuring, casting, even necromancy. It's interesting stuff." Nick had never been what you would call "studious." He wasn't stupid, don't get me wrong, but he'd never had much interest in the craft until recently.

"This *is* interesting," I agreed, glancing at the moving illustrations in the book.

"The Children of Endor have one of the most extensive collections of esoteric texts on the craft in the world." He indicated a stack of books. "And these are just the hardcopy editions. They have a whole freakin' Guttenberg-style database of lost or nearly-lost texts online."

I paged through the book, surprised by some of the glyphs and spells I saw. This wasn't amateur hour, that was for sure.

"I'm trying to do better—to better control my craft..." He stopped as if he'd said too much.

I looked up. "Did something happen? Something bad?"

He opened his mouth, closed it. "Things...have been challenging lately. There was this spider from Mars, and it was being controlled by this dude, and he was a really bad dude..." He stopped. I waited for him to elaborate on this really bad dude of his who controlled spiders from Mars. Instead, he started cleaning up his mess, muttering, "I know what all of this looks like to the outside world, but the coven is serious business, Viv. I promise it's not all partying up here in the House on Haunted Hill."

I stood there, watching him stack the closed books neatly and carefully the way you do when something means a lot to you. He looked tired. Troubled.

Old.

I'd never known Nick to look old before, and Morgana's warning came back to me.

He has changed, she said. Suddenly, I believed it.

Reaching out, I laid my hand on his arm.

He stiffened in response as he turned back around. He was pressed against the big oaken desk. Nowhere to go. So, when I ran both hands over his tense shoulders—I couldn't help but touch him;

he was like a drug I couldn't live without—he slowly relaxed and his posture changed. Opened to me. I moved closer and ran my hands down the front of his body, over the soft white undershirt. His muscles were hard, his nipples peaked. His entire rangy body seemed to melt a little at my touch until his head was canted downward and his breath was touching my face. His eyes were closed, his lips sweetly parted.

I turned my head to kiss those lips. They weren't at all soft or full or giving like in the romance novels. His mouth was hard, his teeth inhumanely sharp. It was like kissing a predator, but I felt my entire body melt against his as I sought more. As we increased the pressure of our kiss, his hand cupped the side of my face, holding it with heart-tripping intensity. He had big hands; they encompassed the entire side of my face, and his strength was startling. Suddenly, he was growling like an animal coming awake from hibernation.

Grabbing me, he stood up and turned, unceremoniously dumping me on the edge of the desk. He then shoved my legs open so he could fit himself in between and bent to kiss me again, but he was fiercer now. Hungry. His teeth snapped at my lips and his hands dug into my sides. I wriggled in his embrace, wanting him close...closer. Inside me.

As we moaned and bit our way into each other's mouths, a thought came to me: *This wasn't the relationship I wanted.*

The thought was unexpected, and I wondered if he was having the same one because he stopped kissing me and just stared down at me for a long, hard moment.

"It's not," I told him breathlessly, putting words to my last thought.

"Yeah. I know."

I swallowed hard against the lump in my throat. The lump that was so much want. "We have to stop doing this, Nick. All this wanting, followed by all of this hating of each other and ourselves. I didn't want to live like this anymore."

"Yeah," he agreed.

"We..." I gasped for breath. "We need to try something different. Something new."

"Yeah. We do."

It was the hardest thing I had ever done. Turning him down. But we managed it. He let go of me and put distance between us—not a lot. I didn't want to lose him. I wanted my brother! So, I put my hands on his shoulders to stop him from moving too far away, then slid them behind his neck and pulled him to me once more—but only for a long, tight, and utterly asexual hug.

"I'm sorry. So fucking sorry, Viv..." he cried on my shoulder.

I didn't answer, but that was because I was crying, too.

| 35 |

AFTER WE PULLED ourselves together, we spent time looking through about two dozen rare texts on divination that the Children of Endor owned, hoping they would give us insight into the Devil's Tarot. I'd never even heard of it, and neither had Nick, even though he should technically own the cards as part of his birthright, which included an extensive infernal arsenal.

"Maybe they're not some ancient, magical artifact," I suggested as my confidence in Nick's books—many so old that I was afraid to handle them—started to flag. I set one down gently on the desk.

Nick turned away from the bookcase, a question on his face.

I sat down on the edge of the desk. "I mean, maybe they're just cards that John owns. Cards he bought somewhere or had made."

"John?" Nick said, his brow furrowing.

"John Englebrecht," I elaborated. "Our dad?"

Nick's lips part slightly in an "ahh" gesture.

"You didn't know that was his name? The name he used when he lived on Earth?"

Nick looked stunned. "No. He never told me..." For a moment he seemed to be at war with his own bitterness. Our dad had never gone easy on him. "Seems so...mundane." Then he added, "He never gave me cards. Never gave me anything, in fact, except the pokey stick—and I don't think he had control over that."

I pressed my lips together. "Well, they're technically yours. You're his heir."

He shook his head vehemently. "He gave them to you. They're yours, Vivian."

He picked the cards up off the desk's blotter. "But maybe you're right. We could be overthinking this. They might not be an artifact like the Morning Star. They could just be his cards."

Nick shuffled them, cutting a finger on them as I had. Frowning, he stopped to turn a card over. Like me, he got the Devil card. Then again. And again.

"They do that," I explained. "That's *all* they do."

Nick cleared a spot on the desk and retrieved a second chair from the corner of the room. We spent the next hour sitting on opposite sides of the desk, turning cards over, but they just kept doing that thing where they showed the same card over and over no matter what Tarot pattern we chose.

"Try thinking of someone you know," he suggested.

I did. I thought of Sebastian as we laid out a three-card draw.

All of the cards come out Death.

Then Nick did it. I knew he was thinking about Morgana because all of the cards turned up the High Priestess.

Nick finally stopped. "Maybe this is all they do."

"Point out the obvious? How exactly does that help me?" I asked, recalling our father's words.

He glanced up, his eyes shifting to me in concern

I shrugged to cover my awkwardness and gave him a condensed version of what was going on. "I mean…the people after me," I concluded, meaning Tupoc and the Toltecs, "…they aren't going to just sit there patiently while I do a reading for them and get a spiritual awakening. How does any of this help me?"

I waited for him to voice his concern, but he surprised me. "Yeah," he responded instead, tapping his temple thoughtfully. He suddenly looked wise. Were he wearing glasses, he would resemble our father. "We're missing something here."

He picked the stack of cards up and dropped them. They suddenly shift across the table toward me.

"Interesting," he said. He picked them up again and moved them closer to himself.

They immediately shifted across the blotter toward me again, this time making a fan of all Devil cards.

"Wow," I said. "That's new." I reached for the fan of cards and they shifted back into a neat stack. I lowered my hand. "Okay. I don't know what that means."

"Move them again," Nick said.

"I don't know how!"

"Make a fan," he commanded. "Imagine it."

I did.

It took a second like there was a glitch, but the cards did shift again, fanning out.

Nick nodded. "It's a start."

There was a knock on the study door. It was Henry. "We're ready to begin the esbat, Nick," he whispered.

| 36 |

UPSTAIRS, I FOUND the Children of Endor had cleared the common room of all furniture and rolled the carpet back to reveal a complex ideogram etched into the wooden floor. Though more complex than the ward on the wall of Confessions, it was essentially the same symbol—a series of lesser wards surrounding the big kahuna, an elaborately carved symbol of the House of Lucifer. Perhaps a hundred black candles filled the room with somber dark light. Black candles. The color of spellcraft and conjuring.

The Children of Endor had gathered, but this time they were all completely and unashamedly naked. They padded barefoot across the floor, joining hands as they formed a circle around the candles.

Amber and Henry stood to one side like sentinels.

Nick treated all of this as if it was perfectly natural. "I'll change and be right down," he told the twins with an amiable smile and then turned to me. "Would you like to change as well, Viv?"

I didn't know what to say. I had no idea what he meant by that. Change into something or change out of everything?

Sensing my hesitation, he took my hand and led me up a flight of stairs to his bedroom, which I quickly learned was remarkably mundane. No black bed sheets or goat-headed pentacles on the walls or anything. It was very homey and comfortable in a post-Victorian type of way.

"Do I have to be naked?" I asked at last. If it was just him, I'd probably be okay with that. But I was not big on group nudity.

"You can be if you want," he explained, "but it's not a requirement."

There was a huge walk-in closet against one wall that he threw open. I noticed it was full of expensive-looking formal suits.

"You have changed," I muttered.

He glanced over a shoulder. "What's that?"

"Nothing."

I watched him change into a black silk suit for the esbat. He eschewed a shirt and simply shrugged the matching jacket over his bare shoulders so that when he turned to glance at me, freeing his hair from the man-bun, I was left speechless at the change in him. In the black suit and long blond hair, he looked incredible, like some dark, malevolent elf prince from a fairy story not destined to end well for anyone involved. I didn't know why I ever doubted he could do the job of reigning Lucifer.

"What happened to your hair?" I asked because it had been bothering me all day.

"Oh." He brushed the silky, shoulder-length skein out of his eyes. It glittered like a pale gold curtain and fell over one eye Veronica Lake-style. "Did a big spell. Got blowback."

"You got long hair out of it?" I gaped, nearly laughing.

"*Fast-growing* long hair," he corrected me with a biting smile that suggested he didn't enjoy the extra grooming, which was just like Nick. "I cut it. It grows back overnight. I cut it again, it just grows faster. I got tired of cutting it every single morning." He shrugged self-consciously.

I'd lost count of the ways Nick's life had gone sideways. I was about to ask him the specifics of his longhair blowback when he pulled a long black dress from the closet. It was a bit glittery, and he seemed to realize this. He dropped it on his bed and reached in again, this time pulling a slim, short, red trapeze dress from the depths. It was not flashy. Simple and short, but with very long bell sleeves and a sweetheart neckline. The moment I laid my eyes on it, I loved it. It was so incredibly kitschy in a 1970s sex-kitten kind of way.

"You like?" he asked.

"I like." I was already half out of my clothes so I could put it on.

Minutes later, we were descending the stairs to the common room. Nick had graciously offered me his arm as if he was escorting me to the prom, and as we made it to the bottom of the staircase, I really did feel like a princess. The coven lifted their heads collectively, following us as we approached. Their eyes sparkled like cats, and, as we stepped into the circle through the narrow opening left for us, they began to sing that wordless dirge to celebrate the impromptu esbat. The sound of their voices made the little hairs on the back of my neck stand on end.

Nick looked at me and offered me his hand. I took it. I could feel the magical charge between us.

The song ended and the twins called the four corners of the circle before going to their knees before us and obediently bowing their heads. Soon, their singing changed, becoming a chant in a language I didn't recognize.

Their voices were beautiful, almost surreal, and the soft sound of the ancient language seemed to charge the air around us. I could smell the magic gathering within the circle. It smelled like electricity and rain. Hell, I could almost see it as it intensified and lifted our hair up off our shoulders with its sheer force. Nick looked like he was glowing.

"Feel it?" Nick asked me, our hands still entwined.

"Yes." It took me a moment to realize our lips hadn't moved. We were speaking to each other entirely in our minds.

I looked down at the twins, suddenly, incredibly, curious. *Who are they?*

He told me.

I gaped. I couldn't believe their parents were such important people.

Before I could ask anything else, the energy in the room seemed to redouble. It felt like a thousand hands were caressing me, but not in some sexual way. Rather, it was a warm, comforting feeling. As the coven's singing increased, I felt better. I felt good. I stood there amidst our worshipers, bathing in what felt like angelic song. It felt like love. And it was wrapped tightly around me, keeping me safe from all harm.

"It's the well," Nick explained aloud. "The well of power."

"I don't understand."

He laid a hand flat to his chest. "*We* have limited power. Or that's what I've learned from the library downstairs. Those of the Lucifer line, like all Old Ones, are natural channelers. We absorb the power of others through the act of worship. With brides—that is, a coven of dedicated followers acting as our well of power—we can be rendered virtually invincible."

"Brides." All of this was brand new to me, but I could feel it was true. I felt that in my bones.

I looked around at all of the bowed heads surrounding us. There was power in the people gathered here, but I could also feel it in him. In Nick. Like a battery, he was absorbing an enormous amount of his worshipers' power. I turned to him and said, "Will you hold me?"

He slid his arms around me, holding me against his suit. The warmth and power and love increased. The feeling of *family* hit me as it never had before and nearly buckled my knees. I'd never felt so loved. It was an incredibly addictive feeling.

"This can last," he told me, his voice brushing softly against my ear as his arms tightened around me. His voice was strangely sleepy. I knew he was feeling what I felt—this incredible rush of goodness and love.

"How?" I needed to know!

"Ceremony helps. But so does having brides to draw from."

At that moment, Amber and Henry looked up and smiled serenely before getting to their feet. As they joined us in our little huddle, I felt their power, their worship, and their love surrounding us. It increased the good feeling swirling around us. I didn't even need to ask him what a "bride" was. I knew innately what that was. And I never wanted anything so much in my life.

Nick let go and edged back so the twins could embrace me freely. I turned to him because I didn't want to lose him. But he hadn't gone far. Someone had placed a chair in the space where we first entered the circle. He sat down in it as if it was a throne. He looked elegant and vaguely threatening. He had brought the Devil's Tarot with him, and he set the cards on the floor at his feet. Then he raised both hands and clenched them into fists, one over the other. The Morning Star burned into view in his hands, and, seconds after that, his wings shushed open like long shadows behind him.

It threw me a moment. He was so beautiful.

Then the twins were back, embracing me front and back. I loved the soft, warm feel of their satiny skin. They acted like big kittens as they stroked my face and over my body, murmuring soft words of love and devotion in my ear. I found myself touching them, delighting in the way they purred against me.

Henry scooted down and slid his warm hand up the inside of my skirt. Amber was whispering little endearments in my ear and trailing her lips over my cheek and down the slope of my throat. She stopped when she reached my cleavage and lifted her head, looking at me with such devotion that I felt devastated by it.

I didn't want her to stop. I raised my hand and cradled her face, drawing her close. She kissed me—sweetly, gently. She tasted so good that I plunged my tongue into her mouth. I'd never really been into girls. No, seriously. But I liked Amber. I liked the way she felt under my fingers. She felt like home.

Henry was feeling left out. He had curled his toned young body around my legs, his hand still under my hem as he worked his way up the inside of my legs to the juncture of my thigh. The moment he touched me...there...I stiffened and let out a gasp.

"Let us love you, Princess," Amber entreated me, and I couldn't help but give myself to them. I loved them both so much as they sighed and slithered over me, working in tangent like a primitive tribal dance of desire. Amber kissed my mouth, then my throat, and then moved downward, finally sucking a hard nipple into her mouth right through the thin material of the dress. Meanwhile, Henry had dropped to his knees and pushed the fabric up my legs so he could kiss the heart of my desire.

He glanced up at me briefly, begging for access. I scissored my legs apart for him, and he, clutching my hips, kissed me right *there* just as he might my mouth. His tongue swept over my sweet center, and I closed my eyes and arched my back as he entered me a little ways. Were it not for Amber's support, I might have fallen to the floor.

Soon enough, the twins started working me from two different ends. Licking, kissing, sucking until I could feel the pressure of my orgasm building. The coven's song increased. The pressure increased with it. The twins sucked harder, pushing me toward release. My heartbeat ramped up and my hands clenched and unclenched at my sides as my body jerked and danced for them. Seconds later, my body exploded in an all-over shudder, and I heard the coven's song fell silent.

Opening my eyes, I saw the Devil's Tarot hanging over the three of us in a circular pattern. The shining metal cards were levitating just beneath the ceiling and moving slowly in a whirling, fan-like motion. I turned my head from side to side, admiring them. It was absolutely surreal. Everyone in the room was now watching them, including Nick, who looked impressed with my trick.

I could feel the magnetic pull between myself and the cards. It was as if we were connected in some arcane way. Raising a hand up in front of my face, I spread my fingers wide. That caused the cards to drift apart a few inches. I moved my hand to the left, and the cards drifted that way. Then I moved my hand in the opposite direction and they followed. Swirling my fingers caused them to move faster...then faster still.

I'd been using the cards the wrong way all along. They were never supposed to predict anything.

I felt a flush of power burning through me. The coven, this place, the cards...it was amazingly potent magic.

I wanted to test a theory, so I shifted my hand to the right. The cards flew in that direction, spinning like a deadly metal dervish. They sliced right through a metal standing lamp as it was made of papier-mache, then hit a lighted portrait of Anton Lavey on the wall. The cards cut easily through the portrait and into the wall beyond, but they didn't stop there. They continued to saw right through the wall until they hit the studs.

When I made a come-hither gesture, they tore a huge chunk out of the wall and knocked the portrait to the floor as they returned, landing in a neat stack on the floor at my feet.

| 37 |

EVEN THOUGH NICK wanted me to stay the weekend so we could work with the cards, I decided to drive back to Philly as soon as possible. With all the dark stuff coalescing around us, I needed to check on Sebastian.

"What you said before about being in over your head..." Nick reminded me as he walked me back to my jeep.

I cut him off. "I know. You want to help."

"Let me. The Children of Endor are incredibly powerful and connected."

I looked at his dear, sweet face. His concern for me was etched across it. He had been my guardian devil for so long. But I wanted to stand up on my own now. I didn't want to keep running to Nick Englebrecht for protection. That was not the witch—the woman—I wanted to be.

"I can't let you guys get involved," I finally confessed. "I have to do this on my own. Understand?"

It took him a moment to cave. "But there's no shame in asking for help. And I care about you, Viv..."

I put a hand on his arm. To my surprise, he looked near tears. I thought he could sense some of the things to come—some of the things I had seen. Our Vulcan mind-meld was probably responsible for that. But that was not all of it. I would never be free of him. I had given him my heart, my soul—quite literally. We were bound together in our darkness in a way few people were.

To lighten the mood, I took the cards out of my hoodie pocket. "I have these, remembered? And they're pretty badass."

He nodded, but I could see the deep concern brewing in his storm-grey eyes. "I can send a few members of the coven back with you—at least until you gather some brides of your own and expand your well of power. I knew Amber and Henry will go."

"Thanks, Nick," I told him truthfully, "but I think I have that covered." I thought of Mac. I was surprised to find I missed him. "I've already begun that process."

He tilted his head slightly. "Is he cute? Can I meet him?"

"No!" I laughed, terrified he'd steal him away from me.

We spent the next few minutes talking and giggling about Mac. I was buoyed to see how much my relationship with the detective pleased Nick. I was even happier to be able to laugh over a love interest with my half-brother. Somehow, we had carved the jealousy and pettiness out of our relationship. We'd completely rewritten it.

Before I left, he hugged me. "If you need me, you need only call me. Or even call *on* me."

"I know," I told him. "I'll summon you up if I need you."

That got another round of laughter out of us.

I got into the jeep and Nick scooted down to put his hand inside the window.

I took it. "I've enjoyed my time with your coven. And with you. I like this thing we have."

"Me, too," he said with a crooked grin. "We put the fun in dysfunction."

I laughed as I drove away.

| 38 |

I GOT BACK to the Seaside Motel all foggy-eyed from lack of sleep. I hoped to find Sebastian passed out in bed—or even the bathtub; I'd found him in there a time or two—but the room was empty and his bed looked like a war zone full of empty bottles.

Sighing, I pulled my phone out and pinged his cell. Both of us got the app in case one of us was ever stuck on the side of the road—a bad winter storm or an accident. Pennsylvania roads were hell on Earth, especially in the winter. Well, that was what I told Sebastian, anyway. But the reality was that the man needed a fucking animal tracker.

After I got an address, I checked us out and went back out to the jeep. Along the way, I got a bottle of water and a Snickers bar from a vending machine before I passed out where I was standing. I was running on virtually no sleep and little food. I drove to the dive bar in downtown Philly. It was a smoky little Irish pub with peeling yellow wallpaper, an ancient jukebox, and a broken Budweiser lamp over the single pool table in the back.

The barkeep—a large man with tattoos down both arms and those earlobe-stretching rings that always give me the heebie-jeebies, looked up from wiping down the bar. He took one look at my face and easily read my expression. "You here for Willard?"

"Willard?"

He raised his hand to Sebastian's height. "A hundred pounds dripping wet? Thinks he's a goddamn rat?"

I opened my mouth, but I didn't know what to say to that. "That...sounds like Sebastian," I said as I followed him into the back room. There were shelves full of boxes of booze, as well as huge kegs stacked against the wall. Sebastian was curled up in the corner, his head twisted into what looked like a pretty uncomfortable position. Bruises dotted his face, and he smelled like cheap, bottom-shelf gin and vomit.

"Kept telling folks he was a rat and was crawling along the floor. Then he started a fight, so someone dropped his stupid ass."

I swallowed. "You didn't throw him out?"

The barkeep looked at me, appalled. "I'm not a monster. I've got kids, lady."

"Sorry."

"He yours?"

"Yeah."

"Get 'im the hell outta here. He's stinking up my joint."

That turned out to be harder than I expected. Sebastian might "weigh a hundred pounds dripping wet," but that was still a lot of deadweight for a gal like me to haul up. Plus, I kept sliding around in Sebastian's vomit. Oh, yuck!

The barkeep finally took pity on me, grabbed my partner like he was a damned rag doll, and threw him over one burly shoulder. We took him out to the jeep and the barkeep dumped him into the backseat. Sebastian moaned but didn't stir.

I got into the driver's seat and pulled the collar of my hoodie up over my nose to cut the stink filling my car.

"For god's sake, lady. Get 'im some help," the barkeep said, slamming the door closed. "He's going to get himself killed one of these days."

| 39 |

AFTER DUMPING SEBASTIAN into bed—by now, he was at least stumbling even if he couldn't walk a straight line, which helped in getting him up the stairs—and kicking a wastepaper basket close to his inflatable bed (just in case), I trudged back downstairs to start cleaning up the shop. I was wasted from driving and punch drunk from lack of sleep or real food. I went to the prep room to put the little coffee machine on and get the cleaning supplies assembled since it looked like this was all on me.

I went out into the ruins of our shop, took one look around at all of the debris, sank to the floor, and cried my exhausted eyes out for about five minutes. I was still sobbing like a baby when I saw a tall shadow approach the shop. The glass in the door was gone, but someone—Safa, maybe—had thoughtfully pounded up a piece of cardboard, so I couldn't see who it was.

Naturally, I worried it was the Toltecs coming back for round two. I'd had about enough of those bastards. I reached into my pocket and pulled the Devil's Tarot loose, spreading the cards in my hand. They felt warm and seemed to vibrate with anticipation.

"Go away!" I shouted at the shadow behind the door.

And so it did. Suddenly—like smoke.

I was just wondering what that was all about when a tall figure manifested in the shop by the broken glass display shelves. I threw the cards at it impulsively and they cut through the air as if they were a circular saw.

A second too late I registered that it was my dad standing there. He raised his hand and the cards stopped on a dime inches from his larynx. With a flourish, he snatched them out of the air like a card sharp. He didn't look upset. "You've mastered them," he said, a smile in his voice.

I swallowed hard and quickly rubbed at my hot, tearful face before climbing to my feet. "Uh...sorry, John...I thought..."

He waved it away. "It was excellent form." He crunched over the broken glass to hand me back the cards. He even smirked as he turned to glance over the mess of the shop. "You made someone very angry, daughter."

"I'm good at that."

"As am I." He turned to look back at me. His face, as always, was expressionless, but I could see something new in his eyes. I wondered if he could tell I'd been crying. I half-expected some kind of criticism to come out of his mouth. Instead, he said, "Have a broom? I'll help you clean up."

My mouth dropped open and I had to close it. "O...kay."

I hurried back to the prep room, gathered up my cleaning supplies, and popped back into the shop.

To my surprise, he hadn't run off. I handed him the broom and dustpan and we spent the next two hours cleaning the floor. I had to drag a large trashcan into the shop for all of the broken glass. It was heavy by the time we were done, but John carried it out to the dumpster and turned it over with no trouble at all. We then proceeded to swab and disinfect the whole room. That took another hour and a half.

We were both exhausted by the end of it. We hadn't spoken much. Once, I asked him why he'd stopped by and he said he was hoping for that daddy/daughter date he'd talked about. I laughed.

"Not much of a 'date,'" I said as we finished up. We'd cleared the debris and I'd dumped all of the candy in the shop since I had no idea if any of it was contaminated.

"This was interesting," John said while he sprayed Windex on the display window and wiped it away. The Toltecs had broken the door but had thankfully overlooked the display window, which would have cost a lot more to replace.

"Not what you saw yourself doing today," I said as I stood there, staring at the jagged remains of the glass display shelves. They were custom-made. I didn't know how I would replace them without going bankrupt. Maybe after we were through here, I'd get drunk like Sebastian and pass out in some dive somewhere.

John came up behind me. "I know a guy who can take care of that and the other damages. I'll send him over tomorrow if that works for you."

Although his offer was kind, I turned around and eyed him suspiciously. "I couldn't pay for it."

"Did I ask you for money?" He made a face. "Humans and money. I don't understand the appeal myself."

"Why are you being so nice to me?"

He frowned as if my question was ridiculous. "Why shouldn't I be?"

I gestured wildly. "You told me you don't love me!"

He raised his eyebrows at my statement. "Yes, I never said I didn't *like* you, firefly." He smiled at me gregariously. "I'm starving after that workout. Do you want to blow this pop stand and get some food?"

So, that was how I wound up going with the Devil in his convertible to an uptown sushi bar where they made the food right in front of you. It was while I was seated at the counter, struggling to use my chopsticks, that he said, "Have you decided on how you will kill Tupoc?"

A sushi roll slipped through my chopsticks and wound up on the bar top. I ignored it. "No. I mean, how am I supposed to do that?"

"I suggest brute force." He paused and used his chopsticks to pick up a sushi roll with expert precision before popping it into his mouth. "You strike first. When dealing with a *brujo verde*, it's important to exert your dominance. It's the only way your enemy will respect you."

"You want me to start a turf war with the Mexican drug cartel?" I glanced around the sushi shop to make certain no one was listening in on this madness, but everyone was preoccupied with the sizzling hibachi grill where their food was being prepared. "I'm not sure I can handle that."

"You can if your well runs deep enough."

The magic well stuff again. "Yeah, well, mine's kind of shallow at the moment," I admitted with a nervous laugh. "More of a child's wading pool."

"It's deeper than you think," John said, expertly popping another sushi roll into his mouth. "It's all there. You just have to fill it with the energy of your brides."

I laughed because he was talking with his mouth full, and I never expected that from someone of his ilk. "Is this how real witchery works?"

"No. This is how *we* work," he explained. "We're not the most powerful of the Otherkind, but we can act like batteries, sucking up energy through the worship of our brides. We can then convert that energy into magic. You'll learn how to do it in time. In fact, it will become second nature to you."

"It sounds...kind of like doing superhero stuff. Like we're Rogue or something," I said, referring to the X-men in the comics who could borrow other mutants' powers by touching them.

He smirked at my analogy. "It can be like that, just more elemental. Our magic is very...vampiric in that way."

After we finished dinner, we headed back to the shop and, sensing some movement in the flat upstairs, John insisted on following me up just in case anyone, or any *thing*, was lurking. But it was just Sebastian. He was awake and hanging his head where he sat on the sofa. An old movie was playing on the TV. But he was not listening to what Humphrey Bogart was saying. He had burrito-wrapped himself in a blanket and looked like he would rather be dead than hungover.

"Right then," John said, eyeing my pet necromancer. "I should be on my way. Remember what I said."

Sebastian looked over but didn't say anything about me hanging out with the tall, blond guy. He simply drew his legs up on the sofa and moaned through his hangover.

I walked John back down to his car, parked in the alley behind the shop.

"There's no way I can pay you back for the repairs," I reminded him. "I'm broke. Totally broke." I tried hard not to cry in front of him. I knew he didn't like to see tears.

"You'll have new customers soon," he assured me, leaning back against his car. I had this gut feeling he wanted something from me—some gesture. I thought about hugging him but then decided to shake his hand instead. He was sweet, but we were not that kind of family.

| 40 |

THERE WAS NO point in taking Sebastian to task about his drinking binge. A tiger wasn't going to change its stripes. And a longtime alcoholic like he was wasn't going to wake up one day and turn over a new leaf unless he wanted to.

I finally crashed out for a while, waking groggy and disoriented sometime later. I thought I'd only been down a few hours, but when I looked at my phone, I saw I'd slept round the clock. I thought about going downstairs to start a new batch of hard candy, but then realized it was futile since I didn't have a store to sell it in. I was stuck waiting to see if my dad came through with the guy he knew.

In the end, I wound up lying in bed, watching the Cartoon Network, one of the X-men series. Near midnight, I got the idea. It started as a brief flash of inspiration in the deepest whorl of my brain. I laughed over it. But as I burned through episodes of the cartoon series, it started to take hold, branching out in my head until it filled it like a tanglewoods—just one with plenty of thorns.

I got up and picked through my clothes. I still didn't have a closet, just a big Tupperware tote on the floor with my clothes heaped into it—some of it unwashed. I found the leather jacket I'd worn when I went to see the Toltecs, but nothing else I owned came even close to what I needed.

By morning, I was hyped for my idea, so I jumped into my jeep and drove uptown, keeping my eyes peeled for a particular kind of store. When I spotted it—a small Harley Davidson shop—I parked on the street and went inside. I was on a mission, so I went straight for what I needed and bought a pair of leather biker jeans and boots with low, comfortable heels even though the clerk insisted I'd looked so much sexier in the expensive and impractical stilettos she tried to sell me.

I had one more stop to make. It was a long shot, and it took a bit of googling, but it was worth it, though I had to drive to the outer edge of Philly to find a costume shop. Inside, I looked around at all of the costumes hanging on racks and the masks and various headdresses hanging from hooks on the walls.

A middle-aged woman walked up to me and asked if I needed any help.

"Do you have any Maleficent costumes?"

She looked surprised. "I'm not sure. That went out of style some time ago."

"Could you check?"

She retreated to the back room, returning a few minutes later with one old, ratty costume that looked like it had seen better years, not days. But I didn't care about that.

"I just want the hennin," I told her.

"The...what?"

I point to the horned headdress in her hand.

She looked confused. "I'd have to speak to the manager..."

"Forget it," I told her grumpily. "I'll buy the whole costume."

Buying the costume ate up the rest of my petty cash. I swiftly dumped the ratty black gown in the dumpster behind the shop, then got back in the jeep. I wound up sitting there, looking at Maleficent's headdress, wondering if this was the best idea I'd ever had—or the dumbest.

Either way, I was about to find out.

| 41 |

THE SCREECHY SOUND of an electric drill woke me from a deep but troubling sleep about things burning. The minute my eyes were open, I started to forget about the dream, but there were snatches. A house was on fire and I was running through the rooms, trying to ferret out all of the pets before they burned up in the flames. It didn't take a genius to figure out the psychology behind the dream.

I felt awful—headachey and nauseated—as I headed downstairs to my useless shop, the last of the dream thankfully disappearing from my head.

Sebastian danced into view. He was dressed and groomed and didn't look hungover. He had two lattes from the Starbucks across the street and handed me one. "Isn't it bloody terrific?" he said as he escorted me into the shop.

A handsome young guy in blue jeans and a chambray work shirt tailored to his muscular build was down on one knee, replacing the L-brackets for the glass shelves that were destroyed in the vandalism. Sitting on the floor were several large, but very narrow, cardboard boxes. I realized they contained replacement glass panes.

The young man smiled up at me. "Good morning, Princess."

I immediately knew who he was: My dad's guy.

"We won like a community lottery or something and this handsome lad is doing the repairs for free," Sebastian beamed.

"That's great," I said after I sipped my coffee. I opted not to explain about my dad or what we'd discussed. I was not ready to discuss it. But Sebastian was so awestruck by the young man that he was not even looking at me, so I went back upstairs and locked myself in the bathroom so I could take a long hot shower and try to wash away the sleep and fatigue.

I didn't understand why my dad was doing this. I didn't understand him at all—but I was smart enough not to look a Satanic gift horse in the mouth.

After dressing in a fresh T-shirt and jeans, I went back downstairs, feeling a bit more optimistic about my life. Sebastian was still fluttering around the repair guy when I noticed a familiar figure out on the stoop of the shop, examining the damage.

I stepped through the cardboard door, then stopped when I saw the absolute horror on Mac's face.

"What the hell happened?" he asked, sounding angrier than I expected.

I thought about making up a lame excuse but I was sure he had read the incident report by now.

"It was them, wasn't it? The Toltecs?"

I shook my head. "It's okay, Mac. I wasn't here when it happened."

He turned and stared at the sidewalk for a long moment and then took a deep, shuddering breath. I saw his fists clench as if he was thinking of putting one through my glass display window. "We need to talk."

"All right."

He led me toward his car, then suddenly changed his mind and walked me down the street. I felt a twinge of concern. Up ahead was the pizza parlor Sebastian and I ordered from the first night we stayed in the shop. They serve Chicago-style deep-dish pizzas. Awful stuff Sebastian called "pizza lasagnas." But I let him lead me inside and to the unisex bathroom at the back of the shop.

He locked the door on the tiny room that smelled of cheap, bottled Freesia, but didn't flick on the light. Instead, he turned to me. The space was so small we were almost forced up against one another. The room was dim, but the hunger in his eyes was unmistakable.

I slid backward a little until the edge of the vanity brushed my ass. He followed my motion before pouncing. He grabbed my ponytail of long red hair and kissed me. It was difficult to breathe suddenly. He tasted of coffee and peppermint. He didn't merely kiss me; he bit my lips while growling hungrily. His free hand followed the line of my body, and then he shocked me by seizing my left breast and working my nipple with this thumb. I shifted around, my breasts heaving up as a familiar whimper crawled up my throat and past my half-parted lips. His tongue went into me then, slippery and hot.

I cried out right into his mouth. He responded by attacking my jeans and pulling them down, along with my boy shorts. "Lift your ass," he said in a voice so deep and steely cold that I couldn't help but obey him.

I wriggled around on the vanity while he worked my shorts over my hips and down my legs, then forced my legs farther apart. I shivered and a small cry caught in my throat when he touched me softly—a fluttery touch that drove shivers up my spine. I was about to beg him to take me when he went to one knee and bowed his head like a prince at the end of a fairy tale. But instead of proposing marriage, he flicked his tongue over my clit. I finally cried out and wrapped my arms around his strong neck. Mac licked, sucked, and then ate me out like a man dying of starvation. I thrashed and bucked against him, my climax building like a storm.

The room was filled with soft, dark light. At first, I was afraid I might be burning him, but then I realized Mac was the one who was glowing. I was absorbing his strength or vitality or whatever you wanted to call it while he gently growled against my core and relentlessly drove me over the edge. I came quickly and forcefully, and Mac sucked at my wetness even as he gave me his light. I dug my fingernails into his powerful shoulders and danced against his mouth, giving myself to him, but also taking that light—his very vitality—from him.

After we both came down from our sexual high, we fixed our clothes, unlocked the door, and walked to a booth in the back. I had to lean on Mac since I felt all weak and wibbly-wobbly inside. The lunch crowd had thankfully cleared out, so we had almost the entire place to ourselves. A waitress came by, but we just ordered a couple of sodas. We couldn't stop staring at each other, and I realized we were breathing almost in sync.

Eventually, Mac got himself under control and started in on me.

"Why didn't you tell me they hit you?"

"There were cops here half the night," I said, hoping to reassure him. My voice was a little hoarse from all of my moaning and screaming, and I couldn't help but wonder if the waitresses had heard anything. I took a long sip of soda. "I reported it. It's over."

"It's not over. There weren't any arrests." He sucked in a deep breath. I noticed a bead of sweat at his hairline, and he was doing that thing again where he kept clenching and unclenching his hands. "You should have come to me, Mistress. This was my fault! I never should have gotten you involved!"

I hushed him and put a hand on his. I was reminded of what Nick said about gathering brides. If I wasn't convinced before that Mac was my bride, I was now. I just had to figure out the proper care and feeding of a Satanic bride.

"This isn't your fault," I told him in a soft but strong voice. "And you don't need to take care of me. *I* am Mistress, remember? I take care of you, Mac."

He looked confused. I thought he thought all of this was a game, a sexy little role-playing charade. But we were at a real crossroads. He didn't understand the weight of what was happening to him—and I was afraid that if and when he learned, he wouldn't accept it. I'd never seen a cross on him, but that didn't mean he didn't believe in God or the church. How would a devoutly Christian man respond to being made one of Lucifer's brides?

He needed to know the truth about me, I realized. He needed to be able to make an informed and committed decision.

Taking a deep breath, I said in a rush before I chickened out, "I lied to you, Mac. I'm not a psychic. Not exactly. I'm more. A witch."

He looked confused for a moment, but being an astute detective, he started putting things together like puzzle pieces in his head, his brilliant mind fusing it into something that made sense to him. I could see the wheels turning. But before he could jump to the wrong conclusion, I added, "And I don't mean a Wiccan, Mac. I'm not a goth or a pagan or any of that—not that there's anything wrong with that. I'm just not it."

His lips form words but it took him a moment to speak. "Wha...what does that even mean?"

I bit my lip. "Are you a Christian man?"

"What?"

"Answer the question, Mac. Please."

He frowned but said, "No. Atheist. Why?"

I didn't know if that was better or worse. I started slow, explaining everything about my parents and myself. Hell, I even dived into a brief subplot about Nick as the current ruling Lucifer, though I did manage to bring everything back around to myself—and what Mac was to me now. I didn't hold back, and, as I finished my tale and my soda, my one wish was that Mac didn't think I was a raving lunatic.

After it was all said and done, Mac continued to stare at me, but I couldn't read his expression, which frightened me.

Naturally, I expected him to accuse me of being crazy or lying or trying to manipulate him in some way. I half expected him to bounce up and run from the crazy woman in the booth who thought she was Satan. So, I was surprised when he bypassed all of that to say, "So, what you're saying is...I'm not in control of the way I feel about you?"

His voice was soft and hurt. I felt as awful as if I'd stabbed him in the heart.

I didn't know how to answer his question, and I couldn't meet his eyes, so I just said, "I have no idea. I've only just found out about all of this bride stuff recently."

I raised my head and finally looked him in the eye. "You believe me."

"It...it feels real," he confessed, frowning again. He didn't remove his hand from under mine, but his other balled into a fist. "So...what you're saying is you've made me this. You've made me a...bride. Like a slave."

I didn't like where this was going. "I never meant to make you anything," I told him honestly. "Mac, you have to believe me...all this happened purely by accident."

His eyes shifted downward and he stared at our entwined hands. Slowly, he pulled his own hand back. I thought he was going to explode based on the stunned look on his face, but he didn't. He just looked up at me instead and said, "So, none of this is real. My feelings aren't real."

"That's not what I mean! Of course it's all real!"

A waitress heading back to our table stopped at the sound of my shouting. I ignored her and I tried to take Mac's hand back. "This is all real to me. It was always real to me!"

But Mac rose from his seat, suddenly looking panicky. "I had to go, Vivian. I have to...be alone. Put my head together."

I started to get up, but he moved in a flurry toward the exit. I watched him go, wondering if I should chase after him. Wondering if I'd ever see him again.

And then I wondered if by telling him everything I'd made one more terrible decision in a long line of terrible life decisions.

| 42 |

WHEN I GOT back to the shop, I felt the best and the worst I'd ever felt in my life. At last, I was learning to be honest with those in my life. It left me feeling empowered. Heartbroken. I knew from prior experience that it was a potent—and dangerous—combination for me.

I marched past the ratty secondhand sofa where Sebastian and the repair guy were doing some serious tonsil spelunking and went straight to our shared bedroom. There, I changed into the leather jeans, boots, my red Devil T-shirt, and the leather motorcycle jacket with the skulls and roses embroidered on the back. I snatched up the hennin and my keys and headed for the door before good sense reared its head and I changed my mind.

"Where are you going dressed like that?" Sebastian asked. When I stepped back into the living room, I saw he was wrapped in an afghan we got at Goodwill. His handsome stud was busy in the galley kitchen, cooking dinner at the propane burners. I thought they might be making spaghetti together. "Jordan is making a homemade alfredo sauce…you're welcome to join us…oi, witchy, wait up!"

He followed me to the door.

I turned around and said the first thing that came to mind, "It's a rave. I'll be back late. You kids better not get in trouble!"

He looked at me dubiously as I shut the door.

| 43 |

I ONCE AGAIN parked at the 24-hour Kwikimart and walked down to the roadhouse, tying the hennin on as I went. It was a Saturday night and the dump was packed to the rafters. I could hear the live band playing something loud and frenetic.

By the time I was within eyeshot of the bar, I was tossing the Devil's Tarot from one hand to the other and hyping myself up. I thought of what my dad said. "You strike first. When dealing with a *brujo verde*, it is important to exert your dominance."

A man got out of a pickup truck, took one looked at me crossing the parking lot, and got in again, slamming the door. I guess he didn't like what he saw. Goodie.

Each step made me feel ragey-er. I kept seeing my broken-up shop. Sebastian in the body bag. Mac looked at me as if he was afraid to be in the same room with me. Mostly, though, I saw Tupoc's shit-eating grin, and I thought about how much I wanted to break it. By the time I reached the door, I was breathing harshly through my nose and mumbling under my breath. Instead of grabbing the latch, I swiped my arm out at the door. I was pleasantly surprised when it caught fire in a sudden *whoosh* and burned down to kindling supernaturally fast.

I heard a commotion inside as I stepped through the hole that remained and into the roadhouse. I didn't think they expected me to be the source of the fire because everyone looked surprised by my return. Several of the Toltecs moved away from the pool tables, long cue sticks stuck in their tight fists, but then stopped to assess the situation. A few big guys shoved themselves away from the bar. But no one looked particularly eager to engage me

One guy, smaller but beefier than the others, moved in front of the gathered crowd and eyed me. "Who the fuck *are* you, *gringo* girl?" I saw his hand waver over his belt and I assumed he was packing some heat.

"Your leader knows me. Tupoc?" I looked around the narrow, low building, but I didn't see him here tonight. "Short and ugly as fuck? Likes to bust up establishments like a little bitch having a temper tantrum?"

No one I looked at answered me, so I added, "He called me Lady Lucifer."

A Toltec standing behind Shorty barked out laughter as if that was the funniest thing he had heard tonight. Several other brave souls join in. But Shorty raised a hand to silence them.

"Ain't no Tupoc here," Shorty said after a few breathy seconds. His eyes slid over my getup suspiciously, but he didn't laugh. "And Halloween is in October, bitch. Get out."

I snorted. "I'm not leaving until I get to talk to Tupoc. We have unfinished business."

"He won't talk to you, little girl. Leave!"

That kicked my rage up a notch. I hated being dismissed almost more than anything else.

"No," I told him, standing my ground. I stretched out my arm, spreading the Devil's Tarot between my fingers, and shook the cards at one of the guys armed with a cue who was getting too close to me. The cue caught fire and the biker dropped it with a bark of surprise.

"Tupoc, Shorty," I repeated in a gravelly tone. "Now!"

That pissed him off. He canted his head sideways at two of his bigger lackeys and muttered in Spanish. The two Toltecs moved toward me, a look of business on their faces. I recognized one of them as the big guy I first encountered in the parking lot the first night I was here—the one who bumped me to get past.

As he approached me now, fists clenched in a threatening way, I said in a clear voice, "Stop."

But they didn't. The two reached for me, grabbing me by the shoulders. My heart flitted in my chest. I jerked back with a shout, my right arm going wide. I released the cards in my hand. The kinetic force driven by my sudden panic caused them to slice into the back of the bar and stick there. Suddenly, with the loss of the cards, I felt vulnerable again.

As the men dragged me backward, I made a come-hither gesture to the cards, but I discovered my brain wasn't with the magic. It was too busy reeling, wondering what I was going to do about the brutes dragging me off to who knows where. Then I realized too late that practicing at home where I was safe and sound was one thing; doing it in a volatile situation was something else entirely.

The cards shivered but didn't move from where they were embedded in the wall.

We weren't headed toward the front door, I now realized. We were going in the *opposite* direction, toward the employee door beside the bar. That made my heart beat too rapidly. My rage flagged as my body went into panicky self-preservation mode. Where the living hell were we going?

I started to fight. Hard. I fought the way every woman fights when she's up against a killing male force. Heckle and Jeckle didn't expect that, and as I wriggled around, their hold on me slipped. As soon as I was free, I bolted for the door, but another Toltec slid in front of the entrance. I put the brakes on and eyed him, trying to look tough, but I was frankly scared half to death, and he saw that clearly.

Shorty appeared beside me and grabbed me around the waist. I screamed and twisted to get him off me, but he was incredibly strong and easily lifted me up and threw me over his shoulder as if I were a potato sack. My head down and spinning, I started to thrash in his hold, but his grip on me only tightened, and when I started to scream, he muttered something in Spanish and slapped my ass as he marched back toward the other door.

The blow enraged me. As I twisted and fought like a cat, I lost the hennin pinned to my hair. But I couldn't get free. He slapped my ass again. "Quiet, *bruja roja!*"

He shouldered through the door and into the parking lot behind the roadhouse. The moment I breathed the clean, frigid air, I fought harder, finally making it too difficult for him to carry me. Muttering curses, he swung me down to the asphalt on my back, the back of my skull cracking against the blacktop. That made my vision swim, and, for a moment, I couldn't tell what was up from down.

After the other Toltecs had gathered around, he leaned down to me. I opened my mouth to scream, but he drew his elbow back and pop-punched me in the upper cheek, bouncing my head against the asphalt. I sputtered as pain spread out over my face and deep into my skull from the impact. I wanted to scream but I was choking on the blood in my mouth.

"Quiet, bitch," he told me and stalked past, nodding toward one of the other bikers. The big guy grabbed me by the hair and started roughly dragging me on my ass across the asphalt.

This time, despite all my pride and my desire to go this alone, I started shrieking for help. There was blood in my eyes and it was getting hard to tell which way was up. My heart wouldn't stop hammering and sending my thoughts reeling off into dark places. I just flailed around until we reached the roll-up door of the garage behind the roadhouse.

I was still carrying on while the men pounded on the metal roll door, but the band had started up again, louder than ever, and I knew no one could hear my screams. After a second or two, the door trundled up on its track and they dragged me inside the dark recesses of the garage.

The fucker ripping my hair out at the roots finally let go. I immediately twisted around onto my hands and knees on the oil-stained concrete floor. Pushing myself up, I glared around wildly at the interior of the vast space. There were workbenches full of greasy tools, machine mounts, and several cars and a few bikes up on hydraulic lifts. But there were also several other men here, including Tupoc, who was standing near a box truck parked at the rear of the garage, talking to the driver. The box truck was parked with the back facing us, a heavy chain on the doors.

Tupoc swiveled his horny, vicious head around, and I saw a smile split his face in half. It dragged his piercings in two different directions, giving him an even more demonic appearance. The sight of him made me flinch.

I completely forgot what I was and what I was capable of doing as he swaggered toward me. "I heard you are looking for me, *bruja roja.*"

He stopped inches away and spread his arms. He was bare-chested once more, with his full-body tattoos and various wards on full display. "Well, now, here I am."

I pushed myself into a crouched position but couldn't think of a thing to say, witty or otherwise.

He grinned with that forked tongue. "What's wrong, *bruja*? Cat got your tongue?" He laughed at his own stupid joke. His wards shimmered slightly in the dim lighting—and I suddenly understood why the cards hadn't worked. He must have the whole place warded against outside magic.

I never had a chance.

I was incredibly stupid.

He gestured wildly to me. "I am here. Show me your big magic!"

The rest of his gang gathered around me. "*Show us your magic!*" they chanted in unison. "*Show us your big magic...!*"

But I couldn't! I could hardly breathe, and I was starting to think I was having a panic attack. I leaned over, clutching my chest where my heart wouldn't stop galloping like a frightened horse. I had a throbbing headache from my head injury, and my throat was sore from screaming. I could barely see through the darkness slowly seeping into the corners of my eyes.

They laughed at me. It reminded me of that time in the gym with the girls. Laughter. So much laughter...

"Stupid little bitch," Tupoc said and pantomimed grabbing me by the throat. "Stupid, unlearned little *bruja!*"

I felt his hand there—right around my neck—and made a strangled noise. He was not touching me, but I could feel his fingers applying pressure to my windpipe. I scrabbled at my own throat, but there was nothing to grab! I couldn't even cry out as he raised his hand in pantomime, lifting me easily with it. He was that powerful a witch.

Brujo verde, my father called him. Our fates were entwined.

I kicked and twisted, scratching at the invisible hand around my throat, but nothing helped. Too soon, my lungs were screaming for oxygen. Darkness pooled into my eyes. My heart skipped a beat. I hung there helplessly—pathetically—as he slowly began to squeeze the life out of me. And all the while, he was laughing.

I was certain he was going to kill me. But just as I thought I was about to pass out, he suddenly let go. Hitting the hard concrete on my back knocked the air right out of my lungs, making me panic more than ever, but Tupoc didn't let me flail around and gasp for long. Standing before me, his feet spread, he leaned down, growling something in Spanish. With a shout of victory, he grabbed me by the belt and slid me easily between his legs so he was leering down at me and I could see his crotch inches from my face.

Punch him, I thought. This was the part in the revenge movie where the heroine punched the ever-living shit out of her enemy's family jewels and then wrangle herself free so she could reassert control of the situation and take these thugs out one at a time. I saw it all happen in my head. But this was real life, not a movie, and I was as much my worst enemy as Tupoc.

I couldn't breathe. I couldn't stop the panic attack from rolling over me. So, instead of punching him in the nards the way I should, I just lay there...

Tupoc laughed. The men only laughed harder. They laughed at my pathetic display. They laughed at the fact that I'd literally pissed myself, I was so scared. I could feel the sticky heat running down my legs...

Tupoc grinned down at me with his metallic teeth. "Get her pants off. It's time the little *bruja* learns what big magic really looks like..."

As the men clawed at me, Tupoc grabbed himself through his jeans and shook his balls before unbuckling his belt.

Fresh panic bubbled up inside me. As the men began to rip at my leather jeans, I stiffened up, arched my back, and screamed at the ceiling. I screamed in pain. In rage. I screamed orgasmically—a ridiculous primal need to be heard. But as that raging pain burst from me, it was like no scream I'd ever uttered before.

My jaw cracked wide open. But what emerged was no longer sound but molten heat.

I coughed smoke. And then liquid fire poured forth like a geyser of white-hot death stretching toward the ceiling. It burned so hot it melted the face of one of the men standing directly over me. It burned away his beard and hair and then his skin as if he'd shoved his face into the path of a flamethrower. His laughter quickly turned to screams as his face liquefied and ran like paint off his bones, revealing his skull and grinning teeth beneath.

The sight of him—of what I'd just done to him—stunned me. I'd since stopped screaming, but I couldn't stop vomiting fire like some ridiculous, modern-day she-dragon. The pillar of fire I was coughing up was extensive. Some of the men leaped back, their hair and beards on fire. They turned and raced away from me, beating at the flames encircling their heads like broken halos. But they didn't get far. As the fire quickly ate through their heads, they dropped like toys all over the floor of the garage.

And I couldn't stop…I couldn't even close my mouth! Fire and smoke poured out of me and stretched toward the ceiling, then crawled across it like an angry, many-legged centipede. Shaking my head from side to side only sent the flames flying in every direction and, within seconds, the cars and bikes were on fire as well. Desperate, I flipped over onto hands and knees, head down as I vomited long tongues of white-hot flame that bounced up from the floor and around me—but, interestingly enough, didn't burn my skin at all.

I watched as the fire started moving in a sidewinder pattern across the broken cement. Tupoc had escaped the flames by virtue of standing back from the start, but the flames were winding toward him as if they wanted him in particular, and he seemed to realize that. As they licked at the silver toes of his motorcycle boots, he leaped backward and nearly fell over a bucket in his way.

I no longer cared about hurting Tupoc or getting revenge on the men who destroyed my shop. I just wanted this hell on earth to stop! I pushed myself up, coughing smoke and bits of flame. I was beyond horrified, and all I could think to do was to get to some source of water like a Bugs Bunny character on fire who needed a swimming pool to douse the flames...

Tupoc was encircling me, muttering in Spanish—whether curses or words of surprise and admiration, I didn't know. Didn't care. I was not even thinking about him, but as I scrambled to get to my feet and run, he misinterpreted my intentions. He thought I could control this. That I was coming after him.

So, when I found my feet and tottered blindly toward him like some unlikely walking flamethrower, he swore and tried to punch me again. But his blow never reached me as his fist was engulfed in my flames.

He looked at his burning fist with admiration, then cried out in Spanish as if this had brought him the greatest joy of his life, seeing this "big magic" of mine. It was a short-lived revelation because, seconds later, one last burst of heat crawled out of my mouth, setting Tupoc's skin afire and melting his piercings in a way that made him almost beautiful to behold. I'd never seen anyone die up close. I'd never seen anyone burned to death in front of me—until now.

The flames burned supernaturally hot. They burned Tupoc down to bones so quickly that he didn't even realize he was dead. For a second or two, he was simply a wailing, voiceless skeleton caught in a gigantic halo of blue witchfire before collapsing to the floor in a smoldering heap.

Only then did I cough my last flames and collapse to my knees, my throat on fire like when I had a bad flu as a kid and I couldn't even swallow down chicken soup without it feeling like razor blades going down. But this was worse, so much worse. I could taste the flames like ozone and burned sugar and stomach acid in my mouth.

And the whole garage was full of smoke and the stench of roasting human hair and flesh.

I heaved and heaved onto the floor, but I couldn't rid myself of the terrible taste.

Few of the men were left, and the one or two who remained were running for the door. I quickly saw why. That bucket that Tupoc knocked over? It had greasy shop rags in it and the flames had completely eaten them up and were hungry for more. The witchfire had reached all four walls, and the ceiling was already crackling with flames.

I felt like I was kneeling in an ecclesiastical lake of fire with flames on all sides. I watched, fascinated, as bits of flaming debris dropped down on top of me. The witchfire climbed one wall like a shimmering blue spider, eating through the plaster and studs so fast that I wondered if anything could stop it. The flames had also reached the box truck, and the driver was half-climbing and half-falling out of the cab as he scrambled to follow his friends out the open roll-up door.

I heard pounding on the doors and walls of the box truck. I twisted my head to one side, thinking I'd gone mad. Then I heard human screaming.

With a lunge, I got to my feet and approached the truck. The closer I got, the more convinced I was that someone was in there, pounding against the walls in their panic. I grabbed the thick chains woven through the handles of the door and pulled on them. I heard women screaming and hollering to be let out.

"Hold on," I told them. "I'll get you out!"

The angry, roaring flames had created a suffocating heat that was filling the garage with choking white smoke that even I couldn't bear to breathe. If I didn't get out, too, I knew I was going to pass out and die in this mess of my own making. But I couldn't leave until I knew who was in the truck.

Coughing and gagging, I ripped at the chains, exerting my will over them. I was surprised when they melted easily under my grip and dripped to the floor. Working fast, I grabbed the doors and yanked them wide open. Inside, somewhere in the darkness, a group of young Mexican women, most no older than children, were crouched together, glaring at me with big, terrified white eyes and strained faces. It took me a moment to even grasp what I was seeing.

"Go...go!" I screamed, waving them out. At first, they seemed frozen, too frightened to move. But then, to my relief, one older girl jumped out and called to the others in her native tongue. Together, hands linked, the girls charged past me on their way to the exit like a herd of terrified deer running from a forest fire.

I turned to watch the girls flee, then looked back at the burning garage. Almost every inch of the place was on fire. A daisy chain of flames encircled my wrist and even danced over it, but it felt cool to the touch. The smoke, though, was making me gasp and wheeze. I staggered around in an aimless circle for a moment before limping out after the girls.

| 44 |

THE NIGHT WAS full of fire, smoke, and sirens.

I collapsed against the jeep parked in a dark corner of the Kwikimart and just sat there on the asphalt, watching the flames consume first the garage and then move lightning fast to the roadhouse. No one noticed me as everyone was vying to get as close to the towering inferno down the road as they could to take pictures and video footage with their phones without breathing in too much smoke.

The terrible pillar of fire lit up the darkness like a Fourth of July display. Eventually, something exploded with a muffled, earth-rattling *thump*—and that made everyone scream. I assumed it was a propane tank or the gas tank of one of the cars in the garage. The fire brigade and police worked like hell all through the night to douse the buildings with fire-retarding foam, but the flames were unbelievably hot and the buildings were glorified timber boxes. The fire ate them all like a cancer and, soon enough, the struggle became one to simply keep the fire contained.

I sat there half the night, watching news crews and fire and police vehicles from a dozen other counties arrive. I heard a reporter talking about what was quickly becoming known as the worst fire Philadelphia had seen in more than a decade. A part of me wanted to cry or laugh or rage at what I had done, but I was too numb to feel much of anything. Inside, I could only feel the witchfire—the dragon fire—cooling within the cage of my ribs.

And just how much it wanted to emerge again.

| 45 |

I WOKE THE next morning in bed. I had no clear memory of driving home or what time it was when I dragged myself in, but I suspected I'd only had a couple of hours of uncomfortable, crusty-eyed sleep.

Lying there, I thought about last night. Then I touched my throat. It was still on fire, and the burning taste was still in my mouth. I really had done all of that.

I expected to feel good. To feel heroic for saving those girls' lives. And a small part of me did. But I couldn't get the taste of burning human hair out of my throat and nose. Eventually, I couldn't stand it anymore and dragged myself to the bathroom to brush my teeth. But even after brushing three times with the minty Pepsodent toothpaste, I couldn't seem to cut through the sour, acrid taste trapped in my throat.

I showered to wash away the smell of burned things. Then I showered again. I could still smell the smoke in my hair even though I'd run Selsun Blue through it five times and now smelled like a medicine cabinet fell on me. Finally, I swallowed six ibuprofen and then just stared at my horrible, bloodshot eyes in the bathroom mirror.

I looked traumatized.

Shaking my head, I slunk out into the living room and saw Sebastian and his new boyfriend sitting all cozy on the secondhand sofa in matching bathrobes, mesmerized by the local morning news on the TV. Flashes of horrific images filled the screen.

Sebastian turned to me. "Oi, witchy, had you seen this? The fire in downtown has taken out a whole city block!"

I stared at the screen—at the burning, at last night's footage, at this morning's chaos—suddenly feeling sick to my stomach while Sebastian rattled off an itemized list of the damage.

"A bar, a garage, half a tenement building. Two fast food joints. A petro station. Bloody hell!"

Sebastian's new boyfriend looked over at me. I could see he knew exactly what I'd done. Hell, my dad probably sent him to keep an eye on me. Which was going to suck for Sebastian when he found out he was being used.

The room started to move around me like a carousel before increasing in speed. I weaved on the spot, clutching my bathrobe to my throat.

Of course, there was no mention of the girls I'd saved. Girls turned into drug mules and prostitutes in exchange for passage to America. They were long gone. Honestly, I was glad no one knew about them. The cartel probably thought they were dead in the fire. Maybe they would find a better life here in America. A kinder life than they had known in Mexico. But as I looked at the awful damage to that part of the city, I wondered about the cost of it all.

The room moved faster and faster. I couldn't hear Sebastian's words any longer. It was like I was drowning underwater, listening to the low din of voices from far above but unable to make out any of the words. I wanted to scream but I couldn't. My throat was too scorched. I had laryngitis from breathing fire on my enemies. All I could do was moan while the room whirled around me as if I was standing in the eye of a tornado.

A tornado full of unintelligible words, sirens, heat, and fire...

Somewhere, amidst the chaos in my head, I saw my father. He wasn't smiling demonically as I would have expected but nodding all the same. Proud as punch.

"Good girl," his voice echoed in the private hell that was my head. *My Left Hand of Darkness. My firefly.*

When the blackness finally consumed me, it was actually a relief.

| 46 |

I SPENT THE next two days in bed while Sebastian flitted around me worriedly. He thought I had the worst flu of my life. I was feverish and my throat was too sore to speak. I couldn't eat a damned thing, and he said I looked like death warmed over—which was ironic. Several times over the course of those days, I thought about picking up the phone and calling one of my two brothers. Nick, who could probably advise me on what the hell to do next. Josh, who would just be a familiar, welcomed voice in my ear. But I couldn't talk to them. I couldn't let them know what happened. I couldn't tell them I'd turned into this monster...

"I'm going down to make a new chocolate village," Sebastian said on the morning of the third day. The repairs on the shop were almost finished. Jordan, the repair guy Sebastian was hot and heavy with, had brought two other guys with him, and, together, they've managed to knock out almost everything that needed to be done to get the shop up and running again. We still had redecorating to take care of, but Sebastian had been tackling that while I rested and recovered.

"I was thinking of a prehistoric village. Dinosaurs and cave people. I think the children would enjoy that. What do you think?"

I nodded because I still couldn't talk with my sore throat.

He sat down on the edge of the air mattress. "Poor lamb. Do you need more ginger ale and soda crackers?" Again, I was struck by that odd mother hen thing he did from time to time. It made me recall the vision I had of him and the baby. And the blood. Whatever the hell that meant. "I could run to the CVS…"

I put my hand on his wrist and shook my head.

"Luv, you have to try and get up," he told me, his voice unusually tender.

I saw the tension in his face. I knew he was concerned I was falling into some dark place I wouldn't be able to crawl out of. To reassure him and make him feel useful, I reached for the notepad and pen on the floor beside the air mattress and wrote *Tomato soup?* on it.

After he left to heat me up some Campbell's, I continued to lie there, staring at the shadows moving slowly across the windows while the sun set.

I knew there was something wrong with me. I was too weak and nauseated not to have something wrong. The pain came in waves, clenching my body so hard it felt like an all-over Charlie horse, but I didn't move even when it became unbearable. I just gritted my teeth, gripped the bedclothes, and rode the wave of agony until it passed. I was exhausted, hungry, hyperaware of everything going on around me. I couldn't go to a doctor because I thought what was happening to me was probably supernatural, and they didn't employ witch doctors in the ER.

That evening, Sebastian appeared in the doorway dressed in an actual button-down shirt and slacks and not looking like a carnival barker. "I'm going out to dinner with Jordan. Do you want to come with, me luv?"

I shook my head.

Looking defeated, he left me to my wonderful, awful solitude. I lay back down and stared at the partially opened window, watching the lights of the cars on the street outside swerve by. I was a little surprised when Jordan appeared in the doorway of my room. He didn't say anything at first, just looked at me for a long, hard moment.

Finally: "Princess, you are going to have to refill your well. If you don't, you'll fade."

I ignored him. What the fuck did I care if I "faded?"

"Take from your bride. Or make another."

Thankfully, after a while, he went away, too.

I didn't want to refill my well. I didn't want to make more brides. I didn't want to be Lady Lucifer any longer. I certainly didn't want to be my father's Left Hand of Darkness, whatever that meant. It sounded ominous, and it filled me with such dread that tears welled up in my eyes.

Eventually, I drifted off into disconnected dreams until a wild pounding on the door downstairs dragged me out of my light, troubled sleep. I shuddered with each percussion, but I didn't move. Maybe they would go away.

They didn't. If anything, the pounding became more frantic. And now I heard someone shouting. It sounded like an extremely angry woman. The pounding was making my head hurt, so I dragged myself up, dressed in only a three-day-old T-shirt with soup stains on it and the boxer shorts I usually slept in. It was warm, but I couldn't shake the chill in my bones. I pulled the bed's comforter around me like a cowl and headed for the stairs, teetering on each as I descended. My legs felt like jelly after having lain in bed for almost three days.

The woman was now yelling incoherently. I hurried to undo the double deadbolt on the backdoor and pull it open before someone came around thinking a new crime was being committed.

A pretty, heavyset black woman stood there, her hand, balled into a fist, still up in the air where she was pounding on the door. She was dressed in nurse's scrubs with the Peanuts characters on them, and her hair was carefully set into long braids that flowed over her shoulders. There was a Starbucks cup in her hand, but from the way she was weaving slightly in the doorway, I had a feeling that whatever was in the cup was cut with something stronger than coffee. Her eyes, fierce but slightly unfocused, moved up and down my body critically. Seconds later, she wrinkled her nose up, and I couldn't help but wonder if I smelled from lying in bed, unshowered, for three days.

"You her, then," the woman said, not asked.

I didn't answer. Naturally, I figured she was someone here in need of help like Matilda and Doris even though I was in no state to play Glinda the Good Witch at the moment.

But she surprised me when she shouldered her way into the prep room in her sensible nurse's white Dr. Scholl's and looked around for a long moment before turning her critical gaze back on me. I got waves of anger and emotional agony from her in equal measure. They were almost paralyzingly sharp and kept me rooted to the floor even when she took a threatening step toward me.

"So you're her," she said, her words slightly slurred. "You're the goddamn bitch."

I didn't answer. I was dumbfounded by her hostility.

Reaching out, she ripped the blanket away from me with such force that I flinched. As it fell in a heap on the floor between us, I felt the chill of the night penetrating my raw, bare skin. But I didn't try to cover up. I just stood there in front of her like an idiot.

"Would be a white bitch," the woman mused almost more to herself than anyone else. "No tits...no ass. I take it you ain't got no kids, no family...prob'ly no fucking job, either. Amiright, bitch?"

A part of me wanted to defend myself. But I stayed silent, too exhausted to fight her.

Then she took another step closer so we were almost boob to boob and I could smell the coffee, vodka, and peppermint on her breath. She looked deep into my eyes. "I want you to know something, you stupid white bitch."

I sucked in a small breath and edged back, but she followed me into the room. She never broke eye contact with me as she continued her tirade.

"When you take him...when you fuck him...you take him away from his kids. Not just me. You take him from his kids!" And she threw the container of coffee—steaming hot—at me.

I instinctively threw my arms up to block the burning hot liquid. Mostly, it hit me across my right forearm and splashed down the front of my T-shirt, burning the skin of my breasts through the thin material. The heat of it stung my skin, which was pretty ironic when you thought about it. Three nights ago, I literally vomited fire at a man and didn't receive a single burn in return.

But this...*this* hurt me.

She threw the empty cup at me as well, screeched a "Fuck you!" and then turned to stagger out the door, leaving it open behind her.

I stood there, blinking after her. I waited until she was gone before I sank down to the floor in the puddle of my blankets, wrapped my arms around myself, tilted my head back, and screamed to the godless and uncaring heavens far above me.

| 47 |

AFTER SOME TIME, I walked out the door and down the street, picking my direction at random. Eventually, I found myself outside the park I'd visited some weeks ago. The jogging paths had gates and chains across them, but you could still walk through the trees toward the dog park or the children's area, and I did.

A small, well-tended creek fed into the duck pond, and a large Japanese-style, wooden bridge with a pagoda-style roof spanned it. I'd seen parents and older siblings sit up here on the built-in benches while the younger kids splashed around in the creek below, picking out fancy river rocks.

With just the moonlight to guide me, I crossed to the center of the bridge and stopped to lean against the railing and look down. I thought I saw sleek silver and gold koi fish down in the creek, but I couldn't be certain.

"Oh. I'm sorry."

The voice startled me and made me quickly turn around. My heart thudded once, hard, in my chest when I spotted a man sitting on the bench directly opposite me. He was dressed in a dark windbreaker and had an ebook reader in his hands. But he was sitting so still, I didn't see him when I first came up here.

He stood up when he saw my reaction, and I immediately recognized the young priest with the gorgeous black eyes.

"Father Matt?"

He was dressed in civilian clothes under the jacket—a button-down shirt, pullover, and snug jeans that looked good on him. He half-smiled in a self-deprecating way as if I'd caught him doing something scandalous. "Vivian. I almost didn't recognize you."

I was barefoot and dressed in my sleep clothes and a ratty robe. I couldn't imagine what he was thinking. "I'm sorry too," I said, glancing down at my state of undress. "Didn't mean to interrupt you."

"It's all right. I was done anyway." He held up the e-reader. "*Lolita* by Vladimir Nabokov."

I stared blankly at him—not because of his choice of reading material (that I didn't care about), but because I was still reeling from my encounter with Brenda, Mac's wife. But Father Matt misinterpreted my silence.

"It's really a political novel," he insisted by way of an excuse. "A story about the corruption and death of the American Dream. Perversity, obsessions, but also art. Suburbia and consumer culture. And none of this looks good on me, *si?*"

I smiled for the first time in days. I didn't care that Father Matt broke into parks at night to read scandalous classical literature on bridges. It was none of my business.

He studied me as he approached. He looked at my arm, partially revealed by the robe but riding up because I kept rubbing my burn. His mood suddenly darkened considerably. "What happened to you?" He took my arm and gently rolled my sleeve up to reveal the angry red skin that was starting to bubble up in places. "Did someone do this to you?"

I looked at him—at the mysterious compassion on his face—but I couldn't seem to speak. My throat still hurt. But so did my heart. It felt like it was broken in a way that would never mend.

As if sensing how damaged I was, he released my arm and slid a hand over my shoulder—not sexual but protective. "Come with me? Please?"

I let him take me. I didn't give a rat's ass if he dragged me to some scummy underground leather bar and whipped the hell out of me if that was what he needed to get off. I didn't even feel like a human being anymore.

He didn't do that, though. We went back to the parish in his car, which was parked on the curb outside the park. Once we reached the church, he unlocked the attached rectory and led me inside.

Father Matt's quarters were small and homey, a tiny collection of rooms—kitchen, bedroom, one bathroom, and an office—decorated for comfort rather than show. I saw a green sofa, lamps with fringes, one of those standing ashtrays you only ever saw in antique stores and old TV sitcoms, and a fireplace mantel cluttered with a plethora of family photographs.

He had me sit on the sofa while he gathered first aid supplies from the bathroom. I looked at the large collection of happy Latinx faces in the pictures on the mantel and wondered who they were and where they were living.

"I really should take you to Emergency. But you won't go, will you?" he said as he returned with a medium-sized tote full of medical supplies. From the size of it, I wondered if he was used to patching up his parishioners. It was a rough neighborhood. Perhaps he acted as a healer of body *and* soul.

He sat down and rolled up my sleeve to examine my burn. Hissing between his teeth, he said, "It looks pretty raw. Does it hurt?"

"Yes."

"Why haven't you done something about it?"

I didn't answer.

He moved in closer to examine my face and eyes. I smelled his aftershave—different than Mac's. Lighter. "Are you high? I'm not judging, mind you. I'd just like to know for your own safety."

I shook my head. Then, abruptly, I confessed, "I deserve this."

He didn't look shocked or surprised by my statement. "You deserve to be burned?"

I couldn't respond to that. I didn't know how.

Father Matt didn't push. He just smiled. "We'll do something about the burn now. All right?"

He found some burn cream and started slathering it over my arm. Then he reached into the tote for a roll of gauze. Having second thoughts, he put it back. "That will stick. How about an ace bandage?"

I just stared at him.

"Let's do that," he decided for me and went to work wrapping my burned arm with an ace bandage instead.

I realized he was speaking to me as if I was a simple child, but I didn't care. I liked the sound of his voice, and I enjoyed listening to him speak. I wondered how long he had been in America.

"Were you born here?" I asked, thinking aloud.

He surprised me. "*Si*...yes. But my *madre y padre* were from Guatemala. Villa Neueva. It's a large city, but it has several beautiful national parks. I saw them all when we visited my *abuela*."

I smiled a little as he finished bandaging me up.

"There we go." He gently set my damaged arm down. "You should rest. It's late. You can sleep on the sofa if you like."

He went to fetch a sheet, a blanket, and a couple of pillows and set the sofa up for me like something he was familiar with doing. Once I got into bed, he stood there a long moment, looking down at me with soft, sympathetic eyes. I felt like my troubles were his troubles.

"I'm turning in, but if you need anything, I'm just over here." He indicated his room.

At first, I thought that was some kind of sexual invitation, but then I realized he was sincere. He didn't want me for sex the way most men did, and I felt safe with him. I couldn't remember a time when I'd felt completely safe around a man.

Before he turned in for the night, I said, "Why are you helping me?"

He looked surprised that I should ask. "We've all been in that dark place, *corazon*."

That night, I slept dreamlessly for the first time in what seemed like forever.

| 48 |

"TRY TO EAT something," Father Matt urged me the next morning. He was again dressed in his holy uniform, a cross hanging around his neck. He was sitting on the side of the sofa where I was lying, a tray balanced on his arm. He had taken the time to make me cereal and toast and orange juice. I couldn't remember the last time I'd had something to eat that wasn't soup or crackers. I thought about something I once read, that a human could go as long as a month without food.

I just stared at him, hoping he'd keep talking to me.

"I'll leave it here," he said with a half-smile, sliding the tray onto the coffee table. "I have work to do, but I'll be back tonight around six. I left a number and money in the kitchen for an Uber if you want to go home, and there are menus in the drawers if you want to order something in. Do you have a phone?"

I'd left mine at home. "No."

He nodded. "There's a rotary on the kitchen wall if you want to call someone." He paused, a look of concern on his face.

"I know how to use a rotary phone," I told him.

He smiled at that. "You could also wait for me if you aren't ready to go."

"All right."

After he was gone, I lay back on the sofa. I again felt like I did at home—like my body had all lead bones inside of it. I couldn't seem to move at all. There was a TV in the corner, but I didn't have the motivation to get up and turn it on. Anyway, it would just be full of stories about dead people I'd killed and city blocks I'd burned to the ground. Instead, I dozed for most of the day.

Around four o'clock, I got a leg cramp that forced me to get up and walk it off. I decided to visit the tiny bathroom, where I discovered I looked like some specter of death walking around. My eyes were blackened out and my hair tangled. My skin was whiter than paper, and there were red spots high up on my cheeks. I looked like a crack addict.

I availed myself of Father Matt's shower, then padded naked into his bedroom. It was kept tastefully spare, with just a large bed, nightstand, and highboy. A simple wooden cross hung over the bed. But directly across the bed, I saw posters for Jennifer Lopez and Shakira, both looking particularly sexy in their brief, fringe-laden dance outfits. And I smiled. Peeking inside his highboy, I found a pair of sweatpants and a T-shirt. They fit me well enough, seeing how Father Matt was small and of a slight build, but I felt bad about borrowing his clothes without permission, so I went into the kitchen to look in his refrigerator.

Before I decided to be a pastry chef, I took a full culinary course at Lincoln Technical. I found some raw ingredients and laid them out on the counter, then went through his cupboards for dry ingredients. Finally, I chose a good chef's knife from the block on the counter. I figured I owed him at least one well-prepared meal for all of his little kindnesses.

When Father Matt returned at six, I had a chicken enchilada casserole bubbling in the oven and the aroma had filled the flat. I noticed his interest immediately.

"You're up," he said, sounding cheerful even though he had to be tired from attending to troubled parishioners all day long.

I stood in the kitchen, washing the pots I had used to make the casserole, feeling slightly embarrassed about the way I was wearing his clothes uninvited. I had taken over his kitchen, but he didn't even mention it.

"I'll set the table," he said instead. "You'll join me?"

I didn't eat much dinner—just a few bites to make him happy. I was pleased to see he liked the casserole, though.

"This reminds me of my *abuela's*. Who taught you to cook?"

It took me a moment to answer. His voice was like a hypnotic drug to me. "I did. I went to school."

"Ah." He nodded over his plate. I loved watching him shovel in the food. It made me feel good. "In my family, the women pass it down from mother to daughter. Often, they don't even write the recipe down and that causes conflict."

I thought about that for a moment. "My mother didn't like me. She gave me up as soon as I was born."

That gained me a long stare. I thought he'd asked uncomfortable questions, but instead, he said, "I'm sorry. Family can be hard." He put another bite of food into his mouth and talked through it like you're not supposed to. "This is so good. I may need to keep you just so you can cook for me."

I snorted over that.

He looked pleased to have finally gotten a reaction out of me.

After dinner, he offered to read me one of his ebooks. I didn't know how I felt about that, but after we were sitting side by side on the sofa together—sitting closer than we should, probably—he whipped out his Kindle and started reading *The Hobbit*.

It was never a book I could get into as a kid. Too twee for me. But I liked listening to him narrate it in his accent.

His voice was such a balm. I felt myself sinking against his shoulder in the seconds before I sat up straighter, clawing my way back awake. I wondered what I was doing here, invading his life like this. It was all so ridiculous...

Father Matt sensed my unease and said, "I could get you that Uber now."

I didn't want him to invest more in me than he already had. "I can walk," I told him, getting up.

He followed me across the room and put his hand on my arm to stop me. "Please don't. I'll drive you."

I looked at him touching me. I knew how this would end. Like it always ends with me and my men. Nick. Mac. I told myself I didn't want to make more brides. But as I tried to untangle myself, he said the words that sealed my fate.

"Vivian, I knew what you are."

Getting angry for the first time in days, I turned and showed him my teeth. "If that's true, you never would have brought me here. Invited me in. You're not...you shouldn't..."

"My *abuela* was a witch."

Tears sprang to my eyes. The absolute horror of my life bubbled over and I found myself sobbing, "I'm not a witch! I wish I were a fucking witch! Being a witch would be simple!"

Father Matt was still standing in front of me, still holding my arm. I simply folded against him and started crying into his shirt. I let it all go and cried until my heart hurt too much to continue and I started to hiccup like a fool. Hot, biting pain bloomed across my bare skin above the neckline of the T-shirt. It was then I remembered the cross hanging around his neck. Pulling back, I drew my shirt down a little to show him the burn mark on my skin, hoping he'd understand. Hoping he'd be just as horrified of me as I was and push me away.

He looked surprised—but not as horrorstruck as he should. He took a moment to study the cross-shaped red mark there and even reached out and tentatively touched it with one finger. "Forgive me," he said and reached for the chain, slipped the cross over his head, and set it down on the coffee table.

I shook my head. "Why?"

He looked confused. Then his eyes cleared. "You feel like the closest thing to God that I have ever encountered in this world."

He made the pain in my soul lessen a little. I knew he was craving me—I could feel that. A low, lonely simmer in his soul that was different from the raging, uncontrollable fire I could feel inside of Mac. Since we were almost the same size, I didn't have to reach up to lay a kiss on his roughened cheek the way I did with Mac.

Father Matt sighed in delight. I liked that sound. When I turned my head to kiss his soft, pretty mouth for the first time, he made a different sound. It was as if this was a relief for him.

For me, the kiss made my heart race as if someone was jump-starting my whole system. My entire body suddenly felt the hunger of the last few days. It was as if my hunger debt had found me. It made me squirm, and the taste of his lips—the spices still strong on his tongue—drove me into a delirium of mindless desire. He felt it too. His eyes—huge and radiant as if he had taken a hit of hard drugs—looked full of stars.

I didn't know what I'd unleashed this time, but soft, passive Father Matt pushed me against the nearest wall and growled faintly as he kissed the side of my neck. He even dry-humped me a few times. His reaction frightened and delighted me in equal measure. In seconds, he had gone from a shy priest to a ravenous male animal. I'd seen the same thing happen with Mac. Hell, Nick was the same way at the beginning of our relationship. One moment, nothing. The next...they couldn't seem to control themselves.

"Matt," I said and slapped my hands to the sides of his face. "Matt!"

He gasped, drawing back, eyes dark and seething with desire and terror. "I...I am sorry."

I ran my hands over his prickly cheeks, but that just made this feeling inside of me grow stronger. I watch him react to it. For one moment, he resisted, then his eyes turned all black, with neither whites nor irises, and he started kissing me, pinning me to the wall as the thing inside me took him over, enlivening his lust. I wanted him so badly I could barely breathe. I fumbled with his trousers, which was a little difficult under his cassock. He helped me with that, then pulled at my sweatpants until he was able to find his way inside me.

His first hard thrust knocked the breath from my throat. Father Matt was surprisingly well endowed and, at the moment, almost frighteningly aggressive in his need to rut with me. He groaned, his eyes all blackity-black, and sank his fingernails into my ass cheeks as he pushed up high inside me so I cried out in surprise and delight. He grunted and growled into the side of my neck, his breath hot and fast as he fucked into me harder, deeper. He was surprisingly strong. Each thrust lifted me off my feet and scraped my back up the wall.

I felt his silken wet tongue following the contours of my neck. Then he murmured something so perverse into my ear that even I couldn't wrap my brain around it. "Ohhh..." I said even as my heart began to race and my blood pounded in my ears.

Amidst all this, I saw that dim, dark light manifesting all around Father Matt. It was warm and welcoming and nourishing. I wanted it so badly. The alien luminescence grew as my body absorbed the priest's strength, his power, his vitality. It was surprisingly potent. It drove us both over the edge and we wound up kissing and biting into each other's mouths as we came together against the wall.

It was over quickly, and it left us both dazed and exhausted while he slowly let me down to the floor. As his eyes cleared and became their usual pretty brown color, I started to recognize the horror of what I'd done to him.

For Father Matt, it was a different kind of horror. He looked shocked by what had happened. "Vivian...I am so sor—!"

I put my finger on his lips. There was a small red sore where I'd bitten him. "This isn't on you. It's on me. I warned you..."

He squeezed his eyes shut. "Sister Marie said..." His voice trailed away.

I immediately stiffened against the wall. "What did Sister Marie say?"

He sucked in a deep breath that filled his chest. I wondered if he would cry. If he did, I would, too. "She warned me about you. She said...she said you were a corrupting presence. That you were the Devil. I didn't believe her. I thought she was overreacting."

I looked at him, my heart aching. I felt so ashamed. I felt as if I'd pulled the wings off a butterfly. I couldn't dispute what Sister Marie said, but it still hurt to hear. "She wasn't wrong."

I started to untangle myself from him, but Father Matt surprised me by tightening his hold on my shoulders before moving them up so he was cradling my face. "She also wasn't right."

"I don't understand," I told him honestly because I felt like he was talking in riddles.

"The girls in the van," Father Matt told me. "You freed them, *si?* You did a good thing. Would the Devil have done that?"

I squirmed uncomfortably. "How do you know about that?"

"She told me. She was so upset you put the city at risk, but I told her what you did was pure and good and..."

I stopped him there, a hand at his lips. "So you talked to her? About me?"

He blinked, uncertain. "A few days ago, *si*, just before she left." He looked confused before adding, "She said her mother was ill, so she took some personal time off to see to her."

I hung against the wall, fairly stunned by the news. I had assumed, with the destruction of the roadhouse and the scattering of the Toltecs, that Sister Marie would also be gone, along with her goddess. But now I realized how wrong I'd been. Maybe, I thought, Sister Marie and the woman in the iron coffin hadn't been working with the Toltecs at all. Maybe they were two completely separate entities. Hell, maybe they were even at war with one another and stupid me had blindly stumbled in between them...

The idea made me sick to my stomach. It meant Sister Marie was still out there. It meant *she* was still out there...somewhere. It meant I hadn't done a damned thing to stop that vision of death and destruction I saw.

I breathed out a sharp curse. "Do you know where Sister Marie went?"

"No. She did not tell me."

I had to work to swallow down a new panic attack. "I'm so sorry, Matt. So sorry I dragged you into this. I have to go."

But he didn't release me. Instead, he looked deep into my eyes before canting his head down so he was resting his forehead against mine. It was an especially tender gesture. I wished he hated me. But now I realized that was impossible.

"You knew, didn't you?" I whispered hoarsely. "You always knew...about me...but you let me in anyway."

"That you're a demon as well as a *bruja*? *Si*."

I started to struggle.

He looked up, stroked the side of my face, and kissed me. That kiss immediately calmed me. It helped me think. Whether or not I wanted it, and whether or not he understood the gravity of what he had allowed to happen, I now knew he belonged to me. The same as Mac.

I also knew what I needed to do.

I had to find Sister Marie, and I was willing to tear this city apart if need be. If I found her, I'd find the woman in the iron coffin. And once I found *her*, I could destroy her. Or she could destroy me.

Either worked for me.

| 49 |

SEBASTIAN REMAINED PAINFULLY sober over the next few days. He didn't question what had been happening to me or where I went at night. He didn't ask me complicated questions when I was out all night or when I stumbled home at four in the morning, looking tired and punch-drunk, to grab a couple of hours of sleep before work.

I didn't tell him I'd been hitting the bars and nightclubs—not to drink or to party, but to sit in a shadowy corner for half of the night, the pounding music making my ears bleed, and watch people ignore me whenever I showed them a picture of Sister Marie and ask if they knew of her.

During the day, more and more people visited the shop looking for charms. Many of them were Matilda's friends, though some were not of her circle, I learned. Those people told me they'd heard stories circulating that I could fix things in small but meaningful ways. There were a surprising number of people who needed small fixes. Even though I knew I had to find the witch, I also had an obligation to them. A few good things to balance out all of the bad I was doing.

There was the old woman who asked for a charm so she could forget about her daughter who died as an infant so she could get a few uninterrupted hours of sleep at night. The college boy who begged for something to help him with his ADHD because he was failing his classes. The five-year-old girl who showed up with her deceased green anole in a paper bag, asking me if I could make him alive again. That one was easy. I went to PetSmart and bought a new, matching anole for the little girl. Magic, after all, didn't have to be complicated.

While on break one afternoon, I leaned sleepily in the doorway of the display room and watched some young kids oohing over Sebastian's dinosaur village. He had a chocolate stegosaurus with a cart attached to it to transport his chocolate cave people in, and a chocolate Apatosaurus standing in a chocolate swamp.

A man in a nice suit walked up to my partner the brilliant chocolatier and started talking to him about creating a custom-made chocolate display for his daughter's ninth birthday party. His daughter, Amber, wanted a whole herd of white chocolate unicorns. While they were hashing out the small details, I noticed Mac hovering in a corner of the shop, looking over the gourmet selection of boxed chocolates.

I immediately thought of Brenda and had to steel myself. I then cut across the floor and stopped near his elbow. I watched him pick up a heart-shaped box of dark chocolates, but I reached across him and tapped the box of artisan mocha lattes. "You should give her these."

He looked up at me and sighed. "We need to talk."

"We do."

We needed somewhere private, but not isolated. I didn't want anything happening between us like in the pizza shop. In the end, we walked to Safa's Laundromat next door and sat down at one of the booths near the back where they served hot dogs and soft pretzels. Safa raised her hand and waved to me from the change counter. I waved back.

Mac immediately dove in. "The other day? That shouldn't have happened. I am *so* sorry..."

"It's fine," I interrupted. "That was always going to happen."

He shook his head vehemently. "Brenda had no right...and then she told me about the coffee and, Christ, Vivian..."

I held my hand up to stop him. "She was right. About everything—"

We were interrupted when Safa appeared, carrying two cups of coffee. "For you guys. On the house!"

"Thanks, Safa," I said, trying to sound cheery even though I needed to talk to Mac alone.

She set the coffees down. "Haven't seen Sebastian in a long while."

I smiled up at Safa, knowing she had a minor crush on my train wreck of a partner. "He's been buried in the kitchen."

"That reminds me...I need to buy some chocolates."

"I'll send some over later." Safa looked disappointed, so I added, "Or you can pick them up yourself. Just tell Seb I owe you."

Safa smiled ear to ear. "Cool! Peace out, you guys!"

After she was gone, Mac cleared his throat. "About Brenda..."

I reached out and touched the back of his hand to stop him from apologizing one more time for his wife's behavior. I felt a spark, and Mac jumped a little.

"Tell me that was static electricity."

"Mac..."

His brows knitted together like he had a headache, then he leaned down to sip his coffee. "What you did to me..."

"I know what I did to you, Mac. And I'm sorry. I'm so sorry all of this happened, and—"

"See, that's just it," he interrupted. He sounded angry, but I was not sure why. "*You're* sorry. I'm not." He leaned forward a little.

"This should hurt. I should feel like a shit because I *am* a cheating, no-good shit. But I don't feel it. I wake up in the morning beside Brenda, knowing what I'm doing to her, and I'm *not* sorry."

I saw the tears form in his eyes. I stayed silent; I couldn't imagine what he was going through—the literal hell I was putting him through. He rubbed the heel of one hand over his eyes, and I felt my heart break inside me a little more.

"I don't understand why I don't care..."

Since he was backing me into a figurative corner, I said the only thing I could. "You know why. You just don't want to say it."

"Say what?"

I blurted it out. "That I'm evil. Or, at least, something damned close to it—"

"You're not *evil*, Vivian. Christ!"

He sounded insulted that I should even contemplate it, but I was not done. "Well, let me tell you something, Mac. I'm not good. My father is the former Devil. My brother is the current ruling Devil. I'm a witch, a daemon, and also some kind of succubus. I live off the vitality of men. That doesn't exactly put me in the saint category."

He looked unimpressed with my confession. "So you meant to do this to me?"

"Christ, no!"

He eyed me. "Then you're not evil."

I shook my head, hating that he wouldn't blame me. Maybe if he did, we could resolve this once and for all. Maybe I could just walk away. "This has to end. It's dangerous for you to be around me. Can we agree on that?"

He didn't nod, but he did say, "Yeah."

"Good." I started to get up, but he seized my arm to stop me.

"You can't just leave, Vivian. I'm your bride now. You're responsible for me. You said so yourself."

"I..." Hot tears filled my eyes. "I didn't know what to *do* for you, Mac."

He closed his eyes and thought a long moment before continuing. "If you're done with me, then let me go. But if you love me...if you want to keep me, then you have to save me..."

I swallowed hard against the knot forming in my throat. Christ! "Give me a few days. Let me try to sort this out."

He nodded. We stayed that way for a long moment. It must have made Safa nervous because she winged by our table once more.

"Everything okay, guys?" she asked, looking to me for clues or signals.

"Everything is fine, Safa," I told her.

She looked at Mac.

"Yeah," he agreed, his voice remarkably steady. "Everything is great." After she was gone, he reached under his jacket and set a small manila folder on the table. "You know that case you were helping me with?"

My heart jumped. "Yeah?"

He waited until Safa had returned to the change desk. Then he went on. "Well, the gang...the Toltecs...they're gone. Like magic. Poof."

I took a deep breath, hoping the truth wasn't written all over my face. "That's good, right?"

"Good and bad."

"How is it bad?" Suddenly, I was terrified of what he was going to say next.

"There have been more murders," he said low, sounding angry and frustrated. "Like the last ones. Just not the same type. God help me, I shouldn't give you this folder, but I'm at a loss as to where to go from here. I don't understand this...this witch stuff..."

A cold dread bloomed within me, but I swiped the folder up all the same.

| 50 |

THE MEN IN all of the photographs had been brutally slaughtered. Skin peeled from their faces and bodies, mouths gaping open in silent screams of outrage and pain. Just like before. But unlike before, these were not pimps, rapists, and murderers. Not all of these men belonged to the shadows in this city.

I looked at the picture of the dead vagrant found in the alley behind a tenement building: a slick red skeleton in a dirty, crumpled coat, his afro full of blood. The man skinned and hung from a tree in his backyard, his two children bawling their heads off as they were led away by police. Another man, just a teacher, flayed, his body tossed into a dumpster.

I set the roadhouse on fire. I burned Tupoc down to black bones. I scattered his gang of human traffickers. I'd killed a lot of people on purpose and by accident. And my one, thin, sad little consolation was knowing that maybe something good had come of it. Maybe I had stopped the Toltecs from burrowing deeper into the Philly underground. Maybe I had stopped the murders if nothing else.

But I hadn't stopped *her*.

I set the pack of pictures down on the kitchen counter, covered my mouth, and rushed to the bathroom to throw up all over the toilet.

Afterward, I stood in front of the scarred yellow sink and looked at my paper-white face and feverish dark eyes in the mirror. My tangled hair. My haunted dark expression.
I still didn't know where to find the woman.
The woman who would destroy this city.
The woman who would kill me.
The woman I *knew* would kill me.
I exhaled a sob and the glass medicine cabinet broke into a spiderweb pattern as if I'd punched it.

| 51 |

AFTER THE SHOP was closed and Sebastian had tottered out to complete his nightly binge drinking, I locked the door and set a dozen lighted candles around the prep room. Then I turned the lights out.

The candlelight cast a warm sepia tone over everything. I reached into the drawer where I'd been gathering items for tonight and pulled out the cloth-wrapped package, setting the items out on the prep table where I normally made my charms for my after-hours customers.

A bag of red salt, three black crow feathers, a mini-cauldron I could fit in the palm of my hand (it was difficult to find cauldrons of such size except on Amazon, I discovered), a handful of river rocks I'd collected from the children's park, a votive candle I borrowed from off a memorial for someone who died on the side of the highway, and the Devil's Tarot, which managed to find its way back to me within hours of the fire. Finally, I chose a dicing knife from out of the butcher block because I didn't have a proper athame. But a knife's a knife, right?

I set the cauldron on the countertop and filled it with water from the tap. Then I placed the other magical items around it in a circle—the feathers, the stones, the candle, and the red salt. The pseudo-athame I placed to my left-hand side. I kept thinking of what my father said, calling me his Left Hand of Darkness, and this seemed to fit. Finally, I spread the Devil's Tarot in a circle around all of the other items. I was not following any spell book. I was just going by instinct here—doing the best I could.

I stood back and looked over my impromptu altar. I realized I needed something that was sorely missing.

Going to the beecosystem, I unlatched the series of safety doors and slid them open. My bees slowly drifted out and formed a dark cloud that filled the tiny room. The sight would surely have sent any sane person running off screaming into the night. A few settled on my shoulders, and one landed on my cheek. Their collective hum filled my head and heart.

I reached inside and collected the queen in my hand since she was wingless.

"What do you think? Can you help me, Your Majesty?" I asked as I felt a warm surge pass through my body. The queen hummed in response.

I carried her to the altar and set her down on the edge of the cauldron, where she waited for me to begin my work

Picking up the knife, I raised it above my head and closed my eyes. I tried to find the words necessary to achieve the spell, but I couldn't think of anything mystical to say, and the harder I tried, the more frustrating it became. As if sensing my impasse, the bees moved upward into a cloud over my head. Their hum filled my mind. I listened to it and slowly, with time, I started seeing words in my head—just not in any language I'd ever heard.

I started speaking the language as I heard it. It sounded like an obscure Russian dialect—if it was spoken backward and with a mouth full of marbles. I wondered if it was Divine—angel-speak.

With the knife, I cut a sigil into the air. It didn't surprise me that it was the sign of the House of Lucifer. I mean, what other power was I capable of summoning? Certainly nothing of God or man.

The humming increased in my head. The air suddenly crackled with raw blue energy. And when I opened my eyes, I saw the sigil hanging in the air over the altar in what resembled a glowing blue-white strike of lightning. I sucked in a quick breath at the sight. This was big magic—a big working. I was afraid to move or to make any sudden gestures, lest I break the spell. But as I slowly lowered the knife, I saw the Devil's Tarot drift upward, forming a deadly silver halo around the sigil.

The entire display was pretty to look at, but when I checked the water in the cauldron, all I saw were my own eyes reflected there. They were full of the same energy as the sigil, but that was not what I was looking for. Maybe I need more power for the spell. I remembered what Nick said about the Lucifers being natural channelers. We didn't create our own power. We drew it from our wells.

Closing my eyes again, I imagined a well—deep and dark and full of blue light. Both Mac and Father Matt immediately came to mind.

They felt close—so close, I could smell Mac's cologne on the air. I could hear Matt's sweet and balmy voice. I could even see them. Father Matt was talking with a young woman who was weeping on the pew they were sitting on together. At the same time, Mac was getting his young daughter Charity into her PJs. I felt like my brain was splitting in half as I watched them in real time.

The moment I sensed Mac, he sensed me in return and quickly turned from his daughter and walked downstairs, shutting himself away in his study. Father Matt didn't miss a beat. Ignoring the crying woman, he got up and let himself out of the church and crossed to the rectory nearby. Both men lay down on the nearest surfaces available to them: Mac his leather lounge sofa and Matt the ratty old sofa I'd slept on. Both immediately crossed their arms and stared up at the ceiling as their lips began to move. I couldn't hear their voices, but I thought they were speaking my spell.

I tore my inner eye away from them and refocused on the cauldron. I was surprised to find the water in it swirling clockwise around the small container. "I need to see," I told it. "Show me."

The water moved faster, but that was all.

I needed more. More power. I raised the knife higher and coughed out another angel-speak spell I didn't know.

That made both men jerk as if they had hooks in their flesh and I was yanking their wires. It was not pleasant for them, I knew, but it couldn't be helped. I had shown them a shade of heaven; they owed me this.

"I need to see!" I commanded the cauldron. "Let me see!"

This time, I raised the knife and shouted the spell to the ceiling, putting all of my will behind it. The swarm of bees rose with my gesture, their humming so loud that it drowned out all of the other sounds around me. Both men jerked upward at the same time, still in their supine position, the pull on them so fierce that it actually bowed their backs as a dark light poured from their open mouths. Both of their eyes turned pure black, and even though I couldn't hear them—all of this was more remote viewing than anything else—I knew in my heart that both were screaming as I ripped the power from their very bones.

The water moved much faster now like a miniature cyclone barely contained within the small black cauldron. Finally, *finally*...I saw light in the water. I saw images. And because of my brides' sacrifice—because of the well of power they had opened to me—I recognized the place where Sister Marie was hiding my enemy.

| 52 |

I PARKED IN the front lot of the vast Tyson Manufacturing Company Plant. It was a sprawling, long-abandoned steel manufacturing plant in the northeast sector of the city. I'd read about it here and there in "hunted Philly" brochures, which were incredibly popular. When Sebastian and I first launched Confessions, Safa came in with an armful of booklets she said we could have because she was always ordering too many from her printer. We set them up in the window alongside the chocolates and teddy bears and they were gone in one afternoon. I knew from the pamphlets that Tyson was among one of the more popular hotspots for ghost hunters and tourists who loved photographing abandoned places, a popular sport in this town.

The pictures I'd seen of the Tyson Plant didn't do it justice. Up close, it looked like one of those places you see in post-apocalyptic movies full of zombies and flesh-eating cannibals.

I got out and cautiously approached the crumbling building. The structure itself covered several acres and rose maybe fifty or sixty feet into the air—all broken, eyeless glass and ragged black steel bones with the skin scraped away. I felt a chill that had nothing to do with the darkness, the full moon, or the lonely sodium lamps that lined the vast, broken concrete apron.

The doors and part of the building in the front were simply gone, producing a ragged hole into darkness. I was a little freaked out about going in, partly because of the ghost stories about the steel mill in Safa's brochures, but mostly for practical reasons: I was scared of getting lost and wandering around in the dark until a vagrant grabbed me.

Thankfully, there were plenty of windows and enough moonlight pouring through the skylights and between the catwalks above to see well as I walked to the center of a large, hangar-like space. I found myself gaping at the total ruin of the mill. Old machine mounts and piles of scrap metal lay scattered across the floor. Arcane graffiti covered the walls. Metal catwalks bridged the space above me like weathered bones. From them hung the rotted wiring entrails of ancient electronics. Throughout the space, sheets of ragged plastic soughed mournfully in the cold breeze billowing through.

I was dressed in a short black pea coat. It was far too warm for this time of the year, but I wanted something that made me feel protected. I was happy now that I'd worn it, as I was freezing my ass off as I clumped along, the echoes of my footfalls sounding too loud and intrusive in this space. Shivering, I walked around this huge, abandoned catacomb to turn-of-the-century human endeavors, trying to avoid the pools of oil and stagnant water on the floor, but even though I peered into every corner, I didn't see anything that resembled the vision I'd had.

Still, I knew I was in the right place. In my cauldron vision, I recognized the elaborate Tyson Manufacturing logo painted on the walls.

I could smell the black mold invading my lungs. Somewhere, a cat yowled. After twenty minutes of wandering around aimlessly, I got fed up and started back. But as I turned, I spotted a light ahead and stopped.

A shadow was standing about a hundred feet away, holding up a battery torch.

I swallowed hard and felt my nerves sing. I wanted to say something tough and clever, but I didn't have any spit left in my mouth. Anyway, the figure spoke first.

"It's you, Princess," came a woman's soft voice. She lifted the lantern higher and I recognized her sad, carven face. She was wearing civilian clothes and a long windbreaker, but it was definitely Sister Marie, the witch-nun who first gave me the name Lady Lucifer.

"Y-you..." I had to swallow to wet my throat before I could continue. "I thought you might be here."

Our voices echoed so loudly that it seemed we were shouting at each other.

Sister Marie ignored my statement. "What are you doing here?"

"Looking for you. And for...her."

I still didn't know her name. All this time I'd dreamed of her, feared her, abhorred her, and waited to speak to her again, and I didn't even know her goddamn name.

Sister Marie nodded. "Xtabay."

The name echoed in the vastness of this dead place and drove what felt like a cold scalpel up my back. "Xtabay," I repeated. "That...that's her name?"

Sister Marie only looked at me accusingly.

"Who is she?" When she didn't immediately answer me, I added, "*What* is she? Not a real goddess...?"

"Leave here, little Princess," Sister Marie intoned. "Forget her. Forget all this. Go home and live your sad, lonely little life with your brides and your necromancer."

She started edging backward, but I took a quick step forward. I was angry now. Fucking belittle me? "Stop!"

To my surprise, she did. But she glared hostilely at me as if I'd slapped her.

I took another step, narrowly avoiding an oil spill on the floor between us. "I need to know more, witch. I need answers."

"Answers? Why?"

I wanted to sob in exhaustion and frustration. "Because I've seen things! Things that I think she can do."

"And...?"

"And I need to stop her! *We* need to stop her!"

To my surprise, Sister Marie moved swiftly toward me. I didn't even have the time to react before she was practically nose to nose with me. I could smell her sweat. I suspected she'd been holed up here for days, wearing the same clothes.

Grabbing me roughly by the arm, she used an inordinate amount of strength to drive me to my knees in a puddle of stagnant rainwater. I cried out in response as I went down, splashing stinking water up the front of my coat.

"You stupid *puta!*" she screamed in my face, startling me. "How dare you come here after what you have done to her!"

She slapped me, then...so hard that I wound up down on my ass on the concrete. I cried out, but she wasn't done with me. She grabbed me by the hair and shook me violently while spitting Spanish in my face. The pain and violence made me cry out in surprise. The whole experience was so different from what I'd expected from her. I was left stunned and helpless as she yanked on me and slapped me like some disobedient child, then threw me back down again.

I didn't fight her. I lay there, my heart thudding in my ears, breathing roughly and listening to her raining down her rage on me. In too many ways, I deserved this—someone to hurt me. To tell me exactly what I was. A monster. Something worse...

Finally, Sister Marie, who once seemed so at peace, spat on me.

Her cold saliva hit me in the cheek and partially in the eye. I blinked it away. I didn't know what I had done to her or to Xtabay, but I was sure, whatever it was, I probably deserved it.

Only when she drew a decorative magic athame from under her coat did I start to panic. If it was just a regular knife, I might even have let her continue. But a witch's athame can really hurt another witch—even kill her. And I didn't want to die. I didn't want to know where someone like me went when she died.

With a cry, Sister Marie lunged at me.

I started to move, to roll away, but I knew I was not fast enough, not in this vulnerable position. Instead, I threw my arms up in defense, not that that would save me. But just as she reached me, the athame was torn from her hand and flung away as if by tremendous force. The knife flew the full length of the hangar, hit the floor, and skittered along for a while before disappearing into darkness.

Sister Marie almost pitched over, catching herself at the last moment. Muttering a curse in her native tongue, she turned her head in the direction of the lost athame.

I thought about getting up and charging her while she was distracted, but then I spotted the woman—the goddess—Xtabay standing on the crumbling metal catwalk above us, her arms outstretched to perform the spell that saved me from the athame. She was no longer dressed as she had been when I first saw her step out of the iron sarcophagus. She was still so beautiful that it hurt to look upon her, but she had cut her dark hair short like a boy's so her ears stuck out a little, and she was wearing jeans and a strappy T-shirt of the kind I favored. She was still barefoot, but she sported a white wrap sweater that flowed around her like wings.

All of that was weird enough on its own. But what really surprised me was the look of horror on Xtabay's beautiful face. I hadn't expected that. She put a hand on the railing and, with almost no effort at all, launched herself over it. But she didn't fall like a human.

Instead, she fell like what she was—a goddess descending to Earth—and I couldn't help but be mesmerized by the sight of her floating down to the floor in front of us, her bare toes touching down as if she were weightless.

Sister Marie straightened up and turned to address Xtabay while I lay there on the stained concrete, watching them. "I told you to stay upstairs."

Xtabay narrowed her black, cattish eyes but said nothing. Nothing *I* could hear.

"This is none of your concern!" Sister Marie insisted as if they were holding a private conversation only she could hear. She gestured wildly. "She is *his* daughter. Ha-Shaitan's corrupted blood! And she has corrupted *you*, my lady!"

Xtabay shook her head as if she was not convinced.

"You *must* stay away from her! You must not be tainted by the unholy one!"

Xtabay raised one long arm and pointed her finger directly at me. Then she brought her hand in and laid it to her heart in some arcane gesture I couldn't translate.

"No...no, you didn't understand, my lady!" Sister Marie insisted in some kind of panic, holding her hands up as if to ward her back. "Do you not know what she is?"

Xtabay brought her hand up and then down in a long line. I thought she might be making the sign of the House of Lucifer. She then made the heart gesture again.

Sister Marie blanched as she grew more hysterical. "My lady, she is the Left Hand of Darkness! She is *his* cursed daughter...!" Exasperated, Sister Marie turned and gestured to me. "You do not understand! She is the Heir. She is the fucking Whore of Babylon!"

Those words hurt me worse than any knife. I'd heard them uttered in the past by other hateful people. I'd been called the Great

Whore so many times that I wanted to scream my rage to the sky. "Stop calling me that!" I roared, getting to my feet. I wanted to scratch the witch's damned eyes out for that.

But Sister Marie turned to me. The look on her face stunned me into silence. I'd seldom seen such fear and hatred on a human face. "You've corrupted her! You've destroyed everything I've tried to do!"

I started putting everything together in my head. It took me a moment, but I finally understood. "Sonja...the other girls. You've been using Xtabay to murder those men, haven't you? To kill anyone hurting the women on the street..."

She didn't deny anything. She just moved more purposely toward me, her lantern swinging and casting slanting shadows across her tired, enraged face. Too late, I realized she had a *second* athame in her hand. I don't know where she got it from. Perhaps she'd had it hidden in her clothes or in her boot, but, somehow, it was in her hand now.

"I'm sorry, Princess. I'm so sorry it must be this way. But you cannot be allowed to continue your rampage."

Sister Marie's voice dissolved into another language as she cast a spell. She raised the athame high and positioned it so she could plunge it straight into my heart. I saw it shimmer red hot and more than capable of carving up my flesh.

I tried to move, but I couldn't. She was a powerful witch. A learned witch—unlike me. Her spell had bound me to the floor. I couldn't shift out of the way. All I could do was raise my arms in defense and scream in absolute fear as the blade plunged toward me.

| 53 |

XTABAY RAISED BOTH hands and spoke, but not in any language I had ever heard before. It was certainly not Spanish. I suspect it was much older than any human language.

And I felt the entire world crank down into absolute stillness like someone put a brake on. It reminded me of what my father did at the roadhouse. In the end, only she and I could move. Sister Marie was stuck in her goddess's strange stasis, her mouth hanging open in a scream of insult, her eyes wide and mad, her body canted forward and arm outstretched, the blade of the athame only a few inches from my heart. To me, she looked like a macabre *objet de'art*.

I sucked in a sharp breath. I couldn't believe Xtabay had saved me. She slowly lowered her arms. "Stand up, little flower."

I risked shifting around in the oil spill under my feet. If Xtabay could stop time—or, according to my dad, at least slow it all the way down—what else was she capable of?

The goddess gave me a sympathetic look. "You are afraid. I did not want this."

I looked her over, feeling more than cowed by her queenly presence. She was much taller than I was, and despite the modern clothes, she looked like someone out of mythology. Her eyes were pitch black—no whites or irises at all.

"You're…well, a bit intimidating."

She smiled then, sadly. Raising a hand, she passed it over her own face. When she dropped her hand, I saw her eyes were brown and warm and human. "Does this please you?"

I looked around the hangar for an escape route but then realized the futility of it. If I ran, she'd probably just freeze me and drag me back. So, I turned to face her instead. "Why…do you care?"

Her fingers twitched like she was looking to touch something but was hesitant. Taking a step toward me, she reached out with that twitchy hand.

I stiffened but was immensely proud of myself for not screaming or bolting when she touched my hair. I felt a tingle in my scalp, but that was all. I'd never been touched by a goddess before.

"I never meant to frighten you, little flower. I never wanted you to run from me."

I swallowed hard and looked into those quasi-human eyes of hers. "Why?" I asked because I couldn't imagine one single reason why she should care what I thought of her.

She tenderly pushed a coil of red hair off my face. The contact sent a warm pulse of pleasure through my skin. I didn't expect that. "Is it not obvious? I love you."

Her words confused me. I'd known plenty of people who'd "loved me," but that was not what they meant by those words. They just wanted me. Or they wanted to conquer me. Control me. I don't even think my adoptive parents truly "loved me" in the traditional sense. They were simply too ashamed to dispose of me.

Xtabay looked sad as if she instinctively understood these things. After a moment, she slid her large, warm hands down the sides of my bare neck, resting them on my shoulders. "You are strong. And the world does not suffer strong women. This world breaks such women." Her dark eyes blinked once. "The witches."

I could feel the otherworldly strength in her hands. I was acutely aware of how she could break my body with no effort at all. But, strangely, I was not afraid. I was suddenly, embarrassingly, wet down below. My heart was racing and the tips of my breasts hurt as if she was passing an electrical charge through my body.

"Yes," I agreed because I couldn't argue with her logic.

She nodded almost imperceptibly as if she knew what she was doing to me. Normally, I would have hated that she knew how she was affecting me, but I felt strangely at ease with her.

"But...you..." I stopped myself, afraid I'd sound stupid in front of her. "How can you even know all that? I mean...you don't come from here. Right? You come from...somewhere else."

"I was sent to the far realms." She dragged me closer. Her face—and, more specifically, her eyes—seemed to fill my whole field of vision. Her scent, like soft white lilies after a summer rain, made my head swim, and I suddenly felt the whole world tilt around me as if I'd taken a hit of some powerful acid. "But I was queen here once in the time before. And then *he* came."

"Who?"

"Ha-Shem." The name echoed around the ruins of the mill, making some birds in the rafters take flight. "He arrived with his sword of fire and his fleet of light creatures, and he banished me. I and the rest of the Old Ones." Her eyes blinked black for one second before returning to their brown color. I could feel a vibration from her. I thought it might be her righteous anger. "And he has ruled for millennia, but now his power is lessening. His believers are slowly returning to the old ways, and their worship fills the wells of ancient power. Through them, I was able to claw my way back through the cracks."

Her voice echoed strangely in my head. I felt so dizzy.

"You are the child of his general. You are of the line of Ha-Shaitan."

"I..."

"Left Hand of the Coming Dark."

God, I felt so sick. Thankfully, she was there to catch me when I tipped forward.

Too late, I realized she was casting a spell on me. I wanted to tell her to stop, to let me be, but I couldn't feel my body at all. She lifted me so easily that I felt like a child in her arms. "Let...go..." I said, slurring my words as if I were drunk. My head, so very heavy, suddenly bobbed downward and my chin rested on my chest as she held me against her bosom.

"Sleep, little flower. We have much to do."

Darkness—followed by a rush of cold wind. I didn't need to see to know we were flying. Time had no meaning suddenly. She might have carried me for seconds or years. It didn't seem to matter, and there was no way for me to measure what was happening. But, eventually, the darkness gave out to a pinprick of light that slowly grew in brilliance.

I woke up still in her arms. She was standing in a cold, concrete room of some kind, a bunker-like chamber deep in the embattled remains of the old steel mill. But this one had no windows. Just a row of lanterns similar to what Sister Marie had been wielding hanging from hooks in the walls. They produced minimum illumination.

The room was empty save for a creaky-looking cot in one corner, a table near it with some basic human toiletries on it, and that huge, frightening iron sarcophagus on the floor taking up most of the space in the small room. I shuddered at the sight of it, but Xtabay made shushing noises and ran a hand over my face as she carried me toward it. I knew I should be panicking like crazy, but I couldn't find it in me to care.

The lid shifted and fell to one side with a heavy thump without her needing to touch it. Inside, the sarcophagus was full of soft throw pillows. But it was still a sarcophagus. I heard myself moan in distress once we were standing inside of it and she was setting me down on the pillows.

I wanted to get out of the horrible stone coffin, but I couldn't seem to move. I started to protest, but Xtabay, who was crouched over me, touched my forehead. The smell of rain and lilies increased, and I had to really think about why I was so afraid of her.

She was so beautiful. I hoped she would kiss me. I mean, I was not into girls like that, but I'd been with them to please past lovers. I didn't have any hang-ups about sex with girls. I liked them. And she was so beautiful like some angel come to Earth just for me—to save me. Would an angel really hurt me?

Xtabay smiled. "That's better, isn't it, my little fire flower?"

"Yes," I said and smiled even though I didn't know what she meant.

"You will be my new keeper, yes? You will guide me through this strange new world?"

I wanted to say yes, but I hesitated. What did that even mean?

"If you say yes, I'll kiss you. You want that, don't you?"

"Oh, yes," I told her honestly.

When she kissed me, I sighed. She tasted like sweet sunshine and gardens full of springtime flowers after months of cold white winter death, and her breath was hot and soft against my lips. I was so tired of the darkness. I wanted to drink up her light as if it was wine and I was dying of thirst.

She laughed, delighted with the way I was squirming beneath her. She slid my coat off and dug her hands under my T-shirt, cupping my breasts. She held them and squeezed them as if they belonged to her. Again, she kissed me. Her tongue danced down my throat while she fondled me. She kissed me as if she wanted to crawl inside my mouth and down into my unnatural body and fill it with light.

I moaned against those delicious, sugary lips, and she smiled in response and moved downward, leaving little sticky sugar kisses along my neck until she reached my cleavage. Stopping, she wrestled my shirt off and undid the front clasp of my sports bra. Then she kissed me again, following the contours of my body until she reached the edges of my jeans. I moaned in frustration and wriggled, making it hard for her to undo my jeans and slide them and my boy shorts off. But, somehow, she managed.

She sank down, making approving noises as she licked and tickled her tongue around my navel before dipping lower. Her hot, flitting tongue drove the pleasure deep into my body in pulses that left me breathless and panting with anticipation.

"You taste like honey," she whispered, her voice almost inhumanely low.

I groaned as she pushed inward. With a gasp, I threw my head back on the pillows in the sarcophagus and writhed with her tongue deep inside of me.

"You will be mine? Say you will be mine," Xtabay insisted, her whole face alight with desire when she looked up.

"Yes!"

One last little lick and the orgasm hit me hard, making my legs clench Xtabay's head as I shook all over with release.

I screamed, and the whole factory echoed with my cries of pleasure. It stoked the witchfire between us, and I felt the rush of that primal force as it consumed my skin all over so that, for one second, I was quite literally a creature on fire. The ripple of blue flames licked at Xtabay's body too. But unlike the others I'd touched with my witch fire, she seemed delighted by the sensation. It didn't hurt her at all.

After I fell back, exhausted, Xtabay climbed back up my body so we were lying side by side. I was still trembling in the afterglow of our lovemaking. But, for once, I was also at peace. I hadn't hurt her.

I hadn't taken anything from her or enslaved her. She kissed me so hard I could taste myself on her lips.

"Oh, little flower of fire and pain," she whispered against my lips. "You are mine. And, together, we will rewrite the world."

The lights in the room flickered and went out.

| 54 |

I WAS SITTING in a bright, sunshiney room full of bookshelves. I realized it was the library in White Haven, where I grew up. Before I became a teen and found out what a terrible and friendless place it was to live, the library was my refuge.

I was five or six, dressed in a long purple Barney shirt and leggings. I was still three or four years away from the horrors that would slowly but inexorably manifest themselves in school. The girls who would revile and torment me. The teacher who would ask me to stay after one day, only to bend me uncomfortably over his desk. At the moment, I was still untouched—a virgin.

I realized I was here for Story Time, an event I'd always looked forward to. We couldn't wait for kind Mr. Felix to come in and read us a book. But it was not bent old Mr. Felix who smelled of red licorice who entered the children's section of the library. Instead, it was my father here to read to us.

Not my adopted father. My real one. Dr. John Englebrecht.

He was dressed in a smart tweed suit, the silver glasses on his face. "Hello, children," he greeted everyone gathered on the colorful throw rug. I felt particularly special when he turned to me. "Greetings, daughter."

"Hello, Daddy!" I said, my voice high and enthusiastic.

He tsked. "What did I say about that, Vivian?"

I blushed. "I'm sorry, Da..." I immediately correct myself. "...John."

"Good girl," he said, assuming the big comfy green chair at the front of our little group and opening the thick, heavy old book he had brought. I felt disappointed because it didn't look like the kind of book I was expecting.

"Today, children," John announced, "we are going to read about the Legend of Xtabay, the Demon of Lust and Darkness."

The children cheered at that. I cheered louder than them all.

John smiled gregariously at everyone gathered. "The legend begins in a world very different from the one we live in now. In those days, the world was full of darkness, gods, and monsters. There were no people or animals then. Just blood and warfare as the Old Ones gathered in their masses to battle each other for control of Earth."

I saw the children around me nod, already spellbound by my daddy's voice.

"Earth was very important to the armies as it was one of the few worlds that had not yet been destroyed by either conflict or cosmic cataclysm and could thus sustain life. So, of course all of the Old Ones wanted control of it. In fact, they were willing to destroy one another to possess it, and the battles that raged were long and tiring and very bloody."

He stopped to look at me sternly over the top of his glasses. "I hope you are paying close attention, Vivian. This is important."

"Yes, John," I answered dutifully, my cheeks flushing because I'd been singled out.

He returned to the book. "The greatest army of all belonged to Ha-Shem, also called The One—and, sometimes, The Name. Ha-Shem was strong because the army he created was made up of brilliant strategists and fearless cosmic warriors.

"Perhaps the bravest and most powerful of all was his favorite creation, Ha-Shaitan, also called The Star of Morning, because wherever he went, he filled that place with the light that was his master's dominance. All who faced Ha-Shaitan knelt before his power and judgment. Whole armies were razed to the ground under his two-pronged weapon, the bodies decapitated and then burned in giant holes in the ground, the god-bones scattered to become the foundation of the greatest cities on Earth. This is how it was in the old days.

We all nodded our understanding. This was how it was.

"But then, one day, Ha-Shaitan came upon the Old One who had named herself Xtabay the Flower That Never Blooms. He found her beside a fountain, washing her long black hair in the fragrant waters. He had been tasked by Ha-Shem to destroy every Old One he came upon and burn and scatter their bodies, but he found Xtabay to be quite beautiful to look upon. She smelled like spring and she spoke with great wisdom to the creatures of the night.

"Ha-Shaitan stopped his footman from destroying Xtabay and, instead, went out to speak to her. And do you know what happened then, children?"

The children shook their heads. I shook mine with them.

"Xtabay charmed Ha-Shaitan with her wit and wisdom, and the two become allies and lovers on that day. And as they lay on the riverbank, exhausted from their passionate lovemaking, Ha-Shaitan confessed all of the plans that his master Ha-Shem had for destroying the Old Ones. Naturally, Xtabay was distraught by this news, for she had friends and allies among the Old Ones. As they talked, Ha-Shaitan came to sympathize with Xtabay's plight.

"The next day, Ha-Shaitan asked for an audience with Ha-Shem. Ha-Shaitan, being the favorite son, had the ear of his lord, you see, and Ha-Shem relied greatly on Ha-Shaitan's wisdom. He begged Ha-Shem to spare Xtabay and her allies from the slaughter. He argued that Xtabay would make a much finer ally, and, after much persuasion, Ha-Shem agreed to let Ha-Shaitan pass over her in his campaign to destroy their enemies. But what Ha-Shaitan did not know was that Ha-Shem had secretly deployed a platoon of his soldiers to the river where Xtabay dwelled.

"The men caught Xtabay unaware and trapped her against the rocks. Ha-Shem, who was a very jealous god, was irate that Xtabay had seduced Ha-Shaitan and turned his head. To punish her for what she had done to his favorite son, Ha-Shem had his men rape and torture Xtabay until she was broken and quite mad. Then he had his men banish Xtabay to the Outer Realms, where she would dwell in darkness and madness forever and ever, alone and apart from Ha-Shaitan.

"When Ha-Shaitan learned of what had been done to Xtabay, he questioned his lord's edicts for the first time. Naturally, Ha-Shem was insulted that his general and favorite son would challenge his authority. The two had a terrific row, and, in the end, Ha-Shaitan broke rank and left the presence of Ha-Shem, taking with him a whole host of his most loyal soldiers. As for Xtabay, her fate was far crueler."

The children had begun to cry. One started to scream. But my father continued, unperturbed, his eyes entirely on me now.

"The great goddess dwelled in her darkness and her madness for many millennia before finding a small crack between the worlds, formed when the followers of Ha-Shem began to turn away and seek the counsel of the Old Ones, most of whom had been banished. It took hundreds of years, but Xtabay was finally able to birth herself back into our reality, though she was not the same goddess she once was. She had brought with her many millennia's worth of madness—as well as her hatred and distrust for males.

"It's said she steals the skins of the guilty to wear upon her broken bones. But sometimes she also slays the innocent, her wrath is so great. According to some legends, Xtabay can only be kept in check by a female witch of great strength of will. Such a woman has the power to become her high priestess and servant. But even though this woman may act as a servant, she has enormous influence over Xtabay, for the demon is a wild, mad thing and can be seduced into acting out the high priestesses' deepest and darkest desires..."

| 55 |

I JERKED AWAKE in the iron coffin, the cries of terrified children ringing in my ears.

It was dark and I was soaked in sweat. My heart was hammering in my chest so hard that I thought it might be trying to escape. In my mind's eye, I could still see my father staring over his glasses at me, explaining about Xtabay.

Sitting up, I looked over at the naked woman lying beside me. Her back was turned to me, but I could clearly see her dark hair and the sigils marking the smooth brown skin of her back. They seemed to shift and move. And I knew then that it was no dream; Xtabay was most certainly an Old One.

"The demon is a wild, mad thing and can be seduced into acting out the high priestesses' deepest and darkest desires…" I whispered to myself.

I was overwhelmed with a feeling of absolute certainty that if I didn't get away from Xtabay, we would destroy each other. Or we would destroy this world. I got slowly to my feet, trying not to disturb the goddess, and picked up my clothing, which was scattered. I slipped it on quickly, forgetting about the underwear, and slid my coat and shoes on before creeping toward what looked like a closed door.

I glanced back at Xtabay, but to my relief, she hadn't woken yet. I scratched at the door until it opened. The hinges started to groan, so I only opened it a few inches and slid out, leaving it cracked behind me. It was only then I realized I'd been holding my breath almost the whole time. I let it out in a long gasp, sucked in a fresh breath, and sagged like some boneless thing against the wall.

Jesus Christ. What the living fuck had I gotten myself into?

I was trying to figure out what to do next when my phone suddenly went off. I had the ringer set to Scandal's "The Warrior," and the sound up. I made a strangled sound as I wrested it loose from my coat pocket and saw it was Sebastian calling, probably trying to figure out where the hell I was. I stabbed at the red icon, but I could hear Xtabay's breath from the other side of the door.

She was awake…

I didn't waste any time and took off down a long corridor with rusted fixtures on the walls and more graffiti on the walls. Frightening symbols and painted faces leered down on me as I turned the bend and followed another corridor into an even darker recess of the mill. I had no idea where I was going, or even if I was headed in the right direction. A number of large pipes overhead blocked the light that normally poured through the skylights, so I found myself stumbling along in the near dark as I searched frantically for a way out.

Another bend and I nearly pitched down a long flight of metal stairs—just stopping myself at the last moment by grabbing the rusted railing and hanging on until I found my feet. The railing gave a little with rust and age, and I felt my heart drop down somewhere near my toes as I steadied myself.

The darkness behind me breathed. I could hear *her* coming for me. Slowly. Steadily. As if she had all the time in the world. And perhaps she did…

"Little flower...!" she whispered from down the hall, and her voice sounded like the sough of the wind.

Letting go of the railing, I swallowed down my fears and took the stairs two at a time even though the whole staircase rattled in a horrifying. Halfway down, I passed the support wall and recognized the big hangar where I first confronted Sister Marie. Its vast, moon-dipped wetness looked inviting after what had happened up there in that sarcophagus...

Xtabay moved supernaturally fast. I could feel her closing in before I even reached the bottom. I jumped the last ten feet or so, landing hard—and funny (but not in a ha-ha way)—on the concrete below. I felt my ankle turn and I grunted as I rolled to the floor. Despite the sudden shock of pain, I scrambled up before the goddess could land in front of me and stopped me from leaving.

But I was so stupid. I'd forgotten she could fly.

Long before I limped even halfway down the length of that vast hangar, Xtabay landed weightlessly in front of me as if she was some beautiful pale bird descended to Earth. She seemed taller now—closer to the titan-like image I'd seen in my vision—and her eyes were all blackity-black once more. Her hair, now streaming down over her shoulders, moved in a way that seemed almost alive. But it was what she was wearing that stopped me dead in my tracks.

Not the T-shirt and wrap from before. Not the tight-fitting white dress from my dreams.

This time, she was wearing a gown that I first assumed was buckskin. But it was not. The fabric was crudely sewn together with black thread, but I easily recognized the different shades of human skin. Some of the patches even had hair or distinctive tattoos still inked on them. Around her waist was tied a thick brown leather belt with the flesh of human limbs rubbing together as she moved, and around her neck, a collar with what I was terrified might be made of human penises. Her long earring and the braces on her wrists and upper arms were made of tiny, delicate, bleached human bones, like those you might find belonging to an infant.

She still smelled sweet. But under that odor I detected it—the sweet putrefaction of human remains.

Her presence stopped me dead in my tracks. I knew this beautiful and awful creature of night was going to kill me.

| 56 |

"LITTLE FLOWER."

I expected to see a raging black inferno of rage in Xtabay's eyes, but she only looked on me emptily—sadly. Tears coursed down over her brown cheeks. She looked so despondent that, for one moment, I felt my heart break for her. I thought how lonely it must be for her. To live, but to be the goddess-servant of whichever powerful witch controlled her at the moment. I couldn't help but wonder what terrible acts her high priestesses had foisted upon her.

"You're not...not angry I ran away?" I asked, panting through my shuddering fear.

She blinked away the tears but they clung to her long lashes. "I could never be angry with my fire flower." Moving closer, she lifted her arms slightly and presented her open palms to me as if she were inviting me to step into her strong embrace. I might even have been tempted were it not for her smell or the sight of those ghastly human remains on her.

"Do you not understand? I love you, my little flower. And I would never destroy something I love."

I turned my head as a glimmer drew my attention. At a distance, I saw Sister Marie. She was still frozen in the same position she was in when Xtabay stopped time, body contorted as she lunged toward the place where I was lying, arm fully extended, the gleaming athame at the end of it aimed to pierce my heart. We were still living in the time lock Xtabay initiated a few hours earlier. All the while we'd been together upstairs, the world hadn't moved on at all.

Swallowing my surprise, which felt like a marble in my throat, I point to Sister Marie. "And her?"

Xtabay turned her head slowly and in an entirely mechanical way to look at her servant and high priestess. But her eyes remained emotionless.

"She's your high priestess!" I pressed, hoping to undo all of this through sheer reason. Maybe I could convince Xtabay to return to the witch who controlled her and forget all about me. Maybe we could settle this reasonably. "The two of you were doing so much good! She needs you to stop all of the people hurting—"

Xtabay gestured toward her priestess and a sudden gust of wind drowned out my voice. The wind clawed at the witch with all of the power of a hurricane and flung her statue-like form carelessly against the farthest wall, shattering her into pieces. I gasped at the sight. The impact was so strong that it flung parts of the woman in every direction. A large shard of Sister Marie's head bounced off one wall and flew toward us, jouncing along the concrete floor and shattering into yet more pieces that came to rest, finally, on the floor at my feet.

I was looking down at a quarter of Sister Marie's face, her lips still stretched in a scream of rage, her eye glaring up at me accusingly.

I couldn't help myself. I took one look at her remains and started screaming my guts out.

| 57 |

I WAS STILL screaming when Xtabay grabbed me up in her arms—and her hair!—and, together, we rocketed up toward the roof. The lurching sensation made me sick to my stomach, and I vomited compulsively over Xtabay's right shoulder as my stomach was momentarily slammed up into the bottom of my rib cage. Thank god I hadn't eaten anything in hours. It was just stomach acid, but still...

With a groan, I tilted my head back, which was a bad idea. I saw the skylights rushing toward us. That made me scream again, but the glass exploded outward long before we reached it, falling away in glittering shards, allowing the two of us to pass safely through the ragged hole that remained and up into the sky.

My whole body froze up in fear as the cold night wind ripped through my clothes and hair. All I saw were stars on black night, and I had a horrid fantasy of us continuing upward until we broke through the atmosphere and I could see the Earth drifting far below. The thought made me sick again.

But Xtabay finally slowed as if she sensed my discomfort. Together, we hung in midair. And although I was terrified of her—horrified by the thing I was clinging to with its raw, stinking human skin dress—I found myself too frightened of falling to let go.

"Oh, my little fire flower," she cooed, raising a hand to run it through my hair, which was furiously flying around my face. "Look. See. All this I can give you."

The wind dried my eyes, making it hard to focus, but through the blur, I recognized the whole west end of Philly laid out around us, a mass of blocky and often ugly and unnatural shapes surrounding us on all sides like false mountains full of insignificant pinpricks of light. Traffic and trains cut long rivers of smeary light through the dark metropolis.

"I...I don't want it," I answered her question truthfully. At this altitude, I was so cold that my teeth were practically chattering. "Wh-why would I want *th-this?*"

She drew back a few inches so she could see my face. That made me panic, but she kept her powerful hold on my arms. I kicked out reflexively, but there was no purchase.

"My lovely," she said, tears in her eyes. "All of these things I will give you if you will only worship me. I will give you castles to live in and jewels to wear. The humans will be your brides and your victims." She sighed and closed her eyes as a smile spread across her face. "And, together, we will make it all burn."

I gaped at her in horror. "I don't...I don't want to burn it!"

Xtabay looked as placid and pretty as a picture—some demonic Madonna raised up from hell. But when she opened her eyes, she looked slightly confused. "Of course you do. You have dreamed of the burning. You have dreamed me to your side, little flower of fire and pain. You have summoned me in dreams. And so I had come to find you."

I gaped at her in absolute horror...

"Those...d-dreams..." I said but couldn't continue.

"Those are your dreams. Not mine."

I couldn't respond to that.

Her face grew strangely desperate as she pulled me to her so our breasts were pressed together and our faces were inches apart. The odor of decay made me want to gag. "You are of Ha-Shaitan's blood." She sounded desperate now. Angrier. "And the Ha-Shaitan has always been the ally of the Xtabay."

"I didn't...I wasn't..." I didn't know how to explain that this was all a misunderstanding. "I didn't mean to call you!"

Xtabay lost her serene smile. Now, she just looked disappointed. Scorned. And hell hath no fury...

"You called. I answered. This is how it is."

"No..."

"Together, we will make them all burn. All the humans—and all of the Otherkind." Her eyes flashed with black fire. "We will make all of the worlds burn for us. And it will be a pleasure."

"No!" roared. Panic raked across my brain like cat claws. I even started to fight her embrace even though I knew the fall would kill me. "I don't want this!" I said. "I didn't want you, you crazy-ass fucking bitch!"

Xtabay grew very still. She looked confused. Hurt. "You...refuse me?"

I had a moment where I thought, *Oh, shit. Shit. Shitshitshit...!*

But I'd always been inclined to self-destruction. I'd always had that in me. And perhaps, after all, she was the one who had been sent to punish me for my sins. Perhaps this was all meant to be. So, I told her the truth, "Yes, Xtabay. I refuse you. I don't love you, and I never will."

She closed her eyes, and I saw the blood leaking out from under her eyelids. I thought she would scream. Instead, she said in a maddeningly calm voice, "I have seen many futures, fire flower, so I want you to know this one thing: You will never know real love or happiness in your whole life. Not as I could have shown it to you. Goodbye, Vivian."

As I expected her to, she dropped me.

| 58 |

AS I FELL to my death, I thought about the many bad things I'd done. There was a lot to think about. The fall itself was weightless and almost pleasurable. For a few seconds, I seemed to hang upon the upper currents. But then, inevitably, I plummeted back to earth like the fallen angel I always knew I was.

Strangely, my last thought before impact wasn't of some esoteric concept or love or regret but of Nick, who knew and loved me perhaps best of all. He knew what I was. He knew I was a bad person, but he still loved me despite it all—perhaps because he, too, knew what it was like to be a bad person trying to do a few good things in this world.

I didn't feel the impact. And for that, I was grateful.

Maybe, somewhere out there in the vast, uncaring universe, there really was a merciful god.

| 59 |

I WAS DRIVING my jeep up a rocky, badly paved road. Good ol' PA and its shitty back roads. The winter had been particularly bad, so the roads were all worn down and potholed from salt and the almost nonstop clawing of the snow movers. I thought of a popular joke I'd heard in high school: *We used to have bears but they all fell into the potholes.*

But it was not winter now. It was early summer—Memorial Day. The trees were green and lushly filled out, and the wildflowers and weeds were growing in waist-high tangles on the sides of the road. The mosquitoes were terrible, as usual—and I thought a wasp might have gotten into the car somewhere along the way. I rumbled along the last half-mile stretch of road until I reached the old, restored Victorian at the top of the mountain.

Several cars were parked on the gravel drive. I slid into the last open spot, cut the engine, and got out. The stifling May heat hit me like a fur blanket, and I could feel my tank top sticking to me in a wholly uncomfortable way while I maneuvered the giant Igloo trunk cooler out of the back of the jeep.

"Hey, sis, let me give you a hand with that."

I looked around and saw Nick moseying down the steps of the Victorian. I gave my big brother a big hug and a kiss on the cheek before I let him take the Igloo out and roll it across the driveway.

"What in hell did you make this time?" he asked with a laugh. "It's like a thousand pounds!"

"Cheesecake, key lime pie, and two different puddings for the kids. Banana and chocolate. Don't wreck anything!" I warned him as he dragged the heavy-ass cooler up the stairs to the house.

"You know you don't have to go nuts. You could have just bought a pie from Wawa."

"Bro, I'm a baker. I always go nuts," I laughed, giving him a playful slap on the arm. Like he didn't know me by now.

Inside the house, I heard the thump of footsteps descending rapidly from upstairs. Seconds later, Nick's two boys come rampaging down like kaiju stomping a part of Tokyo flat. One had a Super Soaker and was shooting his brother in the chest while both boys screamed at the top of their lungs.

Nick didn't even look surprised. He just stepped between his sons and snatched the toy away from the older of the two. "That's enough of that. If you get the floor wet, your mom is going to have a fit, men."

The boys groaned in unison so Nick pointed to the door. "Out!"

"He started it!" the younger boy yelled.

"I didn't care who started it. Give your Aunt Vivian a hug and then go outside if you want to roughhouse."

The boys rushed over and I dropped to my haunches to give each of my nephews a quick hug. "I made you guys your favorite," I whispered in their ears. "Banana pudding!"

"Cool!" the eldest said.

The younger one turned to Nick. "Daddy, can we—?"

"No pudding until after dinner. I said out! Now!"

Nick has that deep, strong voice that gets everyone's attention. He wasn't angry, but he did mean business. The boys relented and followed each other out, kicking, moaning, and making a dramatic exit—but not before the eldest grabbed the Super Soaker up and shot his little brother in the ass, making him scream.

I shook my head. "God, they are a handful."

Nick sighed in agreement. "I'd say they take after me, but they're actually stubborn like Morgana most of the time. Or maybe impetuous like Dad. Yeah, they are definitely more like Dad."

"Is he coming?" I asked as I followed him into the kitchen.

The cutting board was set up and there was a vegan lasagna in the oven for those who didn't want to eat off the grill. I could smell it. Nick did all of the cooking in the house because Morgana wasn't talented that way and was usually too busy running their shop to handle the household. The house and the boys were Nick's department—not that he minded. He worked from home anyway, doing Tarot readings online, so it worked out well between them.

Nick shrugged as he started stuffing the refrigerator with my offerings. "Not sure. You knew Dad. Says he might come, then he doesn't. Or says he won't, and then he shows up unexpectedly." He rolled his eyes. "He'll probably show up with some nineteen-year-old floozy on his arm. Remember Christmas?"

I laughed at that. Our dad was a real man-slut. Over Christmas, he'd had one girl on his arm and one texting him on the phone continuously. It was a riot, watching him trying to sort out his tangled mess of a love life. Hell, he was the one who showed up drunk at Nick and Morgana's wedding and had the nerve to try to kiss the bride—not that Nick's wife would ever put up with such lothario behavior.

I sighed, wondering if I'd ever have a relationship like Nick and Morgana's. Honestly, I never thought they would mesh as well as they had. But I was proud of them both—even if Morgana and I had never been what you might call BFFs.

With the desserts cooling in the fridge, Nick led me out to the deck where a long redwood trestle table was set up under a colorful yellow and white sun umbrella. The grill was gently smoking on one side, with a small patio bar on the other. Morgana was mixing drinks, and when she spotted me, she rushed the first—but certainly not the last—margarita into my hands. Down in the large, attached yard, I saw Josh had beaten me here and was running around with his nephews, wetting them good with the Super Soaker while his dog Tiger barked and jumped excitedly between them all.

I sighed as I settled back on a sun lounger and tried to catch an early summer tan. Nick and Morgana laughed about something that went hilariously wrong at work. In the meantime, Josh worked his way up to the deck with the two boys in tow. Morgana got the boys some waters while Nick split a six-pack of Budweiser with Josh. Soon enough, the two men went to work grilling the hamburgers and steaks. Nick called over that the food would be done in five, so Morgana and I slipped back into the kitchen to fetch the salads.

We were almost ready to sit down to our annual Memorial Day family feast when—yep, you guessed it. Dad showed up. Late, as usual—but at least he wasn't dragging one of his many tagalongs with him. Our dad is a real handsome devil even at his substantial age. You wouldn't know it, though. Those sensual eyes. That impish smile. He looked as rakish now as he had when we were children.

He hugged me tight and gave Nick's hand a shake. He had always been more affectionate with me. After all, I was his little girl. His little princess.

I sat to his right at the picnic table and we all talked and laughed about our lives since the last time we'd been together as a family. I listened to my dad's stories about teaching academia at college. He made certain to include all of the gory details of his most recent affairs—PG versions of the story since his grandsons were listening while they stuffed down their hamburgers as quickly as possible in a bid to get back to chasing each other around the backyard with the Super Soaker.

"Dad, are you ever going to settle down?" I asked.

"Are you, my princess?" he asked right back.

I blushed. "I don't know. Honestly, with the shop, I don't have the time to date."

"There's always Tinder," Nick threw in.

"Shut up, you!"

Dad smiled wisely but there was a shadow in his eyes. It was like a twinkle, but darker. "No time to date or get married or have children. And yet you have time to make those brides of yours."

I paused, a forkful of potato salad halfway to my lips. "What?"

"You," My dad elaborated. "No time to date properly, yet you have time to make slaves out of all of your men. How many are you up to by now? Two? Three?"

I lowered my fork and sat up straight on the redwood bench under the pretty yellow sun umbrella. "I don't understand. What are you talking about?"

Dad narrowed his eyes and pushed his uneaten plate of food away from him. He dabbed his mouth with his cloth napkin, but I could see his smile. I could see the terribly sharp angel teeth in his mouth. "You aren't human, Vivian. You don't *date*. Nick isn't human, and he isn't married. There are no children. There is no picnic. No holiday. No fucking yellow umbrella." His voice dropped to a low, uncomfortable growl. "Are you done with this ridiculous charade, daughter?"

His words...his tone of voice...made me glance around. My little family was all frozen in place. Nick was frozen while pouring an equally frozen Morgana a fresh glass of iced tea. The boys were pushing at each other, but now they were sitting there like statues. My brother Josh was throwing a piece of steak to Tiger, who had his mouth open. Josh and Tiger were frozen solid, and the bit of steak was stuck in the air between them.

"What is this?" I asked worriedly. "What's going on?"

My dad rose from the table and leaned against it to deliver his news in a whisper. "There is no house. There is no family. Vivian...you are dead."

I found the news not so much frightening as fatally depressing. I'd had a lot of dreams I'd never fulfilled. I was too young to die without realizing at least some of them. "Dead." I looked around the table. "But what about them?"

Dad nodded to the table. "This isn't real. Well, it is, in a way, but only because it's your Harrow." He eyed the people gathered around the table. "They aren't really here. Hell, some of them aren't even real. Do you really think our family would act like this?"

I looked around the table sadly. I didn't want to ask it, but I knew I must. "What's a Harrow?"

Unexpectedly, my father looked sympathetic. "It's a state the dead dwell in for a time. It acts as a luminal space between the world of the living and the realm of the dead. Living humans, and even Otherkind, enter it after death and, after a time, choose either to go back or to go on. The dead rarely choose to go back."

So, I was in a kind of limbo. And I could see why most wanted to go on. I liked this place. I didn't want to return to the world I had known.

"All right. Let me go on."

He came around the table to touch my shoulder. "If you go on, there will be nobody left to stop Xtabay."

I bit my lip in frustration. Slowly, I rose to my feet, still looking at the family that never was. "I don't want to be the one to take her on. Take me to Heaven, Daddy. Or to Hell." I looked at him. "I belong in Hell, right?"

"I can't." He smiled sadly. Reaching out, he flicked a long red curl out of my eyes. "You have no soul, Vivian. No afterlife. You gave your soul to Nick once upon a time, remember?"

Yeah, I did that. Shivering, I wrapped my arms around myself. Suddenly, I was cold. I stared down at the tabletop before looking back up at him. "So that's it, then? If I go on, I just...cease to be?"

He glanced around sympathetically. "Well...it has to be better than this incredibly boring Harrow."

He meant it to be funny but my heart clenched up. "All right. What can I do to get out of here?"

I was afraid he'd said nothing, that I was doomed to live in this false Heaven forever, but I recognized that shifty look on him. My dad had never been one to stick to the rules. "I can't bring someone back from the dead. That power is not in me. But..." Reaching into a pocket of his grey tweed jacket, he produced a silver pocket watch engraved with sigils that seemed to shift and change before my very eyes.

He shows me the pocket watch on its chain. "This is Methuselah's Watch. With it, I can not only slow time down but reverse it for several seconds. Just enough time to undo a small mistake."

I looked from the watch to his face, suddenly hopeful. "Will you?"

He shrugged. "For a price." His smile grew.

Of course there was a price. No one made a deal with the Devil without paying their dues. "What's the price?"

My dad moved in a slow circle around me. I watched him study me for a long, hard moment before stooping down to point to his left cheek.

It took me a moment to catch on. "You want me to kiss you?"

His smile grew.

"That's it? I thought you didn't love me?"

"I enjoy having you around, daughter. You amuse me."

I leaned in and kissed him on the cheek. I was surprised by how human he felt.

"Come with me." He took me by the hand and guided me down the deck stairs to the patio below. He continued to grin as he moved a few steps away and set the pocket watch on the ground in front of us, where it emitted a dull, flickering sepia light. At first, the flickering was very slow, but as he joined me at my side and took my hand, I saw the pace of the light increase. "This is always so much fun."

The light moved faster and then faster still. Within seconds, I felt a gust of wind lift me easily into a horizontal position in front of him. I nearly giggled because it was like being one of those floating assistants for a magician doing a trick for the audience.

"How does it feel?" he asked as he moved to one side of me so he was perpendicular to my floating form.

"It feels weird. Ticklish."

"Light as a feather. Stiff as a board." He placed his arms under me, palms up, but did not touch.

The light from the pocket watch was flickering incredibly fast now, a pulsing illumination that lit up his face and engulfed the two of us. The ticklish feeling increased.

He chuckled. "This was where it gets interesting."

"What does that mean?"

"It means be prepared: Things are about to happen very quickly. Say goodbye to the family, daughter."

"Goodbye, family," I told them, feeling sad.

"There's my good girl."

| 60 |

AS I FELL to my death, I thought about the many bad things I'd done. There was a lot to think about. The fall itself was weightless and almost pleasurable. For a few seconds, I seemed to hang upon the upper currents. But then, inevitably, I plummeted back to earth like the fallen angel I always knew I was.

The impact was surprisingly hard—but it didn't kill me. I let out a scream of ecstatic fear as my father caught me in his arms. I remembered everything. The Harrow. Our conversation. His pocket watch, which was still on the ground, emitting its shaky, strobing light.

"Got you!" my father cried triumphantly and laid me down gently on the concrete apron where I knew I'd died once, in another timeline.

"Daddy!" I cried, not caring that he didn't like that name.

But he didn't seem to care about that. He crouched low and kissed me on the forehead. "You okay, darling?"

I swallowed hard at his tenderness, overwhelmed by it. "Yes."

"Good." He smiled, showing off his sharp little angel teeth. "Then you know your mission. You know what you need to do. The Xtabay has committed a grave offense against the royal line of Ha-Shaitan. She must be destroyed. There is no other way."

Tears formed in my eyes. I didn't like that I had chosen to destroy Xtabay—I didn't feel she deserved that—but I returned his look, staring into his upside-down face. "What do I do?"

"What you must. This will hurt—and I'm sorry." The Devil grimaced as he reached out and set his big hands in the middle of my chest over my heart, one over the other. I could feel my heart flitting erratically under his hands.

"Make her burn, firefly. Make her burn with all of the fires of hell!"

He roared the last. And as he did, I felt him tear the witchfire out of the center of my body as if it was a rabid living thing made all of hungry teeth and claws. The heat of it singed my cheeks and eyelashes. It consumed him. It consumed me. It rose higher and higher, and, as it did, my back bowed almost to the point of breaking and I screamed in hellish, orgasmic agony, my voice merging with the roar of the flames.

It was such a pleasure to burn, I thought, as I unleashed this apocalyptic fire into the night sky.

The writhing pillar of flame contorted into something winged and almost dragon-like as it stretched all the way to the roof of the mill. The creature's makeshift jaws fell open and flames snapped out of the funnel of its throat, consuming everything in its path. The building...the telephone wires far above...and, finally, my enemy still hovering overhead.

As with Tupoc, my witchfire...my infernal dragon fire...ate the goddess whole and screaming.

| 61 |

IT WAS THE worst noise I had ever heard. It was like the final noise as the Earth burned to death.

I was still screaming even as the goddess, now a flaming bundle of dirty rags, fell to the ground inches away from me. Far, far above, I watched the dragon fire spread its wings into the night sky. As it burned out, it left behind flickers of light burning on my retinas.

I turned my head. Hoarse and gasping, I stared at Xtabay for several seconds, barely recognizing what I'd done to her. The pile of blackened bones and burned cloth gave off a sickly sweet odor like graveyard flowers on fire. I watch it tremble on the concrete. And then, impossibly, a skeletal arm began to rise out of the ashen pile, and I saw a hand with five blackened, claw-like fingers stretch out in a fan.

The Xtabay was still alive. I'd never seen anything survive my witchfire…or the dragon fire…until now.

Slowly—too slowly—I slid backward until I hit a chain link fence, then used it to claw my way back to my feet. I weaved uncertainly but forced myself to back away even as the thing in the fitfully burning ashes began to tremble and rise from its own funeral pyre. A low hiss came from the bones. I was terrified it was her words to me.

Spinning around on my heels, I started to run, staggering like a drunk. I didn't look back, but I could feel her presence. Hell, I could smell her rotting, burning breath on my neck. It just spurred me to run faster...faster...

I hit the street and started heading north, dodging around the cars that sat completely frozen in the street. It was like some bad dream. The cars...the people in them...the few on the sidewalks walking to or from establishments at this late hour. Everyone was still trapped in Xtabay's time-lock from hours ago. As I weaved between the cars as though they were some strange gauntlet set before me, I had a horrifying thought. What if Xtabay never released the world from her spell? What if I couldn't stop her and she left the world frozen forever?

I tried not to panic as I reached the first intersection. I had no idea where to go, but I could hear a dull thumping noise in the street behind me. I could hear *her* coming, each angry footstep like a minor tremor in the street. I made the quick decision to duck inside one of the shops along Broad Street, but as I headed to the door, someone jumped in front of me.

I screamed at the sight of Sebastian, who was running full tilt down the street toward me.

We both stepped back, gaping at each other. "What the hell?" I said, gesturing wildly at him. "You scared me half to death!"

I'd never seen Sebastian so frightened. He looked like he'd just thrown his clothes on—shirt weirdly buttoned, one button on his trousers undone. He was also wearing a thick black dog collar and a headband with long dog ears hanging off it. I ignored that for the moment and said, "What are you doing out here?"

With an angry snort, he shouted, "Oi, bitch, do you *ever* answer your bloody phone?"

I just glared at him, wondering why he hadn't been affected by Xtabay's spell the way everyone else was. I could only guess it had something to do with him being a necromancer.

"I've been busy!" I shouted back, indicating the street around us. And then, sputtering with anger, I added, "What the hell are you wearing?"

He stopped, his eyes rolling upward to the headband. Ripping the dog ears off, he threw them into the street, giving me a sheepish grin. "Jordan likes pup play. We were—"

I held up a hand to stop him right there. "I didn't want to know anything about your degenerate sex life. What are you doing out here at this hour?"

He stopped to glare wide-eyed at all of the frozen people standing around us. "Th-this happened." He gestured toward a frozen couple. "And I tried to contact you because...what the fuckity fuck is this?"

I was not even sure how to answer that. But before I could even think of something to say, I discovered we were out of time.

Several cars in the street shook side to side—and then were forcefully blown back into one of the storefronts across the street as if they were toys. The display window of a shop shattered on impact and the cars crumpled inward, their alarms blaring. Sebastian cringed and looked at the smashed cars in horror before turning his attention back to the street.

I looked, too.

Xtabay stood in the place where the cars once were, glaring at us both. It was obvious she had been using her extraordinary powers to mend her terrible wounds, but she wasn't fully healed yet. Her body was pale and gelatinous like the skin of a newborn baby, with all the veins and arteries showing blue beneath. Her features were strangely unformed, with just two black alien eyes without eyelashes or eyebrows, a rudimentary nose, and an angry, downward-pointing slit for a mouth.

She was completely bald and naked. But, as Sebastian and I stood there, stunned, little tendrils of coal-black hair sprouted from her pale, moist scalp and curled down around her head, growing long and tangled.

It reminded me of time-lapse photography. Xtabay's hair thickened and lengthened until it reached her waist. Seconds later, she sprouted eyebrows, long black eyelashes, and even a small froth of pubic hair between her legs. Fresh new nails, as long as cat's claws, slid bloody and wet from her fingertips, and, seconds later, her skin thickened and darkened until it achieved its customary soft, brown-as-buckskin glossiness.

It was both fascinating and revolting to watch, and when I glanced at Sebastian, he looked like he was going to be sick all over himself. "Oi, who the fuck are you?" he demanded.

Ignoring me for the moment, Xtabay turned her attention to him.

I started to warn him back, but it was too late. With a dismissive flick of her hand, she knocked Sebastian back across the sidewalk until his head collided with the bottom of a metal street lamp. He grunted as he slammed to a halt, his dog collar jingling.

At first, he looked angry...and then he became very, very frightened as Xtabay advanced on him. He tried to scramble up and away from the approaching monstrosity, but he wasn't fast enough.

Xtabay moved with inhuman speed, reaching him and slamming her bare foot down across his neck. Sebastian coughed and wheezed, grabbing her by the ankle, but I could see he couldn't budge her.

"You men," Xtabay said coolly. "How dare you look upon a goddess and not kneel?" Grinning like the demon she was, she applied a bit more pressure. Sebastian choked.

"Stop!" I shouted at her, terrified she was going to kill my best friend.

Xtabay ignored me. Sebastian just barked a laugh as he hung onto her ankle in self-defense. "Oh...darling...you don't...want to kill me..." he coughed out. And then he grinned crazily. "But...if you...insist...I'd...much fancy...being a goddess!"

Xtabay's eyes blazed with anger as she stared down at him. Then, in a sudden turnabout, she drew her foot back, eyeing him carefully. "You are not a man. You, creature, are cursed."

Sebastian laughed maniacally as he scrambled to sit up against the lamppost. He made a come-hither gesture. "Want to find out how, lass?"

Xtabay made a noise of frustration as she backed away from my friend and turned to face me fully. Her eyes were full of fire and rejection. I felt the chill of those ancient eyes deep in my bones and it paralyzed me on the spot. "S-Sebastian, get out of here."

He pulled himself up to his full, lanky high. "Absolutely not! I'm not finished fucking with Aztec Murder Barbie here."

Clenching his fists, he took a step toward the goddess...then stopped as she turned her head and gestured toward the young couple frozen side by side on the sidewalk that he had pointed out earlier. The man was gesturing toward something in the picture window of the bakery they were passing. Their forms shimmered and shook, and suddenly the two of them completed the step they were taking hours ago and stumbled to a halt, looking around in confusion. Xtabay again gestured to them, and both began screaming in hellish agony as the skin along their faces and hands split wide open, revealing their wet red musculature and skeleton beneath.

I screamed too as the skin was flayed swiftly and efficiently from their bodies. The man raised his arms in defense and the skin fell away from it like ill-fitting sleeves. The woman screamed even louder as the skin was peeled from her face like a mask and the flesh of her legs simultaneously fell down to her bony ankles like stockings. Both tottered around in circles in an agonized little dance of pain.

Snarling, Xtabay made a chopping gesture and their screams cut out abruptly as their heads snapped sharply sideways. Their eyes closed. I expected them to drop where they stood like marionettes under the cruel influence of an unseen puppet master, but they merely sagged for a second before standing back up and opening their eyes.

Their eyes were as black and empty as Xtabay's own. I could see her in them as they tottered toward us, their bloody red arms outstretched. Sebastian rattled off a series of British curses I couldn't even begin to follow. I ducked the couple's embrace and raced out into the street, calling to my BFF, but he didn't move fast enough. He just gaped at the scene as if he couldn't believe it. Meanwhile, the two skinless zombies managed to trap him against the door of the bakery.

"Sebastian, got the hell out of there!" I shouted.

He started to panic as the two zombies tried to snag him by the arms, then noticed the blue and white shop awning with the *Dale's Delicacies* bakery logo printed on it. Reaching up, he grabbed the edge of the awning and jumped, kicking the two zombies hard in the chest to launch himself up and onto it. The zombies went down hard in the street, and Sebastian easily turned himself upside down and landed on his knees on the awning. Naturally, the fabric sagged under his weight, so he quickly scuttled up to the gutters and onto the roof, where he crouched low.

The height didn't seem to bother him at all as he stood up. "Acrobat training from me time in the circus," he informed me, giving me a sweeping, professional bow. "Now run! Get the bloody hell outta here!"

"I can't leave you...!"

"Go!" he screamed as the two zombies sprang back to their feet like demonic jack-in-the-boxes and stared at me with those black, skinless, hungry eyes of theirs. "The bitch can't do a damned thing to me and she knows it!"

I didn't want to leave my friend, but I knew he was right. Sebastian was literally the only one in the whole city who was safe from Xtabay's wrath.

Turning to the goddess, I growled out, "Fuck you!"

She just laughed as I ran away.

| 62 |

I WAS HALFWAY down the avenue crowded with frozen vehicles and people when it hit me. What the hell was I doing? Where could I go? *Where* was there to go? If I went home, Xtabay would find me there. If I ran, she'd just follow.

No. I had to stop and face her. I had agreed to stop her.

Xtabay was approaching slowly, but as she passed the people frozen in whatever act they were doing, each started to scream as they were forcibly torn from stasis, their flesh ripped from their tortured bodies, and their necks snapped like twigs. They staggered a long moment before righting themselves, and as soon as their eyes opened in their horrible, skinless faces, I saw her eyes reflected back at me. Then they started staggering after Xtabay, walking in her footsteps.

I flinched each time it happened and issued a low moan in my throat.

Xtabay smiled. Out of her mouth unfurled that black lotus like some alien second mouth. It licked at the corners of her lips, looking like a rotted black starfish. As in my dream of the burning city, she started to speak, but only in my mind.

Little fire flower...come back to me. Let me embrace you.

I stumbled back, colliding with a man behind me, and had to scramble to keep from falling. As soon as I was back on my feet, I screeched, "Why? So you can turn me into one of them?" I nodded at the growing army of Red Walkers staggering after their mistress. "Or a new Sister Marie? Use me until you're sick of me and someone new turns your head?"

The Xtabay and the Ha-Shaitan have always been allies...

"Oh, my god. You need to stop living in the past!"

Her impromptu army of the dead was moving faster, I noted, overtaking Xtabay and moving past her as the bitch continued her leisurely pace toward me. I swung around and looked both ways down the intersecting avenue. My panic immediately edged up a notch; I was quickly losing all sense of direction. Thankfully, I spotted the spire of Father Matt's church.

I didn't know if the holy place would have any effect on Xtabay or her Red Walkers. I didn't know if Sister Marie had chosen it as a hiding place for her mistress's sarcophagus because it was a place of power or because it could contain her, but I was totally out of ideas, so I started running that way. The Walkers immediately picked up their pace like they could smell my fear, and as I started running full tilt toward the church, I heard the sound of their frantic footsteps and ragged breathing.

Racing past the huge cross, I pounded up the steps of the church, but there was a chain and lock on the big, arched, oaken doors. I started pounding wildly on the doors but no one answered. Everyone was locked in Xtabay's time-lock, including anyone who might have been able to help me. I was still pounding and screaming at the top of my lungs when the collection of Walkers reached the bottom of the steps.

I swung around, screaming for my father. It had come to this: I was calling on the Devil for help. But even he didn't show.

Looking down at all of the bloody red skeletons in street clothes gathered around, I felt sick. Xtabay was still half a block away, but the first Red Walker advanced up the steps—a tall man in a business suit, his black eyes wide and trained on me. I heard a whimper gather in my throat as he approached. I started clawing at my coat, looking for anything that could help me, but he moved quickly, and, in seconds, his hands fell on my shoulders. He pushed his gory wet face with its bloody, lipless grin close to mine, hissing.

"Get off!" I screeched, pushing him back. He went down on the stoop of the church easily enough, but another—a woman—was right behind him, and she reached for me. Her claw-like hands tangled in my hair and I grunted in fear as I tried to twist away, but there were too many and there was nowhere to run. Their hissing filled my head. I thought about scooting down and trying to climb between their legs, but a Red Walker no more than seven or eight years old latched onto my leg, nails sinking in. I screamed as the small, dead army swarmed me, trapping me against the doors of the church.

I let my most primal instincts take over and started thrashing and fighting even as the gory meat puppets clawed at my clothes and face. I slapped their hands away. I clawed at their soft, meaty face. But it didn't even stun them. They crowded me, tangling their slick red hands in my clothes, and their hissing sent me into a fresh panic as they dragged me down the steps on my ass. It was all I could do to keep my head from slamming into the concrete walk as they dragged me over the curb and out into the middle of the street. I was still screaming when Xtabay parted her hideous little army of zombies and smiled down at me.

She petted one of the Red Walkers on his bloody head as she said, "I told you that you would be mine forever, little flower."

"Fuck you!" I spat at her, not that it seemed to bother her in the least.

Xtabay just blinked the droplets of spit off her eyelashes and reached out to draw a circle on my cheek with her fingernail. "You fight me now, fire flower, but soon you will have no more will to fight. In fact, you will want to fill every one of my commands."

Looking up at the Red Walkers, she told them, "Hold her."

They clamped those horrible, slimy red hands over my arms and legs, pinning me down on the street. One tore at my coat and shirt beneath, exposing my breasts. I roared obscenities at Xtabay until my throat was sore. I twisted and fought. Xtabay was no fucking different than the endless procession of men who had tried to own me over the years. So many had tried to bend me their will, but she...she was a hundred times worse than they were because she too had suffered. She should know better than this!

Burn her down, my mind whispered. *Burn it all to the ground!*

Before I even stopped to consider it, I felt the heat gathering within me. Really, it was always there, boiling just under the surface of my skin. Waiting for a reason to rise. And now, at last, it had one.

I stiffened up as it seized me. I felt that fierce and hungry fire pass like a shockwave over my prone body. I heard the roar of the hungry flames in my ears. I felt the pleasure of the burning like some massive, body-wide orgasm.

The wave of blue fire rippled out over the Red Walkers holding me down, consuming them like kindling. At first, they just looked with fascination at the flames engulfing them and dancing over their hands and arms. They seemed incapable of feeling it—or caring about it if they did—as the wave of blue flames traveled over their flesh and skullishly grinning faces. Within seconds, my witchfire, hotter than any normal fire, had burned what was left of them down to black bones that fell in clatters to the street.

Xtabay, already wary of my fire, took a quick step backward.

I exhaled a long plume of acrid smoke. With their hands off me, I scuttled backward until I hit the curb. I was shaking violently as I groped my way to my feet.

Xtabay faced me, looking unsure.

I was burning hot. It licked like sharp tongues over my skin and delicate girl parts, and I groaned in pleasure. For the first time, I was not afraid. I felt strong. When I lifted my arms, I saw the blue witchfire coasting up and down my limbs. I felt it shivering through every strand of my hair. I could feel the bite of the fire against my cheeks. I peered past Xtabay and into the dark glass of the bookstore across the street. I was entirely engulfed in blue flames like some walking flamethrower.

Once again, I remembered my dream. I could set the whole city to burning with my dragon fire. Cleanse it of Xtabay forever and ever. Then I would never need to fear her or her undead army again. That idea appealed to me. I was tired of being afraid of others. Of myself. Of what I might become. I thought about what a pretty fire it would make. All those buildings alight...all those people.

It was, after all, a pleasure to burn.

I lifted my arms, prepared to give Xtabay and the rest of this city my kiss of flame, but Sebastian suddenly appeared in the street behind Xtabay. He stood there, panting and disheveled, eyes wide with fright. He shook his head and mouthed, *Don't do it, witchy.*

I suddenly thought of Mac. Father Matt. My brides. The people I'd helped. I didn't want them to burn, but I knew there was no way to control the dragon fire once I'd loosened it on the world.

The last of the burning Red Walkers dropped into the street. Xtabay looked at them sadly before switching her attention back to me. She extended her hand to me. *I could have given you the world!*

A dead world, I thought. A world without people like Sebastian in it. With a wave of my arm, I extinguished the flames dancing around me. Stupid, stupid witch, I thought as a realization came over me. Reaching into my pocket, I withdrew the Devil's Tarot and slid the cards apart, their edges glinting wickedly in the dim light of the burning bodies in the street.

The cards, I had suddenly realized, *were* my athame! How could I have not realized that fact until now? And a witch's athame could harm any other witch threatening her.

Xtabay stared at the cards, suddenly concerned.

"Stay back," I whispered as I turned sideways and drew the cards close to my chest. She was so beautiful that it hurt to look upon her, but goddess or not, she was just another monster. Which was why when she took a step toward me, I swung around, extended my arm fully, and let the cards fly.

They cut through the air like a metal dervish, and the noise they made was enough to set my teeth on edge. I expected them to cut into Xtabay's throat, but she did the unexpected and lunged at me with a cry, moving faster than any living thing should. The cards whirled right over her head and flew across the street, sinking into the bricks of a used bookshop.

I screamed in outrage when Xtabay tackled me, her body pinning me to the ground. I started to twist and fight, but she grabbed my wrists, pressing them to the asphalt. Her body pressed against my legs, preventing me from kicking out. She was so much stronger than I was. All I could do was sob and beg like some desperate child.

"Shhh..." she whispered. Her lips went to my neck, her cold black lotus kiss sending icy shudders up and down my spine.

Over her shoulder, spotted the glint of the metal cards embedded in the bricks of the shop. Calling them back would kill us both. But I suddenly didn't care. I was done being victimized. Anything was better than to never be free of this terrible fear. So, I twisted my right hand so hard that she had to let me go or risk breaking my wrist. She was busy kissing and licking my neck anyway, so she didn't notice when I extended my arm and stretched the fingers of my hand toward the cards, beckoning them to me.

They shivered almost imperceptibly.

Come on! Please! Come to me!

Another shiver. And then they did. The last thing I saw was that deadly, witch-killing blade flying toward the two of us.

Then: darkness.

| 63 |

"WITCHY? WITCHY, WAKE up!"

Someone was slapping me across the face. The voice and the sharp pain pulled me forcibly out of the darkness. Opening my eyes, I blinked up at Sebastian's face. Looking concerned, he tried to slap me again, but I reached out and stopped his hand.

"I'm awake. Stop."

We were still in the middle of an intersection with me on my back and him kneeling over me. Several fires were burning fitfully in the curb. He sat back on his haunches and rested his hands on his knees. "Are you sure? Maybe all of this is a dream. It could even be the afterlife."

I glared up at him. "If it was the afterlife, you wouldn't be here."

"True," he agreed.

I was lying on the cold asphalt, staring up at a sky quickly lightening to that familiar shade of grey just before dawn. I could see the sun rising behind Independence Hall. I heard distant sirens. So, I thought, time was marching on again. I considered that a victory. But how in hell was I still alive?

"Get me up," I said, and Sebastian grabbed me by the arm, dragging me to my feet. I felt dizzy and it took me a moment to orient myself. I was standing in the middle of the street outside the church. Bundles of burning cloth were scattered around like small bonfires.

I looked at them. I had to remind myself of how all of these were once people. The smell of burning hair and human flesh filled the morning air, making me feel queasy.

Leaning over, I waited to heave into the street. But Sebastian came up behind me and wrapped an arm around me, covering my mouth with his hand. "Way to leave DNA at the scene of a major crime," he warned. "We need to get the hell out of here before the police show up."

I swallowed hard and waited for my stomach to settle. When it did, Sebastian withdrew his hand. "What about...?" I had to catch my breath and swallow again. "What about...her?"

Sebastian laughed. "Ding dong, the bitch is dead." He pointed to the sidewalk in front of the church steps. Large ancient bones were scattered across the street, with the skull several yards away where it had been effectively clipped from the body. My cards were lying scattered in the street. They had not killed me—but then, I'd forgotten that too. A witch cannot be harmed by her own athame.

Sebastian walked to the cards and picked one up. When he turned it over, it was the Death card. Because he was holding them, they all were Death at the moment. "What are these?"

I swallowed hard. "They're...my athame."

"Ah, well, that's different." He picked them all up, being delicate about handling them, and returned them to me. "Let's get out of here, cunt. I'm getting too old for this shite."

Together, we limped back to the shop, our arms around each other like wounded combat veterans. The first police car passed us on the way to the scene of the crime, but it was going in the opposite direction and the cop inside never looked our way.

| 64 |

THE INCIDENT RECEIVED surprisingly little coverage. But then, despite the city bringing in the FBI, the CIA, and, finally, the NSA, no one could put together a coherent story about what happened. The multiple car accidents, the burning remnants of people in the streets, and the calcified bones of the decapitated woman that experts had carbon-dated to five billion years—over half a billion years older than the oldest known fossil on Earth—had left everyone stumped.

There was speculation, of course. A Russian dirty bomb. A gas leak. A terrorist attack. A mob war. Possible aliens. The list went on and on. With so little story to pick over, only people like psychics and ghost hunters pursued it. Normal people quickly lost interest and moved on to the latest scandal in the next news cycle.

Mac visited me a few days after the incident. We retired to the Laundromat and he told me the police had no leads, although the ancient bones continued to interest the authorities. I told him the bones belonged in a museum.

He laughed. "You sound like Indiana Jones."

I smiled back at him over my coffee and reached out to take his hand on the table between us. I felt him stiffen and his eyes blanked out slightly as I exerted my influence through our bond. "I trust you'll keep my involvement in your case out of your report? After all, the murders have stopped."

"I haven't included you in any of my reports. Don't want to be laughed at for having a pet witch."

Pet witch. Cute. Smiling at that, I made a swirl over the back of his dark hand, creating a burning ideogram that quickly vanished. Mac's eyes blanked out briefly before returning to their usual brown color. "Are you sure you're not my pet detective?"

He blushed at that. "You had something to do with stopping those murders, didn't you?"

Instead of answering him, I changed the subject to something more pleasant and romantic—specifically, what I wanted to do to him once he got off work. After thinking it over, I'd made the decision to keep him as my bride. I loved him. And I loved Father Matt. I was not letting them go that easily.

Maybe that made me a bad person, a bad girl, but I was learning to live with a lot of new things in my life. *You will never know real love or happiness in your whole life. Not as I could have shown it to you.* Perhaps Xtabay was right, but I was going to enjoy what I did have fully and completely.

After planning our little after-work rendezvous, I went back to the shop and started cooking up a storm in the prep room. We had a lot of confections to replace, and with all of the news coverage in our haunted little corner of the world, the summer tourists had come early to the west end of Philadelphia. Sebastian's exotic British chocolates were drawing a lot of customers, and my Sweet Stix were so popular that a representative from Whole Foods had begun sniffing around the shop.

It was all good news for our little business.

I'd decided to include Sebastian in my extracurricular activities. I still hadn't told him about the devil stuff because I didn't feel the time was right—and, frankly, I was terrified he wouldn't be able to handle it. But he'd saved me that night on the street, and I felt it was important I let him into my life a little more.

When a young, college-age girl visited the shop later that day and asked me to make her a charm to protect her from being raped a second time while on campus, I asked Sebastian to stay after hours and assist me in creating the crystallized honeycomb talisman. After cracking off the excess, the shape reveals itself as a spade.

Sebastian watched my process over one shoulder, saying little until he saw it. "Is there some rhyme or reason to the shape?"

"I don't know. They come out however they want. I trust the magic to know what it's doing." I didn't mention that the spade in the standard French deck symbolizes the medieval pike or halberd, weapons used in medieval society to run evil men through. The magic knew what it wanted to be.

He picked the talisman up by the string and held it up to the light. "You know you didn't have to hide any of this from me. I could have helped you. I might be a dodgy witch, but I'm still a witch."

"You're a necromancer. Aren't your skills mostly…you knew…for dead things?"

"Resurrectionist," he reminded me. "And even if my skills are a bit dodgy, they're still skills, witchy."

I felt blessed to have someone so sweet and non-judgmental like Sebastian on my team. Impulsively, I turned around and threw my arms around my friend's neck, hugging him tight and giving him a big kiss.

"Thank you," I told him. He could have run away that night and saved himself. He could have left the city and started over. He hadn't. I'd never had a friend quite like Sebastian Davis.

To my surprise, he hugged me back. Then, after a moment, he drew back and picked up the talisman again. "Poor lamb," he said of the girl. "Poor, poor little girl."

Yeah. That.

With Sister Marie and Xtabay gone, there was going to be a lot more crime on the streets. Many more women would be hurt and raped and murdered by careless, soulless men. I might have stopped Xtabay from turning the city into a burning hellhole, but—according to Sister Marie, at least—I was the one who'd corrupted her in the first place. I was the one who destroyed her.

I'd wanted to be a good girl. I'd wanted to be a damned superhero. But I'd let a lot of people down along the way. And that wasn't right. I had no business upsetting the balance like that.

"You okay?" Sebastian asked with concern when he sensed my sudden change of mood.

I looked up and nodded and put on a brave face because what else could I do? I couldn't tell him the near-disaster we'd barely avoided was all my fault. I had no idea how to make up for what I'd done except, perhaps, to make more of these small talismans for desperate souls standing on the edge of the abyss.

He gave me a grand smile and said, "You are and will always remain my favorite witch."

"My favorite witch," I repeat. "Sounds like a cheesy romantic sitcom."

And he laughed about that. And I laughed, too.

And, for a little while, all of the pain went away.

Vivian Summers will return in
BURNT OFFERINGS

About the Author

K.H. Koehler is the bestselling author of various novels and novellas in the genres of horror, SF, dark fantasy, steampunk, and young and new adult. She is the owner of KH Koehler Books and KH Koehler Design, which specializes in graphic design and professional copyediting. Her books are widely available at all major online distributors and her covers have appeared on numerous books in many different genres. Her short work has appeared in various anthologies, and her novel series include *The Kaiju Hunter, A Clockwork Vampire, Planet of Dinosaurs, The Nick Englebrecht Mysteries,* and *The Archaeologists.* She is the author of multiple Amazon bestsellers and was one of the founders and chief editors of KHP Publishers, which published genre fiction from 2001 to 2015. She has over fifteen years of experience in the publishing industry as a writer, ghostwriter, copyeditor, commercial book cover designer, formatter, and marketer. Visit her website at https://khkoehler.net.

www.ingramcontent.com/pod-product-compliance
Lightning Source LLC
LaVergne TN
LVHW031609060526
838201LV00065B/4792